the

looking

glass

Henry Holt and Company ~ New York

the

looking

glass

MICHÈLE ROBERTS

Henry Holt and Company, LLC
Publishers since 1866
115 West 18th Street
New York, New York 10011

Henry Holt® is a registered trademark of
Henry Holt and Company, LLC.

Library of Congress Cataloging-in-Publication Data TK.

ISBN 0-8050-6700-0

Henry Holt books are available for special promotions and
premiums. For details contact: Director, Special Markets.

First American Edition 2001

Designed by Kelly S. Too

Printed in the United States of America

1   3   5   7   9   10   8   6   4   2

for the muse this time

ACKNOWLEDGEMENTS

I am grateful to Lennie Goodings and all at Little, Brown/Virago, and to Gillon Aitken and all at Gillon Aitken Associates, for their hard work and support. Thanks to Susie Honeyman and Jock McFadyean for telling me a ghost story and showing me the café in which the haunting happened, to my mother for introducing me to Etretat, and to Paul Quinn for taking me to visit Mallarmé's flat in Paris and house at Valvins. This novel, though it concerns purely fictional persons and events, is partly inspired by details from the life of Mallarmé, as recorded in the biography of Mallarmé by Jean-Luc Steinmetz, as well as by details from the life of Flaubert, as recorded in his own letters, and as celebrated by Julian Barnes in *Flaubert's Parrot*. My gratitude to all these writers. Thanks too to my family and friends.

the

looking

glass

Geneviève

It is the sea I miss most: the music of the dragging tide over the loose shingle, shifting it back and forth; the surge and suck of water. The waves advancing in tall ranks, one after the other, into the little bay between the cliffs, folding over, toppling, collapsing into ruffles of white, leaving just a silver tracery behind; foam lace, that soaks away quickly into the pebbles on the shore. I miss the dancing light, and the energetic wind blowing mist and spray, tiny beads of moisture, onto my clothes and skin. The gulls swooping and crying overhead. The smell of salt and seaweed and fish; the way the curved stretch of water sparkles in the sun, changing from green to dark blue to turquoise; and, clinking under my feet as I slither down the wet ridge, the stones on the beach rubbed by each other smooth as eggs, grey-blue, lavender blue, milky blue in the gleaming intensity of late afternoon.

Could I ever return to the house in Blessetot? I don't think I'd have the courage to try. The nightmares warned me to stay away. Dreams of a ghost who haunted me and wished to punish me for what I had done. A ghost who loitered speechlessly at the tight, twisting turn of the steep stairs. I thought she was drowned and gone for ever but she kept drifting back, that body washed onto the beach like a piece of driftwood or a dead starfish, flotsam and jetsam tossed up by the receding tide. Her eyes were open and staring, her face bruised and bloated. Black ribbons of seaweed draped her shoulders. Water streamed from the sodden rags of her dress. I had not managed to kill her after all. I thought she was dead but she had come back to life and got into the house somehow; she was barring my way to bed; she was waiting for me. She was very patient. She would get me in the end.

I would wake up from this dream crying out as though I were a child again, one who had a mother close by and could be comforted; trembling and sweating, praying desperately to a God I rarely summoned otherwise not to allow me to fall into the ghost's clutches. The fear stayed with me even when I shook myself out of sleep, sat up and lit a candle. Fear can flourish in the light just as forcefully as in the dark. The ghost would retreat, dissolve to the shadowy corners of the room, but I knew she was still there. My flesh still crept. The hairs still stood up on the back of my neck. The night air stayed icy cold as seawater, and now it was I who was drowning.

When I left that house in Blessetot I swore to myself it would be for good, that I would never go back. I thought I could cut myself off from the past and take myself far away from it, out of its power to hurt me, to make me remember what had once been. But the past walks with us, shoulder to shoulder, like an invisible enemy or friend; it kicks inside us like an unborn child; it embraces us like a lover; it will outlive us and lay us out, like a wise woman, when we die. The past has lodged in my brain and cannot be pried loose. It is my country and my prison and my home.

I saw Blessetot for the first time in the spring. A fishing village all year round, it became a holiday resort for Parisians in summer. The railway from Rouen to Le Havre running as far as Etretat, a few kilometres further along the coast, meant that the whole area of the pays de Caux, once written off by outsiders as savage, dull and remote, had become increasingly opened up, and was newly considered to possess a certain primitive beauty, to be just the kind of wild and unspoilt landscape to refresh the jaded palates of city-dwellers.

The painters arrived first, and then the tourists. These summer visitors began exploring northwards from Etretat by pony and trap. Driving along the coast road that ran across the high chalk plain to Fécamp, they discovered the little coves and bays hidden at the end of the steep gullies cutting down through the cliffs. Blessetot was the name given to the settlement that had grown up in one of these, a straggle of houses lining the dust-white road to the beach, and a cluster of homes, two streets deep, sheltering under the curve of the cliff. Too small ever to become as fashionable as Etretat, with no fine promenade, no elegant bars or hotels, no market square or formal flower gardens, less dramatic and picturesque cliffs, Blessetot was nonetheless pronounced charming and quaint.

Its appeal lay precisely in its simplicity. The flint and brick cottages had roofs of slate or of thatch, and shutters painted grey or dark green or a bright blue that celebrated the seaside. In their tiny front gardens, edged with large flints from the beach, people grew any flowers, like sea-holly and sea-pinks, that could withstand the salt winds. Some of the smallest houses, nearest the front, were simply huts of white wood, with tiny verandas and porches. The fishermen's shacks lining the top of the steeply shelving beach were constructed of oak, the warped, salt-seasoned timbers stained a glistening black. Nets and lobster pots sprawled nearby. There was no confining wall to separate the village from the sea. Like an urgent animal the water simply bounded up the pebbles, dashed itself on the tide-line in flurries of white-topped green waves, and ran away again. Halfway up the cliffs a few recently built chalet-style holiday villas made splashes of red; brick faced with white

stone; steeply pitched wooden roofs; and their façades orna-
mented with fake-rustic balconies whose lines imitated the
branches of trees. Two streets back from the sea there was a
café, and it was here that I arrived to take up my job as
maid-of-all-work for Madame Patin.

I travelled by horse and cart. Sister Pauline had relatives
who farmed just outside Etretat, near Bénouville, and she
arranged for her brother-in-law to collect me from the
orphanage early in the morning and take me most of the
way to Blessetot. This was substantially out of his usual
road, and there was no question of his doing me a favour. I
was to pay for the cart hire out of my first month's wages.

I said goodbye to my few friends in the orphanage, and
to Sister Pauline. No one was sad to see me go, for I had not
had the trick of making myself particularly liked. The
other girls thought me stuck-up and standoffish, since I
rarely joined in their games at break, preferring to read a
book. The farmer arrived on the appointed day to collect
me. He wore a blue woollen cap pulled well down over his
head for warmth, and his bushy eyebrows shaded his slits of
eyes. He grunted at me and helped me climb up into the
cart. I sat behind him on the dusty boards, facing sideways,
clinging onto the wooden side with one hand, an empty
sack under me as cushion.

We jolted out of Etretat and onto the coast road. Fine
rain blew into my face. The creak of the worn leather harness, the clopping of the horse's hooves, the clatter of the
iron-rimmed wheels, all made an urgent song and dance in

my ears. The finish of an old life. The orphanage had been my home for sixteen years, but now it was behind me. I was nervous of what lay ahead, but I was also exhilarated. The freshness of the rain on my cheeks pleased me, and the wind whipping my ungloved hands, and the salt tang in the air.

The road ran up onto the plain under an enormous sky of billowing clouds. The hedgerows and ditches were spiky with green weeds and grass glittering with dew. Clumps of pale yellow primroses spread along the banks. All around us were ploughed and sown fields showing the tips of crops. In the distance majestic farms reared up, enclosed by high banks planted with beeches. Through the openings in these massive squares of trees I glimpsed half-timbered houses and tall dovecots, stone-built barns decorated with red stripes of zigzag bricks. My eyes seized on everything: the swaying rump of the horse just in front of me and the strip of leather harness confining its black tail, the crows flapping and cawing above the furrowed earth, the stinging green of hawthorn hedges, the shimmer of bluebells, like stretches of blue water, in the long grass beyond. It was all new to me. I had never stirred outside Etretat in the whole of my life.

The farmer did not bother trying to turn round and talk to me as we bumped along. He held the reins in one hand, and a small clay pipe, at which he puffed from time to time, in the other. His bent back, perched up above me, looked quite remote. He was sunk deep in his own thoughts and left me in peace, huddled on the swaying floor of the cart, to look about me and plunge into mine.

I wondered what I was going to, and wished I had someone to give me good advice. I should have liked to have known my parents. If I had known them, of course, my life would have been different. They would have protected me and seen that I came to no harm. At the very least they would have tried to teach me how to recognise harm when it does come, disguised as love. As it was, I had to get on without them. They had loved each other enough to create me, I could not bear to think otherwise, before fortune intervened and my father went away and my mother was obliged to give me up to the nuns. She had been a teacher. That was all I knew about her. She had been unable to keep me, not being married, and so she had had to put me into the orphanage, in the back streets of Etretat, whose high walls blocked out all sight of the sun, all sound of the sea.

Once a week, on Sundays, we were marched through the town in crocodile, on our way to High Mass, so that people would see us and remember to give generously to the charity boxes in church. We were rarely taken to the beach, except on feast days in summer. But just being out in the street was better than nothing, even when it was raining. You could watch the water swirling over the cobbles and along the gutters at the side of the narrow road, hear the gulls shrieking, and smell the sea even if you could not see it. Freedom twitched suddenly close at hand, that taste of salt on my tongue and the wind tugging my cape and the sun glinting bright on the puddles reflecting the blue sky. Treading through rainwater we trod in bottomless sky that gleamed like mussel shells, the backs of mackerel.

As we plodded back after church, and approached the orphanage once more, my heart would sink. As the heavy door scraped open and we filed in, bending down in turn to take off our wet and muddy boots, my spirit, likewise, had to bow, to shrink itself as though it were being forced into a dark, airless cupboard where it would gasp for breath. Back into that cramped place where we all lived on top of one another, where the furniture was cumbersome and ugly, where the light was shut out and we were shut in. However wild and wet the weather, I would always rather have been outside. I hated the muffled house, its smell of wet wool and furniture polish like a hand over my mouth stifling me.

The nuns enforced strict rules of deportment and behaviour, as you might expect. Walk close to the walls, eyes lowered. Don't answer back. Silence at meals and in the dormitory. Our guardians did not see themselves as unkind. To keep thirty boisterous girls in order they considered themselves bound to inflict severe discipline. If we failed at self-control then the cane was there to teach us better. They were preparing us for the harshness of adult life outside the walls, as they were also attempting to ensure we could reach heaven. Girls to them meant mess, chaos and noise. Qualities to be suppressed. It was impossible to believe they had once been children themselves and had hungered for caresses and understanding. They were not happy women, most of them, and so they could not love us. Even while I disliked them, I felt sorry for them. They would never get out, whereas one day I would. One day I would walk out of that door and never return.

I was convinced my mother had been forced by others to give me away, that she had loved me. Had she not fitted me out in a beautifully stitched and frilled nightgown and cap, a soft shawl, before handing me over? So the nuns said, that I was one of the best-dressed babies they had ever received. Of my father they could tell me nothing, only that he had been considered unsuitable by my mother's parents and sent packing. My mother had loved him, so I passionately believed, and perhaps he thought of me sometimes, and perhaps I looked like him. The nuns refused to tell me my parents' names. They baptised me Geneviève, after the patron saint of Paris, and invented a surname for me, Delange. Saint Geneviève had been a brave woman who encouraged the citizens during a great siege and went up on the ramparts to exhort them. She was a nun, but one with an exciting life. In the picture in the book I was shown she looked beautiful, with a warm, smiling face, a rounded body under her habit, and her arms tenderly cradling a child.

I prayed to St Geneviève when thing went badly, but I was doubtful she heard me. I spent the greater part of my days working my way back and forth along the orphanage corridors wielding bucket and brush, scrubbing the stone floors. The coarse soda blistered and reddened my skin; my palms and knees were permanently calloused; I stank of carbolic. All part of the punishment for being born a bastard. As a consolation for these hardships I day-dreamed. Fantasies of revenge, of wild adventure, of exquisite pleasures in fairyland. At night I became the orphans' storyteller. I whispered my tales to the others in the chilly dormitory and thus secured my safety. Even the bullies wanted my stories, and so they let me alone; they did not steal my food or rub coal dust into my hair or lock me in the privies, their favourite tricks when the nuns' backs were turned. They mocked me by day, in the class-room, when I got all of my dictation exercise right, or came top in the spelling test, but they listened to me, night after night, when I told them stories and led them wherever I chose, into a world where I ran on just ahead, towards the unknown. They always wanted more. For the story never to end. When I started each evening's instal-ment I would feel their attention pressing onto me in the darkness. I would shiver all over and then language would fly out of my mouth and it felt as though we all held hands and jumped off the cliff together and then above us the great silk wing of words would flare out and float us away to the magical island across the ocean where we were free.

The nuns always warned against storytelling and day-dreaming, which they said meant lying, an escape from truth. To me it was the opposite. Those bright pictures were the most real thing. Now, daydreaming again, letting myself dwell on all those hardships which were over and could therefore be looked in the face, I had forgotten where I was. I was brought back to the present by a change in the horse's gait, the floor of the cart rocking less abruptly. We were slowing down. There was a crossroads just in front of us, marked by a tall Calvary, with fields stretching away on four sides of it, and here we stopped. The farmer held his pipe away from his lips and jerked his head in the direction that I was to go, then waited while I clambered down over the tail of the cart. He threw my little cardboard box of possessions after me, clicked his teeth by way of goodbye, then shook his reins and grunted at the horse. I stood for a moment, watching them lurch off, the cart wheels tilting as they ground along, the farmer's shoulders slumped forwards, his whip trailing from one fist. Then I shook straw from my skirts, and straightened my wind-buffeted cap. A gull flapped, crying, just above my head: The whole landscape blinked and winked as the sun darted out of the skidding clouds. The patch of blue sky that appeared meant, I was convinced, good luck. I picked up my box and started off towards Blessetot.

The rutted road dropped through a tiny, steep valley, the cliffs rising up on either side. Two kilometres' descent or so and I turned a corner and suddenly saw a blue-green triangle of sea dipping below me in the gap between the chalk bluffs. Nothing could be too difficult if the sea was nearby. I fell down that last narrow stretch of road as though I were being born.

The mirror covered part of one of the side walls in the bar. Every time I came in to sweep and dust I looked at myself in it. I had not lived in a place with mirrors before. This particular one was a tall oblong, surrounded by a black plaster frame painted with curlicues of gold, very fine. While I blew on its spotted surface then polished it with my cloth I would squint at myself. Being able to see my reflection made me feel different. When I wanted to forget myself in safety, and daydream, I could, and then when I needed to know where I was again I had only to glance in the glass and see the frowning girl that was me. A skinny hazel-eyed girl with short fair hair, more like a boy, who appeared, then disappeared, then returned again. I could hide in the mirror. In the orphanage, in the daytime, under the nuns' sharp gaze, I had not felt able to vanish, even when daydreaming. It was only at night, in the dark, that I had been able to let go of myself and disappear into stories. But here the mirror kept a friendly eye out for me; it tolerated my going away and coming back; and I could behave as though it were night, climbing over the black frame and jumping down into a secret room on the other side, whenever I felt the need. The mirror doubled everything. The café, the bar, me.

The bar was simply the front room of the café. It had green walls and a sanded plank floor and was furnished with a few wooden tables and benches, a black iron stove with a tall chimney, and the mirror. The front door opened straight onto the street. Two small windows looked out the same way, veiled in cotton lace that blurred the view. Another door, in the back wall of the bar, had been cut in half horizontally to make a hatch which flapped open and shut for the drinks to be handed through. A piece of plywood, nailed on top of the bottom half, made a makeshift counter. Madame Patin kept all the bottles and glasses in her kitchen cum storeroom. People walking into the bar came up to the hatch, banged on it, and shouted their orders. Madame Patin would open up, slide the glasses across, and get on with her other work on the other side.

The café also functioned as a shop. Since there was no grocer in the village, Madame Patin sold dry goods, such as sugar and flour and salt, which she kept in built-in compartments, like a boat's lockers, just inside the back door. She would lift up the lid of the relevant box, delve in with her wooden scoop, and then pour the contents onto the brass pan of the scales. She had to be very exact with her measurements of rice, or macaroni, or whatever it was. Her customers watched closely, determined not to waste a single sou. Mostly it was women who came to the back door and men to the front. Madame Patin, seated beside her open hatch, could keep an eye on both. She kept an eye on me too. I was only allowed in the bar in the early mornings, when I went in to clean, and at night, after she'd locked up, when I tidied. For the rest of the day I

worked elsewhere. I was certainly not supposed to talk to
the customers.

—If you turn out decent and honest and hardworking,
she told me when I first arrived: then we shall get on. If not,
then it's back to the orphanage.

She stood waiting.

—Yes, ma'am, I said.

What else could I possibly say? I did mean it. I wanted
to please her and for her to love me. That, of course, was the
cause of my undoing.

She had stood in the café doorway, hands folded across
her waist, to watch my arrival. She inspected me with her
keen eyes as I tramped towards her, my box under my arm.
Keeping my head down so as not to seem familiar, I peered
at her. She looked to be in her late thirties, a sturdy woman
with grey-blue eyes, egg-shaped cheeks, and a wide, thin
mouth. A large brown linen apron protected her blue check
dress and a white cap shadowed her face. I found out how
beautiful her hair was the first time I helped her wash it,
and she shook out her hairpins and let down her thick fair
plaits. Unravelled, the hair sprang out in glistening ripples
like something alive.

Sometimes when she was in one of her anxious moods, at
night, fretting over money, I'd brush her hair for her, gathering the thick tail in one hand and drawing the brush
through it with the other, over and over again. It calmed her
down. Then I would re-plait it so that she was ready for bed.
It is soothing, to feel someone else's hands arranging your

hair, stroking and patting it. You don't have to do anything but sit there, leaning back, your whole self flowing away with the brush as it sweeps back from your head. Like being a cat whose owner loves it and grooms it. Her hair was her fur and she liked me arranging it because I was gentle and did not pull hard or snag the brush on tangles. She would sigh with pleasure and close her eyes. When she helped me wash my hair it was quite different. My straw crop was too short for fussing over. Soap rubbed briskly in, water tipped over my head from the jug into the tin basin, then a towel thrust at me and my face plunging into its rough folds, my hands trying to mop the cold trickles down the back of my neck that made my chemise itchy and damp.

On that first day she showed me around the house. We peeped into the bar, where a few customers slouched over their tables. Nobody said a word. Just raised their heads and glanced at us. Then Madame Patin took me around the back, which was divided into two small rooms. One of these was the shop-and-kitchen, and the other was her bedroom. She nodded her head towards the door but did not open it to let me see in.

—Too untidy, she said: I haven't made the bed yet. I haven't had a minute.

From the kitchen a narrow staircase, boxed in, coiled up to the attics. Here, three little rooms opened off a low-ceilinged corridor just wide enough for one person to squeeze through at a time. Each small cabin was panelled up to the ceiling in varnished golden plywood. They were so neat and so snug. The floors were likewise of golden wood, and small casements had been let into the roof so that you could see the sky.

—My husband did all this work, Madame Patin explained: to be ready for the children we would have. But the children never arrived.

She sighed.

—It's God's will. God's will be done.

The words were said mechanically. They were what I'd been taught to say, too, when sad things happened. It meant it wasn't your fault; it couldn't be helped; and the best you could do was just get on with things. I wondered where her husband was now. Perhaps he was dead, or perhaps he had gone away and left her, like my father did. The nuns had told me nothing about my new place, save my employer's name.

The first two rooms disclosed themselves as storage places, piled with sacks of provisions, boxes of biscuits, trays of apples, racks of preserves. She led me past these, and pushed open the farthest door.

—This is where I thought the maid should sleep. This is your room now.

Thanking her, I stammered with delight. The room, the smallest of the three, enchanted me. For a start, it was all mine. I did not have to share it with anyone else.

Its simplicity was its charm, and its soothing colours. Worn blue rag rug on the glistening floor, bleached sacking curtains at the little window, faded red and yellow paisley quilt. For furniture there was an iron bed, an iron wash-stand holding an enamel basin, and, set nearby, a jug, a chamber-pot, a three-legged stool. A cupboard with a sliding panel door had been built in under the far eave, like a little cave. I had practically nothing to put in it but I did not care. I had a cupboard of my own. That was the main thing. I wondered about the previous inhabitant of the room, if there had been one and whether she had liked it as much as I did. What had she been like, the last maid, and why had she left? Or was I the first person ever to sleep in here? These were questions I knew I could not ask. Curiosity was not polite. That had been well dinned into me, along with not staring, eating up everything on my plate, and curtsying every time a nun came by.

Madame Patin did not seem to require to be curtsied to. She was tugging at the casement catch, showing me how to work it. The window being opened, sounds of the outside rushed in: a cock crowing, a dog barking. The air was very fresh and damp and brought with it the smell of the sea. The window was on the side of the house: immediately in front of me were the blue slates of the neighbour's roof, which was lower than ours, and then, when I peered out, one way I saw an orchard, with sheep grazing in it and hens pecking about, and on the other the steeple of the church and a cemetery full of graves. We placed my box on the bed and returned the way we had come, shutting each door behind us as we went. The door handles were of white china, solid as eggs, cool and hard in my palm. They turned back and forth very springily, though the door hinges were a little stiff, and the doors, opening and closing, scraped across the golden wood floor. I thought that would be something I could do for Madame Patin: bring up some oil and a feather and oil the doors. She was ahead of me, grasping the banister rail and setting her foot on the top step.

—Mind how you go on the stairs, she warned me: they're very steep and it's easy to slip.

Downstairs, she showed me the privy, which was at the far end of the tiny courtyard behind the house, and the woodshed and wine cellar which were next to it. I liked the cool darkness inside these windowless caves, the smell of their earth floors. Outside again, we looked at the hen coop, the rabbit hutches, and the dog kennel. The dog, a brownish mongrel, was asleep. In the centre of the yard was the well, flanked by a couple of pots of ferns. Behind the yard was a little meadow, with fruit trees, and a cow grazing. The kitchen garden was on the other side of the road, down an alley in between two other houses. An iron gate squeaked open to reveal tidy rows of dug earth inside low stone walls. Not much was showing yet. A few blue-green cabbages had survived the winter on long scarred stalks and looked very tough. Another gate at the far end obviously gave you a quick route to the church. You could just see a pointed grey porch beyond it.

I decided I liked the house and the garden very much. It was all so complete and so compact, like I imagined a doll's house would be. Yet it was real. I liked the way the café tucked so neatly and quietly into the street, the village. I envied Madame Patin with all my heart. For a moment I disliked her thoroughly, almost as though she were an enemy. Pain shot through me: I had nothing and she seemed to have everything. She was like Saint Geneviève protecting her own city from the foreign rabble like me; she was the house itself, perfect and full; and she was the garden, blessed with richness. She held the whole place like a tiny castle in her arms; she bent towards it possessively, as though it were her child. I could not believe she was going to make room for me too. I thought that more than anything in the world I should like to have a little house like hers, to be mistress of such a neat place I could call my own. I wished that her house were mine, and that she were not there. I wanted to steal her house and push her into the street and let her be the orphan, the vagabond. And at the same time I wanted to sit companionably with her in the warm kitchen and be her friend.

These feelings bursting out inside me were like flowers blooming and then rapidly being torn to pieces by the wind. I wanted to get rid of them because they made me want to cry. I almost wished I were back in the orphanage, inside its cold walls, where I had never felt like this.

Luckily for me, the church bells now banged out half-past eleven. Duty distracted my thoughts as my employer exclaimed how late it was. We hurried back inside the café. I was set to peeling the vegetables for dinner while Madame Patin stuck her head through the hatch and checked on her customers. There weren't many. Sunday noon, I subsequently learned, was the busiest time for the bar. The café being so close to the church was very good for business, for after Sunday mass people stood to gossip outside and the men soon got up a thirst and flooded in. And when there was a *vin d'honneur,* after a communion or a wedding or a funeral, it was Madame Patin who organised it and provided the glasses and the drink. Everybody would squeeze in and stand packed, shoulder to shoulder, the air thick with tobacco smoke and the smell of cider, and the curé as pleased as anyone else to be inside in the warm. The proprietors of the church and the café, I soon discovered, supported each other, their clients flowing back and forth across the road.

On this occasion, hearing the bells, a quarter of an hour later, ring out the Angelus, the call to prayer I'd obeyed all my life at the regulation three times a day, I stood stock-still as I'd been taught, dropped the potatoes I was peeling, crossed myself, then fell on my knees and began to recite the well-worn words. The angel of the Lord declared unto Mary. And she conceived by the Holy Ghost. I stopped for a moment, wondering. At this time of year, just after Easter, we said the Regina Coeli, instead, didn't we? Which had we said yesterday? I could not remember. I had not been paying attention. I began again. The angel of the Lord.

Madame Patin did not join in and make the response. I looked up, puzzled, and saw her staring at me.

—For heaven's sake, child, we haven't got time for that. On your feet and on with your work, if you please.

I got up gladly from the cold tiles. If there was to be an end to so much kneeling I would not be sorry. Nonetheless I was shocked at how an outsider was encouraging me to drop the orphanage ways. That was what made me feel I had really left.

Madame Patin was whirling around the kitchen, stirring soup, chopping bacon into dice, heating fat in a blackened frying pan. Her back was defensive. I was surprised when she bothered explaining to me. As though it mattered to her what I thought.

—God takes care of those who take care of themselves. If I don't have time to pray then he's not offended. He understands. He knows how busy I am.

—Yes, ma'am, I said.

I'd never thought of God as being so kind and ordinary. For me he had always been a distant figure to be placated, a judge who dished out punishments, a baffling father who let his son be tortured and killed. For the first time in my life it occurred to me that perhaps people saw God the way they wanted to. How did I want to see God? I wasn't sure. I put the problem aside, to think of later, because right now I was too busy, just like Madame Patin.

I was clumsy that first day, being more used to scrubbing than cooking. Also, working in a new place, with pots and tools I did not know, made me feel awkward and slowed me down. It's much easier to cook well, I discovered later, once your utensils have become old friends, when you know exactly which battered knife with a worn, thin blade is actually the sharpest, which blunted wooden spatula the best for scraping sauce out of a pan, which spoon holds precisely the right amount of flour. I had to learn how the range worked, which of the several little ovens to use for which dish, how to keep it fed with wood and firing at a consistent temperature. I ended the morning with red burns striping the backs of both hands, fingers scalded from the steam rushing out of the saucepan when I tipped the potatoes into the colander in the sink, and several large grease marks blotting the front of my apron. I had dirtied two of the best linen tea-towels by using them as oven clothes when I shifted the shelves inside the hot range, and I had soaked three others with vegetable water when draining saucepans. Madame Patin raised her eyebrows at my ineptitude. I could see her deciding not to scold me on my first day and hoping to heaven I would improve.

—Once you've done the weekly wash, she remarked: you'll learn to keep your things clean. You don't want to go giving yourself extra work.

We got the dinner onto the kitchen table by half-past twelve. I hadn't been sure she would want me sitting down to eat with her, and was pleased when she pointed to the chair opposite hers. She did not cross herself and murmur a grace, so I did not either, mindful of my earlier lesson about the Angelus. We ate cabbage soup with a bit of bacon in it, and potatoes fried in bacon fat. It was good food, and she let me eat as much of it as I wanted. I had three helpings. She didn't talk to me. She poured us a tumbler of cider each and nodded at me to start. We both got on with eating while the meal was hot. I was so hungry I could think of nothing else, and then when I was finished I felt ashamed at having gobbled like a pig in front of her. She didn't seem to mind. She sat with her elbows on the table, yawning.

I decided to abandon another of the nuns' precepts and to satisfy my curiosity.

—If you please, ma'am, I began: may I ask you something?

She jerked her head round to look at me.

—Depends what it is. Go ahead.

—Did you have a maid before me? I asked.

She shook her head.

—No.

This pleased me. I was emboldened to put another question.

—Where is Monsieur Patin?

—He's dead, child. He was a fisherman. He drowned at sea.

She heaved herself to her feet and began clearing the dirty dishes and plates.

—That's quite enough chatting. Curiosity killed the cat. Come on, there's work to do.

For the rest of the day she kept me busy cleaning the range, sweeping out the yard, and drawing up water. Customers came in and out of the back door, chatting, shaking the coins out of their purses into the palms of their hands, counting them out carefully, one by one, onto the table-top. Their eyes flicked over me and they nodded at Madame Patin as though to say: so the new help's arrived, then.

For supper we ate the rest of the soup. I was tired out. There had been so much to learn and I had made so many mistakes. Now my tasks were coming to an end and I was longing for my bed. After the last customers had departed and the café was locked up for the night, I swept out the bar and was dismissed upstairs. My employer stuck a new candle into a candlestick and lit it for me, bidding me to be careful not to splash hot wax over my hands. She gave me a quick, small smile.

—Tomorrow it will be better. You'll see.

The stairs rose up abruptly as a cliff face. I climbed them awkwardly, my skirts bunched over my arm so that I did not trip on the high treads, the candlestick gripped in one fist and the fingers of my other hand groping for the stair above. I inched up inside my tiny pool of light, until I reached the attics. Inside my little room I blew out the candle then fell into bed exhausted. The mattress was not too hard. Straw-stuffed, it rustled underneath me in its linen cover. The coarse sheets and the cotton quilt were clean, and had the sweet, fresh scent of outdoors. I wasn't too tired to thank heaven that my new place seemed so comfortable, to hug myself with the pleasure of going to sleep so near the beach and so far from the orphanage. When the wind got up outside I felt I was rocking along on a fishing boat that had just put out to sea, and when the timbers of the roof began creaking it sounded like rigging and sails, to my sleepy brain, all part of voyaging out into the night.

The mermaid had long, golden hair, green eyes, and cold white arms. She was half-woman, and half-fish, a beauty who was also a monster. She seemed to promise men pleasure and then turned dangerous. You couldn't see at all, at first, that she had a tail, because it was concealed under the water, a mosaic of silvery green scales, a thick, lively muscle that slapped to and fro as she waited for her prey. She appeared far off, naked and slender, behind a mist of spray, sprawled languishing on the jagged black rocks guarding the entrance to the harbour. You changed tack and sailed closer, unable to believe your eyes, thinking the sun dazzling on the water had deceived you, that the pale girl was indeed a phantom composed of dissolving vapour, a trick of the light. Then your boat was dancing and plunging, almost on the rocks, and you saw her clearly. In one hand she held a pearl-encrusted mirror, and in the other a silver comb. Her song, in a high, sweet voice, coiled about you, a snare of enchantment, a net to lure you into her watery world, to plunge like a dolphin down into the translucent green waves, following her, lost to reason. You wouldn't call it drowning. You'd call it bliss. Only when you were lying trapped in the cold waving arms of the seaweed on the deep seabed would you realise that you were capsized and dying and that you would never come home again; only your bones, perhaps, washing up years later on the beach, white and polished as cuttlefish.

One young man did manage to escape. He burst from the mermaid's clutches and swam ashore; he fled dripping through the town and into his house. And when the mermaid followed him, hauling herself on her arms, with painful slowness, up the hill of stones and into the street, the young man came back with his friends and caught her in a net. He cut her throat with his knife. She jerked and thrashed, then died. The wide wound gushed red, the blood flowing over her as though it dressed her in a red vest. Still streaming blood, she was hung up in the church porch for all the world to see. And the next morning she had turned into a great coil of seaweed, shiny and sticky with salt and seawater. On days of rain this rubbery knot was wet and on fine days it was dry. Which is why people hereabouts still hang seaweed outside the back doors of their houses, to foretell the weather and to warn their sons to keep away from bewitchment.

Did the mermaid have the secret nameless opening between her legs like ordinary women? That was what I wanted to know, but could not say so, since there wasn't a word for it, and anyway it was filthy even to think about it let alone try to refer to it out loud. Did men fear mermaids because of drowning or because they couldn't make love to them? Or both? The tale was baffling and did not tell. It kept its mouth shut, just like the mermaid, who could not talk. She had a mouth but could only use it for wordless singing or kissing.

Stories like these were new to me. I'd never heard of such things, which made me a breathless audience. Madame Patin's tales were far more alarming than the ones I'd told my listeners at the orphanage, because I was not in control of them. And an adult telling them, rather than a child, made them especially powerful. My stories had had murder and violence in them, certainly, but because I was their author I had been in charge of who did what to whom. I had hooked my listeners into my world and felt triumphant. This mermaid story frightened me, because I thought I knew what it meant, and also I didn't know. My body seemed to know, in silence, but not in any words that ever came easily into my mouth. The mermaid could not speak and neither could I.

The only stories I had heard about women in the past were the lives of saints told by the nuns. Carefully chosen tales about heroic struggles to be good, with angels helping, and God rewarding virtue in the end. These folk tales, here in the countryside, seemed to belong to a different order of things. Their narratives were harshly expressed. Their contents were cruel and bleak. They seemed to be outside morality altogether, for they invoked no familiar or recognisable world; they were set in wild landscapes of swamps and forests where wolves roamed looking for prey and huntsmen slaughtered one another and children got lost and starved in the snow. Cunning and malignity and doom were hidden under beauty. You were lulled by the enchanted land under the sea shot through with iridescence and jewel colours, where swimming was like flying, where you rode on the backs of herring and wore bracelets of coral, only to fall prey to enchantresses and witches and wicked queens who had funds of exalted and magical knowledge, who cursed people in hatred and ruined their lives.

I couldn't put into words how these figures troubled me. They weren't like any women I had ever met yet they existed and were real. Their meanings were sealed under a skin of silence, as you seal pâté under fat. They were as mysterious as a foreign language I couldn't comprehend or translate and yet they spoke to my bones.

As a lonely child I had needed stories but now, I decided, I had done with them; childhood was past; I had a job and a home and no hunger for such rigmaroles any more. Another part of me was not so confident, not so sure, and wanted to stay safe for ever by the stove, in the warmth and the dim light, and not to have to get any older, not to have to grow up. The price of that, or perhaps its cause, was immersing myself in the stories, which so repelled and attracted me.

Even though she did not believe in displaying pleasure too openly, Madame Patin smiled a flitting, triumphant smile at my shudders, for I could not resist her deep voice beginning: once upon a time, long, long ago. I always begged for just one more story. I wanted to hear every single tale she had to tell, to discover just one or two with happy endings. But all her stories were sad. She said they were the ones she had been told as a child. Stories about witches stealing black cockerels to sacrifice, about the Devil snatching miserly widows down to hell, about dead twin boys floating along the river in coffin-baskets, about women giving birth to imps and snakes, about change-lings. She told me these stories on Sunday evenings, when we took time off from the usual round of work and did the mending by the fire. Sometimes while I brushed her hair she'd tell me a story. Sometimes we were knitting. It was the one time in the week when she talked to me at length. I believe she enjoyed it. She was proud of her stories; she held them out for me to inspect and I duly admired them even as I shivered.

Sometimes she told me fragments of her own life too. How she was an only child, how she had met her husband at the fair in Yvetot, how they had borrowed the money to buy the house and open the bar with such high hopes.

—You wouldn't believe what a wreck this place was when we first saw it, she boasted; that's why it was so cheap, but my husband fixed it up, all of it. Then he went back to being a fisherman.

The stories went on, Sunday by Sunday, for three months, but in July they stopped. The oats and barley har-vest was being got in, and Madame Patin now had a double amount of cooking to do every day, for she helped out the farmers' wives with their twice-daily task of taking food and drink to the labourers in the fields. Additional seasonal workers had arrived to do the harvesting, and they too had to be fed. Madame Patin gave a hand with this not only to make an extra bit of money but because it was a way of meeting her neighbours from the farms and having a chat. She would go off with two loaded baskets, stay to help with the harvesting for a couple of hours or so, and then come home again. She liked doing this in the early evening, when she rarely had customers in the shop and had got everything done in the house.

—You're to guard the place, she said to me: I trust you. You're the guardian of the house while I'm out.

She left me minding the bar, now that she had decided I was competent and knew what I was about. On my first time alone I did what I had been wanting to do for weeks. I opened the door to her bedroom and peeped inside. Wallpaper flowered with pink roses, a picture of the Virgin above the big bed, a photograph, of a man I assumed must be her dead husband, on the table next to it. He had wavy hair and a beard.

My curiosity satisfied, I got on with my new job. Summer visitors who had driven over from Etretat for the afternoon would drift in for a drink, and I would serve them. Walkers making along the cliff paths would drop down into the village and find a café and happily come in. I found myself serving food as well. People asked for something to eat and so I gave it to them.

At first it happened by accident. A couple of tourists walked up the road from the beach, came in, and called through into the kitchen that they were hungry and could I cook them anything? I was washing up. I shouted back that I was coming; to wait just a minute. I heard them laughing, amused and impatient, as I dried my hands on my apron and hurried over to the hatch.

She had dark eyes and hair, almost black. She was little, but she looked imperious as a queen in a fairy tale. He was more of a typical Norman, solid-fleshed and blue-eyed, with brown hair sticking out all over his head, and a moustache. She looked less happy than he but perhaps that was because her beauty made her seem more serious. He smiled like a boy. They were smartly dressed, she wearing a big flowered hat and carrying a flounced parasol and he twirling a straw boater in one hand. The boater looked brand new, as though he'd bought it specially to go out with her.

I gawped at them and opened my mouth to say no. I was flustered by this new demand. But then I remembered there were plenty of boiled potatoes in cream sauce left over from what we had eaten at midday, and that surely Madame Patin would not be angry if I made us some money by selling it to customers who wanted it. I put the re-heated food on a tray, with some bread and ham on the side, and a jug of cider, and carried it through the hatch door. I was amazed at my nonchalance, but the couple accepted their meal as though it were the most natural thing in the world that a café should serve them with food. When my employer returned home that evening she nodded in approval.

—Good girl, she said: I don't know why I didn't think of that before.

With the business so expanded I was kept very active. Since I was now an adequate cook, I often made the midday *déjeuners* we ate ourselves and then also gave to people, and if we ran out of what we had eaten there was always some *saucisson* or terrine to serve them, or an omelette, with a bowl of salad from the garden. It was the sort of food city people expected from a country café, simple and rustic, and you could see them relishing what felt like the informality and spontaneity of it all. We fed the harvesters well, because they worked so hard, and then the tourists also benefited from any leftovers in that direction. To them a slice of potato galette, a glass of ice-cold cider, was a quaint luxury. They wouldn't get that from their cooks in town. Oh my dear, they exclaimed happily to one another: isn't this delightful! And then when I charged them so little they would often give me a large tip on top.

—You're coming on, Madame Patin remarked to me: you're becoming quite a businesswoman.

She and I remained technically employer and servant. She was my mistress. We both acknowledged that. She paid me my wages and could turn me out at any time if I slacked at my work or misbehaved. I knew she felt obliged to concern herself with my wellbeing, as part of her duty towards me. She checked that I changed my clothes regularly and put on a clean chemise and stockings when I should; she sent me down to run on the beach every day to get some fresh air; she provided me with plenty of good food; she made sure I got enough sleep. I worked very hard, but then, so did she, and so did everyone else in the village. Like all the other women in Blessetot she was responsible for cleaning and cooking, making and mending the clothes, growing the vegetables, raising the poultry, milking the cow, as well as keeping her shop and running her bar. She had done two people's work. But now I had come she had someone to help her and share her work. She had begun to feel she could rely on me and I was proud of this. We had become a team, yoked together, tugging our plough side by side. I had some dignity in my own eyes now, because someone needed me and what I had to give.

One morning in early August I was walking back from the beach with a basketful of crabs I had just bought from the fisherman unloading his catch, which we were going to cook and then serve in the bar. I swung my basket to and fro, enjoying the strong, fishy smell of crab, and the way that the fisherman knew me well by now and called me by name, and the fact that the damp salt wind was blowing off the sea and the clouds were scudding along overhead in the blue sky. I had a place in this world; my feet traced connections between the house and the beach, back and forth between them, or to the *potager* and back, or to the church. I might have made no friends of my own age, but nonetheless I was a part of the village; I belonged in it; people knew me and accepted me. The local boys left me alone because I was so odd and so skinny; they reserved their aggressive teasing for prettier girls; but their parents, when they saw me, greeted me as a matter of course, as though I'd always lived there. And when I entered the kitchen Madame Patin looked up from the mayonnaise she was whisking and nodded at me in her matter-of-fact way, with one of her quick small smiles.

We stood at the table together, she whipping her glossy yellow streak of yolks and oil, I cracking open and cleaning the crabs. We often worked together like this, without speaking. It was a busy, goodhumoured silence, which she would break with some comment or other, swearing at an egg-thickened sauce if it threatened to curdle, or exclaiming at how much we still had to do, or instructing me on a better way to pull the beards off mussels or gut fish. She was often brusque, which somehow pleased me. I liked not needing special treatment. She never praised me much, certainly not regularly, and I didn't mind, for I knew that this taking me for granted indicated that she considered me to be like herself, capable, competent. On the other hand, whenever I proved for the first time that I could do something well, whether it was making a bed properly with sheets mitred at the corners or planting out onions, then she would compliment me. She recognised the learning of a new skill, a job well done.

The crab shins were flecked red and white, flaring with bristly hairs. I cracked them off one by one, tearing the muscly joints. I piled the meat, mixed with mayonnaise, back into the shell. Sunlight moved over our hands busy on the table. Suddenly I felt as though I were like the room, filled with light. It made me want to cry. It was happiness, flowing into me and filling me and spilling out of my eyes down my cheeks. I was floating like a cloud in the sky. I loved Madame Patin. I had never loved anyone before. This was what it must be like to have a mother, I thought, this loving her and being allowed to be near her; normal and real; the most ordinary thing in the world. Love was so precious, yet it was so strong. It lifted me up and made me want to do great things. It made me capable of enduring anything.

Tears ran down the side of my nose and over my cheeks. They collected at the corner of my mouth where they tasted salt. I kept my head down and went on working, so that Madame Patin should not see me crying, but she noticed anyway.

—What are you crying for? she enquired: you silly girl, crying never helped anything.

She did not sound as irritated as the words she spoke. She would often do that, say something harsh then soften it with a smile. She felt obliged to utter the wise dictum, whatever it was, but her sympathy lurked underneath, and she would measure it out carefully if she thought you merited it, like putting a spoonful of eau-de-vie into coffee to give you courage on a cold morning. She waited while I found my handkerchief and blew my nose, and then she started talking, telling me some story or other to take my mind off what she supposed were my woes. I couldn't find the words to tell her I had been crying from happiness. It went on moving up and down inside me, like the waves swelling and breaking on the beach. I contained it. I held it carefully, so that it should last and not leak away. Now that it had arrived I wanted to keep it safe. Happiness would be my fuel. It would keep me alive, like air, like water. Happiness came from loving and feeling loved. Love fed me; love dandled me; love made me want to run and fly. That was what I thought then, before Frédéric Montjean arrived to turn my life upside down and teach me how destructive love can also be.

By the end of the first week of August the oats and barley had all been got in, and the wheat harvest was in full swing. The weather held. People laboured in the fields under canopies of blue, day after day, until late into the night. Madame Patin came home from her trips to the fields with a sunburnt face. She wore a big white linen cap to cover her hair, like all the women did, with flaps hanging down to protect her forehead and neck, but the sun found its way under these and turned her skin brown. Her forearms were brown too, and the little V at the base of her throat.

We were beginning to prepare for the village fête, which was always held on the second Saturday in August. Being a newcomer, I was interested to see how everything was done. At the same time, wanting to be more than an onlooker, to demonstrate that I felt part of village life, I was looking forward to joining in the celebrations. Small as the village was, these would be elaborate. High Mass mid-morning would be followed, after everyone had eaten their feast-day lunch, by a procession, which, as far as I could understand, was a combination of a pilgrimage to a shrine to the Virgin in one of the fields and a walk beating the bounds of the parish. Later in the afternoon there would be a puppet show for the children, and then in the evening a big supper followed by a dance. The old people were put in charge of the preparations, with the younger children to help them, while everybody else continued to give a hand in the fields. Madame Patin and I were to organise the food: the *casse-croute* of bread and ham taken around in baskets after the walk, when everyone reassembled in front of the church, and the roast-mutton feast at night. We were going to eat outside. Tables made of planks on trestles were put up next to the temporary dance floor, and barrels of cider set up alongside. People would bring their own benches and chairs, and their own knives and forks and plates.

I decorated the bar the day before, because we expected a lot of thirsty customers to flock in after mass, and we wanted to create a festive atmosphere that would encourage good humour and, let's be honest, the plentiful consumption of drink. I put a tumbler of white daisies and pink dahlias, picked from the flowerbed in our vegetable garden, on each table, and then climbed on a bench to drape blue paper streamers around the frame of the big mirror. When I stood back to check that the fluttering ribbons hung as they should I looked at my reflection at the same time.

She was a thin, fair-haired girl who put out a finger and rubbed the glass. My double's fingertip met mine. She gazed at me consideringly, pursing her mouth. It wasn't vanity, exactly, more a sort of anxious query, that kept me there, closely regarding her. Would anyone ask me to dance? Did I want them to? I could not be sure. To me boys were strange creatures, foreign as mermen, and I did not know what to say to them. They hadn't interested me much so far. I had been quite content with my life as it was. But seeing the wooden dais being built in the little square outside the church, for the dancing, had given me a sudden idea of a new form of pleasure, a different element in which I might sink or swim. I thought of the mermaid, who had no legs and therefore couldn't walk let alone dance, hauling herself slowly and painfully up the beach. I shrugged at myself. I blew out my cheeks, huffed and puffed, to turn the worry into a joke. Then I polished off the cloud of mist my breath had made and turned away. I left behind me, in the swimmy depths of the mirror, that mermaid-girl intrigued by the possibility of dancing and flirting. I stepped out of the buoyant water, onto dry land. Madame Patin was calling for me, and I slipped happily back into my place at her side where by now I knew exactly what to do. Here I was certain of what needed to be accomplished.

She was standing at the kitchen table, rolling out the pastry for the apple tarts we would serve the following night. I set to in a hurry, oiling tart tins with a brush dipped in melted butter, and then peeling the apples. I'd been dawdling in the bar, her sharp glance reminded me, and I had some catching up to do.

I quartered and sliced a basketful of apples, sprinkled them with sugar and set them aside. I hadn't done as many as we needed, so I ran upstairs to fetch down another tray from the storeroom next to my bedroom.

The door to the first storeroom was open. I went to close it, thinking as I did so how I still hadn't got around to oiling the hinges after all this time, and glanced casually inside. The bed which stood under the window, piled with old curtains and sewing-things, had been cleared, and freshly made up with sheets, pillow and quilt. The sacks and boxes of dry goods that normally crowded the centre of the floor had been moved and neatly stacked against the wall. The seat of a wooden chair, which I recognised as one of our kitchen ones, supported a basin and jug, and a white towel, neatly folded, one of Madame Patin's best, had been hung over the chair's back. I stared, wondering, then went into the neighbouring attic and picked up a box of apples.

Back downstairs Madame Patin was fitting circles of white pastry into tart tins. She did it very fast, picking up each floppy halo by pushing her flour-dusted palms half underneath it, lifting it off the table-top, up into the air a little, flapping it dangling over the rolling-pin and then flipping it forwards. The pastry landed softly, slumped, and she shook and eased it in, a loose white covering that hid the tin in drapes of dough. She inserted a knife at the edge of these folds and ran it round, cutting off the plump overhang with quick strokes, then pressed the remaining disc lightly down and against the fluted sides of the tin. Finally she crimped the top edge, pinching it between finger and thumb to crease it into ripples, and pricked the base with a fork. The pastry went into the oven for a few minutes to bake blind while I sliced apples for the filling as fast as possible, my hands clotted with sweet juice I paused from time to time to lick off.

She knew what I'd seen upstairs, of course. She also knew I wouldn't ask her about it. Her life and her house were hers. It was none of my business.

Oh but it was. It was. It was in her house that I had started living for the first time. Up until then, because I had known no better, I had been merely existing; holding my breath; until my real life could start. At the age of sixteen, when others start to feel grownup, I had been allowed to have a second go, a childhood all over again, with her at its centre as the person I loved. Her well-kept little house, and every object in it, was saturated, for me, with the most tender feelings and memories, my earliest experiences of joy. Everything in that house was beautiful, to me, because I looked at it with love; the house held me; and I held the house inside me at the same time. The twig broom with which I swept out the poultry sheds, the wire basket in which I swung the salad dry, the little porcelain dish, oval and white, in which radishes were served for the hors d'oeuvre, the pierced tin bowl next to the sink that held the nail brush and soap, all these were precious to me. They were themselves, simple and pleasing and useful, and also they glowed with particular meaning. They constructed my self; they had witnessed my beginnings in that house; they preserved my history. When items in the house got moved or disarranged, something in me moved too. I didn't want other people coming in and disrupting us. Madame Patin was the house, and I had begun to believe that I was also. The house was us, was ours; we shared it. So a guest coming in snarled up our pattern like a snagged thread. I wanted to wield my scissors and cut off the loose end, make the weave smooth again.

I loved her too much. It wasn't obvious to me then. I had few words for what was happening inside me. I'd had little practice in thinking about what I felt. I hadn't known it mattered. In the orphanage we were merely brutes, to be kept docile and clean, to be of use. No one there, for all the lip-service paid to religion, had ever suggested that the individual soul had any importance. Now, loving Madame Patin, I discovered I had a soul.

Looking back, what I also see is the ferocity of my love. My desperation; my possessiveness. That wasn't her fault. She'd seen how starved I was, and had been kind to me. She hadn't bargained for me to cling to her fast as a limpet to a rock. It wasn't her way to scold me directly or prise me off. Ever since that day when I cried over my basket of crabs she had tempered her briskness with moments of gentleness.

She accepted my peculiarity, which made me love her all
the more; she was trying to help me grow up, to teach me
better by treating me as a sane person worthy of affection
and esteem. But, God knows, I was not sane; I was a hungry
child; I was a lover; I wanted to stay with her in her house
for ever; I wanted nothing to change; and I wasn't ready to
admit there were others she might love.

I watched her eyes flicker as she considered whether to
say anything. Her face was slightly pink, which meant that
she was embarrassed. She gave a tiny sigh, which I trans-
lated easily. She had decided it would make her life easier to
tell me and just get it over with. It was characteristic of her,
at the rare moments she felt awkward about something, to
announce it obliquely, as a fact she was not responsible for.
She owed me no explanations, after all, yet obviously she
wanted to give me the information. So she tossed it in, like
a pinch of sugar onto the apples. She pretended it was
something I knew already. Her hands were very busy picking up leftover strips of dough and kneading them lightly
into a ball. Her voice was casual.

—After this I want you to grease the spits and take
them over to the square ready for putting up tomorrow
afternoon. Have you ever roasted lamb on a spit before? It's
quite a skill. But I dare say my cousin will give us a hand.

I kept my eyes on the blade of my knife, the coil of shiny
peel looping over my fingers. I made my voice sound as off-
hand as hers.

—Your cousin?

Now, since I'd asked her, she could tell me. It was my fault for exhibiting curiosity, not hers for inviting strange men to stay in the house.

—Yes, of course. We'll be one extra tomorrow night. My cousin is coming to stay for the fête, as usual, for a few days. Go and fetch the apricot jam, will you? I want to start making the glaze.

A little later we stood back and admired our handiwork. We had filled the sweet-pastry shells with flat spirals of apple slices tossed in butter and calvados; we had glazed them with apricot jam boiled down to a syrup; we had lined them up in rows on the kitchen table, to cook in batches of four at a time. Now Madame Patin left me in charge of the oven while she went off to the wine cellar to count out bottles of cider. I checked that the first lot of tarts were turning the requisite biscuity gold. Then for some reason, driven by an impulse too strong to ignore, I walked straight across the kitchen, opened the door of Madame Patin's bedroom, and slipped inside.

In all these months of living with her, I had opened that door only once before, and that without permission. She guarded her privacy, and I had respected that. When we needed clean tablecloths or towels, it was she who went to fetch them from the linen cupboard she kept in there. The bedroom was her domain which I did not enter, just as she let my little attic room alone and left it to me to clean and tidy it. We had our own, separate places, which was impor-tant in such a tiny house. You would have been forever tripping over each other unless you had learned, as we had, how to dart and swivel round each other, that kitchen ballet of being handy and neat, that other gift of knowing when to be silent and not talk, leaving each other in peace. But the most sensible rules tempt you, at some point, to break them. The most fascinating rooms are the ones you are forbidden to go into. My urgent and sudden need to see again what the room was like cut across my knowledge that what I was doing was wrong, I said to myself that I just wanted to take another tiny look; I wouldn't be doing any harm.

This time I went right inside. It was a small, square apartment, which the double bed nearly filled. The linen cupboard took up almost all one wall, and the small night-table next to the bed was wedged in alongside the wash-stand under the window. The shutters were open and folded back, and the casement was pushed wide, to let in the sum-mer air. Her two big square pillows lay quietly side by side, like two friends sleeping next to each other, resting on the bolster with its starched cover fastened by drawstrings threaded through its frilled edges. The white coverlet was folded back over the wooden foot of the bed, revealing the blue quilt. I quickly put out my hand and stroked all these things just so that I could say to myself later that I had. An urge inside me dictated what to do, and I obeyed it. I inspected her billowy white nightdress, which was flung across the corner of the bed, the stencilled pink geometric pattern on her enamel basin and jug, her brush and comb and bottle of eau-de-Cologne, the pair of black ankle-boots that stood under the window, the photograph of the dead sailor that graced the night-table. A second framed photograph, that I had not noticed when I looked into the room before, was propped behind the first. I lifted it up to see it better. It showed Madame Patin standing stiffly and unsmilingly next to her husband. They both looked very young, and as though their clothes hurt. I thought perhaps they had posed for that picture on their wedding day. I looked back at the bed. I walked quickly round it, and pressed my face briefly onto each of the pillows in turn, cheek to cheek with the smooth linen, resting my head on its softness that smelled of her, just for a moment, then smoothing out the traces with my hand. Then I went out, closing the door gently behind me, back into the kitchen. When she came in, I was squatting in front of the open oven, removing a tray of perfectly browned and gilded tarts.

Next morning we went to High Mass, along with everybody else. We slipped out just before the end, to open up the bar. First of all, though, since we had been fasting from midnight in order to go to Holy Communion, we made ourselves a feast-day late breakfast. Hot chocolate and a piece of brioche. More substantial than the papery host I had received on my tongue twenty minutes before. The brioche, leavened with yeast, had been baked in a tall flared tin from which it had burst exuberantly like a mushroom, with a domed top that was shiny and brown. Under this crisp crust the brioche was fresh and spongy, tasting of eggs and salt and butter, a yellowish wedge of lightness, spun holes, in my fingers. I tore off soft shreds one at a time and tried to eat as slowly as possible, to make it last.

Madame Patin laughed at me and cut us both another piece. We drank strong, bitter black chocolate that had been sweetened with sugar and whisked to a froth with milk. Sunlight streamed through the open window and sparkled on the blue and white tiles surrounding the white porcelain sink. This was my holy mass; this was my praying and my Communion; sitting for ten minutes with Madame Patin in the light-filled kitchen; goodness and plenty in the land of milk and honey; the land of spices; paradise. Then we jumped up, put on our clean aprons, and went into the bar.

When I turned round an hour later, picking up a tray packed with glass towers of tumblers, to carry it through into the kitchen, there he was. The bar was starting to empty, as people began to drift away for the midday meal. The door onto the street was open, curtained in a transparent haze of blue tobacco smoke with the sun striking through it. Sun patched the wooden floor and held dancing motes of dust in its beams. Sun haloed the men's heads and burnished their profiles. They were red-cheeked and smiling, telling each other jokes, making friendly digs, teasing Madame Patin as she darted in and out of the little groups with her jug of cider clasped in her hands, a cloth tucked by one corner into her waistband, her face flushed under her starched cap. She gave as good as she got, shooting back repartee smartly as she passed, turning her head, as she went off, to have the last word. And there he suddenly was next to her, his head bent to listen to what she was saying, his hands rolling a cigarette. I hadn't seen him come in. He stood in the middle of the floor as though he'd been there all morning, relaxed, completely at ease. He was tall and solid, with eyes black as sloes in his weatherbeaten face. He had closely cropped black hair, and a black moustache. His mouth, under that silky mound of blackness, looked very red. He was dressed in town clothes, some sort of tweed suit, as though he'd been travelling. I spotted his valise, which he had put down by the door.

We ate in the bar that day, with the curé, and a couple of old people Madame Patin had invited because they were on their own with no family to go to. We pushed two tables together, end to end, and flung a cloth over them, and put benches along the two sides. I did the serving, which pleased me, because it meant I could watch everyone's faces and try to work out what was happening. Madame Patin sat composedly next to the curé, and Frédéric Montjean on his other side. The two men seemed to know each other, and exchanged politenesses.

—So how's life in the china trade? You're looking very well on it.

—Not too good, father, in fact. I'm tired of being a salesman, on the road all the time. I'm thinking of looking for a different job altogether.

I passed round the plates of rabbit terrine, then sat down to eat mine at the end of the table, next to our neighbours, the old lady whose house abutted ours on the left-hand side. She didn't speak to me and I didn't expect her to. I was too young for her to be interested in anything I might have to say; I was not related to her; I was a servant; and, besides, she was concentrating on the delicate task of chewing her rabbit with the few teeth she had left. I ate my helping as fast as possible, then got up and went into the kitchen to dish up the roast chicken. When I came back in with it, I hesitated, not sure whom to give it to. Madame Patin caught my eye and jerked her chin. I set down the platter of chicken in front of Frédéric Montjean and watched him carve it as though he were indeed the man of the house and dished out the food as a matter of course.

Cider foamed into tumblers. There was silence while food vanished off plates and then everybody talked at once. The curé, protesting in order to save face, accepted a tot of calvados in between courses, just like everyone else. Finally he took the old people off with him, sleepy and pink-cheeked, back to their houses, to have a nap. I got on with the washing-up, of which there was plenty. Frédéric Montjean lounged on at table in the bar, his chair pushed back, his legs stretched out in front of him. Every time I turned round and glanced back through the hatch I could see him in the mirror, talking to Madame Patin.

She had moved up a place, into the curé's seat, and sat leaning forward, her face animated and dreamy by turn, her left elbow on the table and her hand supporting her chin, the fingers of her right hand playing with the crumbs on the cloth, sweeping them into little hills. They chatted companionably together, relatives who got on well, two apples off the same tree. I reasoned that she had known him all her life; they had perhaps grown up together; of course she would treat him like a friend; they had news to exchange, family gossip to pass on and enjoy. But I felt dull and heavy, as thought I'd eaten too much.

He accompanied her when she brought their coffee cups into the kitchen. I'd left the pots and pans till last and was up to my elbows in creamy black suds. My apron was wet; my face was hot; I was sweaty with effort; I was tired. I glanced round when they came in then got on with what I was doing. He reached a hand past me for the matches, which we kept on the right of the sink, just as though he were in his own home, and lit his cigarette. His freedom with her things really affronted me but I was determined not to show it. I concentrated on scrubbing grease off the bottom of the roasting tin.

—So you're Geneviève, he said: hello Geneviève.

I thought that he'd had all lunchtime to be introduced to me, only he hadn't bothered. I didn't like him making so free with my name, either.

— Geneviève Delange, I corrected him.

—What kind of angelic name is that, he said, laughing: Mademoiselle Delange, you must have had a heavenly conception like the Virgin. Too much of a mouthful for me. I think I'll call you Jenny.

Madame Patin unloaded the cups and saucers one by one onto the draining-board.

—She's not a pet, she said: her name is Geneviève.

He went out, still laughing. He came back, carrying his valise, and she helped him lug it upstairs. I heard their footsteps tapping to and fro across the wooden floor as she showed him his room and where everything was.

I got through the rest of the day. There was plenty to do, and to see. In the evening I took my turn at the spit; I helped fry vats of potatoes; I ran back and forth in between the long tables with dishes of meat, baskets of bread, serving all the villagers. The café was closed; we had set up a makeshift bar near the cooking place. Everyone stayed at table for a long time, until it began to get dark and the Chinese lanterns were lit. Later on, withdrawn into the shadows, well away from the lights, I watched the fiddler and the accordionist tune up, and the dancing begin. Later still, while the ball was still going strong, Madame Patin found me sitting on a cider barrel yawning my head off, and shooed me away home.

—Go on, she said: you've worked hard all day; you're not dancing; go to bed. Next year we'll find you a partner. Trouble with you is, you're too shy.

She clapped me on the shoulder and smiled at me. I went without a backward look. I fumbled my way upstairs, pulled off my clothes, extinguished my candle and fell gratefully into bed. Tired as I was, I lay awake and listened for the music finally to die down and announce their return, the back door opening then shutting, the bolts being drawn across. His footsteps did not clump up the stairs. The door of the room next to mine did not creak open and shut on its unoiled hinges. The only creaking sound came from her bed downstairs, directly under mine, as loud and regular and rhythmic as the dancing in the square.

We kept the coffee-pot on a shelf to the left of the stove, along with the jars of flour, sugar, salt and spices we used every day. The jars were of palest green enamel, with a gold stripe running round the upper and lower rim of each, and loose lids topped with little buds you grasped between finger and thumb when you wanted to lift them off. I liked these jars, drawn up in a row like soldiers doing their duty, each one with the name of its contents printed on its chest in dark green and gold. Over the years they had become bashed about a bit, in places the enamel knocked off and patches of black showing underneath, but that only added to their charm. Every item in that kitchen was like a friend to me, quirky and helpful; there was nothing in it that didn't attract and please me.

I tried not to have favourites too obviously, for that did not seem fair; all the utensils deserved to be in regular use; I made sure I rotated the usage of saucepans from one meal to the next, so that each one in turn saw the light of day outside the cupboard; and when I laid the table I used different knives and forks every time from our motley collection. I knew in my heart that my favourite fork was the one with the thin tines and the worn black handle studded with tiny gold nails, but I didn't pick it out for myself every time it came to hand. I let the other forks have a go at being serviceable too.

The coffee-pot was single, one of a kind, and so could not invite comparisons or suffer from preferences. I loved it because its pale blue enamel surface was mottled and swirled in the manner of seawater. Even the black bruises that patched its battered lid and rim had curved shapes. It was generous-sized enough to make three big bowls of coffee, and so now it came into its own.

The day after the fête was a Sunday. I got up as I always did when I heard the Angelus bell ring out just before seven o'clock, and went about doing my habitual chores: milking the cow, feeding the dog, riddling the stove then carrying the tray of ash outside. Usually even when I was tired I liked being in on the start of a new day: all its emptiness and promise stretching ahead. I liked smelling the invisible sea on the breeze; hearing the cocks crack the silence like an egg with their exuberant crowing; shivering a bit in the cold, fresh air; seeing the sun glimmer gold behind the mist. All this beauty was renewed each dawn; perfect, because nothing had happened to spoil it. But this morning I felt out of sorts and glum. My insides were knotted up like a bag of stones. Everything was too bright; the brick wall of the yard glared and hurt my eyes. When I stumbled blearily back into the kitchen there he was clattering down the stairs, shameless, as though he'd slept in his own room all night, and calling for his breakfast.

He had put a clean shirt on, but not a collar. The bulk of white linen flowed about him like a smock, open at the throat, not tucked into his trousers. He was yawning and unshaven, his hair sticking up on end. Great gusts of yawns he was sending out, his hand going up carelessly to half cover his red mouth and caress his black moustache.

—Make me some coffee, will you, Geneviève, he said through a yawn: there's a good girl.

We didn't always have the treat of coffee on Sunday morning. It was expensive; a luxury. On other mornings we might drink broth, or perhaps chicory, or watery chocolate. It depended on Madame Patin's mood, and on the state of our finances. Broth was, obviously, the cheapest, being homemade, and capable of being endlessly thinned down. So on lean days that's what we had. On feast days we had chocolate enriched with milk, and on days of medium rejoicing, days off, which is what Sunday was supposed to be, we had coffee if our finances could stand it.

I always made the coffee. It was a task I enjoyed, involving the rituals of measuring out the dented, polished beans into the wooden grinder then energetically whirling the metal handle round on top before extracting the grains, minced to a rough powder, from the little drawer below. I put this brown rubbly heap into the top part of the coffee-pot, resting on its black mesh, and poured boiling water through it. Then I removed the filter section from the tall pot, replaced its lid, and carried the coffee over to the kitchen table where Madame Patin would be waiting. I loved the smell of coffee being made, and I had learned that you had to make it strong, or it would never taste as good as it smelled. Fresh hot coffee was as fragrant as some kind of black flower. In your mouth it was both bitter and rich. The hot milk we added to it in our bowls made it taste smooth.

—We don't always have coffee on Sundays, I started saying.

Madame Patin's voice spoke calmly behind me.

—This morning we'll have coffee, Geneviève.

I whirled round. She closed the door of her bedroom and came into the kitchen on neatly slippered feet. Her hair was covered by a fresh white cap, and her face was glowing from its wash in cold water. She looked absolutely as she always did in the mornings: ready, capable, self-possessed. Confident and normal; as usual. She caught my glance and spoke more sharply.

—Wake up, child, you're half asleep.

From then on he had coffee whenever he felt like it. I hated having to wait on him and serve him but I had no choice. It became one of my jobs. He had moved in without anything having been said, not to me at any rate; he was living with us; and I had to treat him with respect as though he were my boss, which he was not. I especially dis-

liked having to make and then pour him coffee. The weekly
ritual of Sunday morning was overturned and knocked
aside. The mottled blue coffee-pot was less special now.
When I glanced at it during the week it didn't signify, any
longer, the prospect of a precious moment shared with
Madame Patin. It was now just a utensil to which he had
access whenever he wanted. He didn't love the coffee-pot
like I did. He just made use of it. To him it was simply
there to serve him and that was that. I hated him for make
me love coffee less. For not respecting it. One morning he
was late getting up and then complained his coffee was
cold. He blamed me, but it was his fault. I said nothing,
just tipped the contents of his bowl out of the back door
and put a saucepan of water back on to boil. Re-heated coffee tastes horrible, so I wasn't going to serve him that and
give him the chance to criticise me again.

He was a fussy and demanding eater. He had a way of
sticking his fork into a dish, picking up a mouthful, and
tasting cautiously, that really drove me wild. I thought he
should be grateful that we cooked him such delicious food,
but he treated us as though he were a rich tourist eating in
the café, always ready to complain. There he was at every
meal, prodding, chewing, considering. Then commenting.
The stew was overcooked and therefore tasteless; the fried
potatoes were not crisp enough; the salad leaves were too
coarse and fit only for the pigs. He would only eat the hearts.
Madame Patin mostly laughed at him, but she looked anxious too. She wanted to please him and he was destroying

her confidence. From my end of the table I glowered at him in silence. My way of showing how much I hated him was not to speak to him. I didn't think he noticed my sulks and frowns, but it gave me a small, bleak satisfaction to ignore him. In my private, inside world he did not exist. No words attached to him, so that if I concentrated on looking down at my plate I could pretend he was not in fact there.

This defence was not enough. I overheard him saying to her more than once: having to eat with that sullen girl glaring at me all the time gives me indigestion, why can't she learn some better manners, for Christ's sake? Anyone would think she wasn't the servant, the way she carries on.

Madame Patin would reply soothingly that I was just shy, that I needed time to get used to having him around, that I did not mean to be rude, and so on. It was almost worth having to put up with him in order to hear her stick up for me. But even her patience wore thin eventually. I had been pushing her to see how far I could go and she had had enough of it.

One Saturday morning in early September she said to me: Geneviève, you ought to have some more regular time off. From now on you're to go out on Sunday afternoons; that's going to be your half-holiday every week; you take your lunch with you, some bread and cheese wrapped up in your pocket, and do whatever you like. I don't need you on Sunday afternoons; the bar is closed then as you very well know; you need to get out more.

It was my own fault. Who could blame her for wanting to get rid of me for a bit, for wanting to spend time alone with him on the only day of the whole week with some leisure in it? They had to get up reasonably early on Sundays, in order to open up the bar for the customers coming in after the first mass and then after High Mass, but if I was sent out of the way on Sunday afternoons then they would be able to go back to bed together in peace without having to worry that I was listening to them in the kitchen and hating them through the wall. That much was obvious to me.

—Yes, ma'am, I said.

—Try and make an effort, will you? she asked; you've worked very well here. I should be sorry to lose you.

We were tidying up the vegetable garden for the end of summer. We still had some rows of late-sown lettuces, some pumpkins swelling up orangey-red, some marrows trailing their huge hairy fans and yellow trumpets along the ground, some early-planted leeks coming up to full maturity, fattening nicely next to the last of the feathery-headed spread of the carrots. It was a golden day, full of sweetness, clear light like blown amber glass, the air sparkling like cider, tart and tingling on your tongue, with a cool wind blowing through the heat of the sun. Yellow leaves had begun whirling down from the trees. The earth smelled of ripeness, of fruits. I was harvesting the beetroot crop, carefully digging up each one with a fork, loosening the soil around it and then tugging it up by its purple leaves.

Outdoors, working side by side with my employer, my face caressed by the sun and cooled by the wind, I was happy. Nothing else mattered except the autumn day, full in my hand like a bunch of grapes running with juice. The delicate sunlight, the scent of pears ripening nearby, the rough perfume of the pink and rust and salmon dahlias blooming against the lichen-encrusted wall, filled me with peace. I'd forgotten, for the moment, all my sorrows, my jealousy. I'd been able to forget him, because he was back in the house, sprawled smoking in the bar. But at Madame Patin's words fear filled my heart. My eyes flew to her.

She was picking over the parsley patch, harvesting bunches of frilly greenness and grubbing up the weeds that grew in amongst it. She was concentrating, as she always did, on what she was doing, wheedling out the roots of docks and stinging nettles and casting them into a pile at her side. To perform a job well, she always told me, you had to pay it sufficient attention. So her voice sounded as calm and detached as though she were pointing out to me how well the brass-coloured marigolds planted around the herb bed were still doing, flowering in their dark yellow profusion as though it were still July. As her fingers, probing for weeds, disturbed the marigolds' petals, I caught a sudden waft of their powerful scent and sneezed, so that I was not obliged immediately to reply.

She sat back on her haunches, wiping her forehead with one hand and looked severely at me.

—If you go on misbehaving like this, she warned me: I shan't be able to keep you. You must realise that. Be a sensible girl and stop being silly.

Her house was my home and she was threatening to turn me out. I was drowning in panic. She'd snatched my oars and thrown me overboard and I could not swim. I managed to get a few words out, because clearly she expected me to. I would have said anything she wanted at that point. I blurted out some kind of apology and we returned to the café, carrying our tools and our baskets of vegetables. I felt anger sowing itself inside me, then rapidly ballooning like a monster pumpkin; I could not prevent its growth; it was the season of bitterness; rage was my prize and I watered it in secret and hugged it silently to myself.

The next day was Sunday. I made the coffee and left the pot standing on the side of the stove, to keep warm. Before they appeared I poured out a bowl for myself and took it outside. I drank it sitting on the back step. I ate some bread. I was too hungry to keep my fast, and so I didn't go to Holy Communion. I sat as far away from Madame Patin and her lodger as possible.

As usual, we did brisk business in the bar after High Mass. Customers crowded in, and I poured, fetched, wiped, carried. I listened to the conversations going on around me and replied cheerfully to all the greetings thrown my way. I knew everyone there, and was used to the men, when they were in the mood, teasing me and poking fun. I just got on with the task in hand, banging down their orders onto the counter on top of the hatch. This particular morning I felt obliged to be on the alert, that it would be wise to watch out for possible danger. I was a little too late. I was using my eyes rather than my ears, which meant that all the village knew what was going to happen before I did. Gradually I realised that there was an additional amount of back-slapping and ribaldry going on. Watching the curé raise his glass in a toast to Madame Patin, and to Frédéric Montjean who stood at her side, and standing on tiptoe, straining to catch what was being said, I finally understood.

—May God bless this marriage, the curé droned: may you have a long and happy life together.

Their Sunday dinner was a *pot-au-feu* resting peacefully in the oven. I carved myself a thick slice of bread and cheese, wrapped it in my handkerchief, and fled out of the kitchen door, down the road, and onto the beach. I walked to the far end of the little bay and sat down on the pebbles to eat, tucked in out of the wind between two rocks, the cliff at my back. I tossed crumbs for the gulls and watched the waves tumble in onto the shore. No one else was about. They would all be in their houses, eating. If you were a mermaid, this would be the time to slink ashore, when no one was watching. But the sea tossed up no amazing creatures, only its foamy chin. It licked the beach, nuzzled and bit it, then retreated. I decided that I would go on, like the sea, and that I would do whatever was necessary to survive. Then I stood up, dusted the remaining crumbs off my skirt, and walked back and forth along the edge of the sea until I judged it was time to go home, back to Madame Patin's house.

That evening I made the soup with especial care, so that it should be exactly as he liked it, the chopped leeks tossed in butter before the potatoes and stock were added, the cooked potatoes well mashed in so that there were no lumps, a spoonful of cream added at the end, and the whole thing served just hot enough so that he did not scald his mouth. When I placed the steaming pot in front of him I arranged my face so that I did not glower. I tucked myself away at the far end of the table, keeping my head down and my elbows in, and jumping up to clear the plates as soon as we had finished. I washed up as quietly as possible, so as not to disturb their conversation, then smiled when I said goodnight and went off early to bed, leaving them comfortably ensconced by the warm stove.

I kept this up in the following weeks. Acting the contrite maid got easier with practice. He certainly swallowed my reformed behaviour, while she was too much in love to notice anything beyond the fact that I had ceased being such a nuisance. Playing the hypocrite demanded a certain skill, I felt, and I took some pride in it. Small comfort for what felt like the end of the world.

—What I love about our weather, Madame Patin told me at the beginning of October: is the way that it weaves the seasons one into another. Like a good darn. You can't see its threads in the knitting, and you're not sure it's there. It keeps you on your toes all right. You never quite know what will happen next. One day you think it's summer and the next you discover it's autumn.

Later on I realised this was her way of talking about hope, a certain secret wish. Farmers and gardeners here in the country had one way of thinking about time; the yearly cycle of seasons of growth, ripeness and decay. Women, in addition, had their own time, like a layer on top, which was not quite the same. You wheeled through life and death every month, not just once a year. As Madame Patin spoke she was examining a blue stocking she'd pulled out of the heap on her lap. It had large holes in both toe and heel, and all I thought then was that it was perhaps the prospect of mending such wear and tear, making things good in preparation for the coming winter, when warm stockings were needed more than ever, that caused her to link the different times of the year, and their subtle changes, to darning and weaving. I couldn't imagine, really, what she meant. Sometimes these days her train of thought was hard to follow, when her mind jumped about all over the place.

Here in the pays de Caux, she went on, the seasons were not sharply distinct, as their names made you suppose they ought to be. Summer, for example, as we both knew, was a capricious time on our high chalk plain. In August it often rained, a fine rain that drove at your face and wetted you thoroughly, your hair and your clothes. Your feet slid this way and that in your sabots and so made holes in your stockings, such as these. Here she held the stocking up and tutted, then threaded a large-eyed needle with matching blue wool. The sea might be so rough that you dared not go near it when you walked on the beach, for fear of being knocked down by a wave and sucked into the undertow, and the fishermen waited a day or two for the storms to calm before putting out. Too many men's lives were lost at sea for them not to be cautious.

She was in a thoughtful, dreamy mood often, these days. More chatty than I'd ever known her. As though she'd begun learning a new language; new words were bursting up in her; and she needed to spell them out to herself, practise a new grammar. She was the pupil, reciting her lesson, while I listened. Frédéric had largely taken over running the bar, so that she spent more time in the kitchen, where, as of old, I was once more her willing audience. Now she was thinking of her dead husband, it was clear; she was ruminating on the past, remembering her life as a younger woman and how it had changed. She paused, and stared at the tin thimble on her finger. She wouldn't have to worry about Frédéric drowning at sea because he was not a fisherman and never would be. He was a fisher of widows, that was all, particularly good-looking widows with nice little houses, nice little businesses like cafés that brought in regular money and contributed towards a nice little nest egg for your old age.

—You've only seen the good weather here so far, she said to me: you've been lucky. The weather was lovely this summer. But we'll have to wait and see what winter will be like.

She was sitting by the stove, the basket of mending at her feet, while I stood at the kitchen table and cut up marrows for jam. Frog jam, she called it, because it looked so green. We'd had a glut of marrows in the garden, and we had all grown tired of marrow soup, marrow slices deep fried in batter, stuffed marrow, marrow rissoles, marrow purée. So jam it had to be. The rough greeny-yellow skins of the gourds were tough to peel off. I hacked at them with my knife, pretending they were the bodies of enemies. Frédéric was in the bar, as usual, where he sat after our *déjeuner* with the newspaper and his cigarettes, and a tot of calvados. Today he was playing dominoes with one of the neighbours. He'd shouted for me to bring him the box from where we kept it on the kitchen side of the hatch. So his wife and I could enjoy a peaceful time together. Like being back in what I now called the old days. Short and precious; the spring and summer weeks before he arrived. That was my idea of time. Time with her and time without her. Time before him and time after him, as rigidly separated as the Old and New Testaments. Except that he was not the Saviour. Only in the sense that he brought not peace but a sword. I heard those words read out in church one day and thought how exactly they fitted our situation, his and mine.

October was also the time of spiders. They obviously felt the cold outside, the frosty nights, and swarmed into the house. Every day, more or less, one would jump out at me from its hiding-place close to the stoves. Big spiders, on bent, hairy legs, that could move swiftly. They lurked overnight in the folds of towels and tea-cloths, wrapping themselves in these snug little tents to keep warm and dropping out of them in the morning when I shook them or got too close. At first I jumped and shrieked, and Madame Patin had to come with the dustpan and brush to sweep them away. Then I progressed into less fear. I became able to pick them up by dint of inverting a tumbler over them and sliding a playing card underneath. Then I would carry them to the back door and fling them out into the yard, admonishing them not to return. I felt they simply waited till my back was turned and then scurried back into the house. It was so cosy inside, with the red logs flickering inside the stove.

During the autumn you felt the summer cool down. It slipped away. You couldn't exactly say when it was gone for good. Day by day the sun grew less warm, the evenings chillier. The late mornings and early afternoons were still golden and sweet, very often, but their light seemed paler and more fragile, nibbled at each end by darkness and cold. The orchard grass became crusted with crackling leaves which we swept up. The winter came closer, like the spiders, like an animal wanting to be let in. You felt it rubbing its nose on the windowpane. You didn't know whether it was a foe or a friend. You felt it enticing you to go out and meet it. Something dark and mysterious waited there outside for me. It prowled up and down. It pawed the ground. I felt as though I heard it growling at night, behind the calls of the owls, but I hadn't yet caught a glimpse of it. I hadn't seen its face and didn't know its name.

I accidentally banged my knife noisily on the table. This brought Madame Patin out of her dreamy trance. She became businesslike once more.

—We need to do some more work on the house, she remarked: that middle attic, for example, badly needs repainting. I'd like you to get on with that as soon as you can.

Now that they were married, Frédéric no longer had to pretend to sleep in that little room. He openly spent his nights downstairs, with her, without fear of scandal. And she, I kept forgetting, was now called not Patin but Montjean. He called her Jeanne. I stuck to the title I'd always used.

—Yes, ma'am, I said.

—There's some whitewash in the shed, she instructed me: left over from doing the room next door. You can use that.

—Yes, ma'am, I said again.

Frédéric had insisted on painting over the wallpaper in her room. He didn't like the opulent pink roses that clambered vigorously about, twining above the mirror and blooming all round the window. He complained it was like sleeping in a flowerbed. Smothered in roses. He wasn't having that. So he had bought the whitewash, and a big brush, thrown a sheet over the furniture, and transformed the room from one day to the next. I peeped in one day, while they were both in the bar, to see how it looked. Very clean, and more bare. His brushes and shaving things stood on the *table de nuit* next to the washstand, jostling her brush and comb, and his clothes were piled neatly on the chair. His nightshirt peeped from under the right-hand pillow, and his boots stood in a row at the end of the bed. The two photographs had vanished. Also the picture of the Virgin had gone, replaced by one of two hunting dogs with pheasants in their mouths. The room smelled different to, of his sweat and soap, his hair oil and eau-de-Cologne.

He was a person who liked everything about him to be done in a particular way. He was now the master in the house, and so he made the decisions about how things should be organised. The farmers here roundabout tended to leave most domestic business, except for major decisions, to their wives, while they ruled things outside in the fields, but because Frédéric worked at home, running the bar, he supervised almost everything that we did. He had a low opinion of our ability to see to the upkeep of the house, and it is true that even in the few months I had been there I had seen its physical state deteriorate without anything being done about it. We had been too busy to do more than simply notice ceiling corners with peeling paint, or damp patches under windowsills.

He took us and the house in hand. As we entered November, rain began to fall more often, and the winds to blow more fiercely. Once or twice a slate whirled off the roof and Frédéric had to climb the ladder and fit the slate back into place. He took a long time over the job, making sure he got it exactly right. He fixed the shutters downstairs, so that they did not bang and rattle so much at night and keep us all awake. He replastered the kitchen walls, which were cracked in places we hadn't noticed. He put up new shelves, and oiled the hinges of all three attic doors, nailed down some planks in the stairs which had come loose, and gave a ferocious cut to the garden hedge.

—It must have been so hard for you, Jeanne, I heard him say one day: all on your own, with no man about the house to help you.

She had me to help her, you fool, I wanted to shout: she wasn't alone. She had me.

I couldn't do and be everything for her. There were things he gave to her, and did for her, that I couldn't. That was the lesson I was learning, day by day, and it went on hurting. I knew this pain was all my fault, because I was still such a child, refusing to accept how the real world actually was. I hated this grownup world, in which women always loved men more than girls. I wished she and I could live together at the bottom of the sea, in a cave made fast with coral and guarded by dragons.

I didn't say a word. I made up my stories in my head, where I could keep them intact, safe from being spoilt or laughed at. I didn't tell them to anyone. I watched him at his jobs around the house, reluctantly admiring him, at first, and then also determined to learn from him so that if ever he left I'd be able to do what he had done. I didn't say:

take this place. It was he who had taken mine. I made myself useful to him, fetching and carrying his chisels and hammers, hanging about to see how he fitted pieces of wood together or got screws into walls.

He was pleased by these attentions I paid him. He would grunt out his thanks when I held the ladder or rinsed out his paintbrushes. Sometimes he would stop the tuneless whistling with which he accompanied his sawing and banging, and smile at me. I caught myself acknowledging, at those moments, that he was indeed a handsome man. Even through the mists of my jealousy I could see that she felt he was good to her, doing all these things about the house. Caring for the house he cared for her too. He restored and renewed her. I could have done that, I told myself fiercely. Nonetheless, he did it, and made a good job of it. I got a glimpse of what had attracted her. I began to see that in her eyes he was more than able; he was kind.

At the same time I carried on with the tasks she set me. I whitewashed the walls of the middle attic upstairs and polished the floor. I hung new muslin curtains at the windows and turned the old ones into caps, peg-bags and jelly strainers. And babies' nappies. By December, she had the news she desired, that she was three months pregnant, and she could begin openly to talk of how she wanted the baby's bedroom to look. At first, of course, he would sleep downstairs in a cradle next to his parents' bed, but then later on, when he was weaned, he would be up here, and she would get him a little iron cot, and a nightlight, and a picture book. And so on. I didn't always listen attentively to her murmurings. They were a song she was singing to herself and did not necessarily require an audience.

Frédéric embraced her when she told him he was a father. At the same time he looked almost aghast. You could see he thought it was too soon, that he had bargained on their enjoying married life a bit longer on their own together without a child arriving to disrupt their intimacy. I was expert at reading faces by now, and I thought I understood what he felt.

She was in his arms, her face against his shoulder. She hadn't waited until they were alone together. She told us both at the same time, which did please me. She dropped the news into the conversation in that casual way of hers, as though she were discussing the price of matches or candles. I stood behind her and saw the frown flash across his eyes. Then he leaped up from his chair, where he was lounging waiting for dinner, and hugged her.

—Open a bottle of wine, Geneviève, he said to me: only wine will do for this occasion. We're going to drink to the mother and baby's health.

I fetched a bottle of the burgundy she kept for really special occasions. I pushed our tumblers aside and got out the best glasses, the stemmed ones, wiping them with a cloth before setting them on the table. After a moment's hesitation I set out three. This was not a moment for sulking. I knew she would want me to join in and celebrate her happiness. We smiled and raised our glasses. It was the first time I had tasted burgundy. A dense sweetness cut with spice. It was an autumn taste: woody; almost burnt; an elixir of all the fruits of the earth. The wine tasted of her, and of love, and of all the things I could not say. I thought that if I were not the servant but the mistress I would drink it every day.

All through dinnertime he fussed over her, being very tender and attentive. He really was doing his best to give her the reaction she wanted. She kept smiling with delight. Once or twice she reached over and patted his hand. I sat with them and joined in all the toasts they drank to the future. It was almost like being a family.

In the afternoon he vanished into the bar and drank toasts with every man who came in. By suppertime he was well drunk, lurching about the kitchen, singing, to convince himself, I thought, how really delighted he was.

Over the next four months the three of us went on shaking down, more or less, into being able to live peaceably together. I still hated seeing them kiss each other, which I thought they should not do in my presence, as though I were no more than a ball of dust in the corner, not worth bothering about or being embarrassed by, and I still found excuses to leave the room when they were sitting cooing together like a pair of wood pigeons. But I went on being polite to him, and in return he sometimes thanked me for what I did for him, when he remembered to notice that it was I who served his meals and washed his clothes and ironed his shirts.

During the winter, while the weather was very wet, when the washing could not be carried outdoors and pegged on the line in the yard, we turned the future baby's bedroom into a temporary *lingerie*. Here I hung the sheets and clothes to dry, and here I started doing the ironing, carrying up a heated iron from downstairs, so as to keep out of the way. On Sunday afternoons, if it was too rainy to go to the beach, if I grew bored sitting in my little room, hearing the rain pattering onto the roof just above my head, I would get on with the ironing.

I always liked ironing, because at the end of an hour or two I felt I had really achieved something. It is a satisfying and sensual job, your hands stroking and folding cloth, your dexterity creating neat piles of smoothed and flattened linen. Soothing too. It sets your mind free to roam about; it lets you daydream, as your arm moves to and fro and your fingers know without you telling them just how to tweak gathered edges into place, how to press collars and glide over starched shirt fronts. At the same time there was a confused pleasure in sorting out his clothes for him; I felt I dominated him when I pushed my burning iron into his handkerchiefs and held it down on a checked corner as though I were branding his flesh. While one of the few ways I could show my angry love for her was to iron her things as carefully and exquisitely as possible. I caressed her chemises devotedly then twisted their arms behind their backs; I bowed them over, captive, and they could not resist.

Out of doors I was less crazy. The sea consoled me. It cured me temporarily, like a blue fizzing dose of medicine. It sent off sparks into my brain which filled me with energy. On Sunday afternoons when it wasn't raining I worked off my sorrows by wrapping myself in a cloak and ploughing up and down the stones of the beach, pitting myself against the gale and enjoying the violence of the wind stinging my face like slaps or tears.

On Christmas Eve we went to midnight mass along with most people in the village. The crib was set up at the top of the nave. The priest came in procession with the alter-boys, carrying the china baby in his arms, and laid it in the straw-filled manger. Madame Patin sat beside me, smiling and calm. She looked like a madonna already. I remembered the picture of my patroness, St Geneviève. I thought I should pray to her, beg her to help me fight my jealousy, but I was too ashamed of how bad I was; I thought she could not possibly want to bother with a sinner like me. Also I did not want to let go of my jealousy, which was my love, my attachment. Green and bitter, perhaps, but the only fruit that grew on my tree. I didn't go to confession and ask for help there, either. I couldn't put my sin into words that I could say to a priest. I hung onto it instead. So to wilful hate and jealousy I added arrogance and pride. God was so very far off, so very high up in the sky, that he was no use to me. I didn't dare bother him. Madame Patin had been my god for too long, but now she had abandoned me.

As Madame Montjean, as I must call her, got bigger, she tired more easily. In her seventh month she took to working mostly indoors. She did all the cooking and light kitchen cleaning once more, while I continued to look after the cow, poultry and garden, and went on doing the scrubbing and washing. Also I gave Frédéric a hand in the bar so that he got a break from time to time and could sit with his cronies and play cards or dominoes. I would do the sweeping up and dusting, which I'd always done, stand at the hatch serving drinks, and come in with a tray, when he shouted for me, to clear away dirty tumblers. Occasionally I glanced into the shining surface of my old friend, the mirror, and caught sight of him watching me. A considering gaze, that I returned.

—Hasn't Geneviève got anything else to wear? he asked his wife one dinnertime in April: she needs some new clothes. Those rags she's got on are falling apart.

Those rags were the ones I'd brought with me from the orphanage, just over a year ago. I was shocked to realise that I'd never written to Sister Pauline, nor to any of the girls I had once thought of as my friends. I had forgotten all about them. I had cut myself off from them as completely as though that old life had never existed.

Madame Montjean put down her soup spoon and considered me.

—They're not just falling apart, her clothes, she remarked: they're much too small for her. My goodness, child, how you've grown. You're positively bursting out of that dress.

—You should have noticed before, her husband told her: you should get her something more decent.

I kept my eyes on my plate. I knew what he meant. I was still thin compared with other girls my age, but I had suddenly started growing. I had turned seventeen, and at this advanced age I finally looked less like a boy and more like a woman. I had brought two changes of clothes with me from the orphanage. Everything was too tight.

—And another thing, Frédéric observed: her hair is a terrible mess. You should cut it or something.

Madame Montjean looked at me thoughtfully after dinner, when we were alone together in the kitchen doing the washing-up. She was measuring me with her eyes, running them up and down and round.

—I know what we'll do, she decided: we'll cut up your two dresses to see whether we can get one new one out of them put together, and I'll alter a couple of mine for you as well. Goodness knows I can't get into them at the moment. You might as well have them.

She would be sewing for me as well as for the coming baby. I was very pleased. I was even more pleased when she helped me to wash my hair, less roughly than usual, and then sat me down in her fireside chair and snipped at my wild crop with a pair of scissors. In the past year my hair had grown to shoulder length. I wore it loose, pushing it inside a cap when necessary. Now she tidied it up. She was puzzled how to do it, at first, and so she took her time. Her comb tugged gently through the wet tangles, easing out the knots. The cool blades of the scissors brushed the back of my neck and made me shiver with delight. She left me with a curly fringe and pulled the rest to the back of my head, coiling it into a tiny chignon, the style worn by all the women in the village.

—Very nice, she said, standing back and considering: now you'll need a new cap too. I'll give you one of mine.

Wearing one of her altered dresses, and her cap, I made my appearance in the bar that Sunday. I watched myself in the mirror. I had borrowed not only her clothes but her mannerisms, her gait. I walked as she did, my tray balanced easily on one hand. I imitated her way of threading quickly and smartly between chattering groups without upsetting my burden. I turned my head and put up my chin as she used to do, when the men teased me. I thought I might borrow not only her gestures but her husband too. He might loan himself to me. He had taken my place. Now I could imagine taking hers. It was a way of being close to her again. Stepping into her shoes, fitting my feet to their shape. Pressing myself as close to her as her shadow. I was her young ghost, dancing along behind her and imitating her every move. So I smiled at Frédéric when we passed each other; I followed him with my eyes; I preened for him. I liked him looking at me and discovering that I was a pretty girl. There was a very sweet and confused feeling in all this. He had thought I was disagreeable and awkward, a misbehaved child who had to be tolerated because she was useful around the house. Now he discovered that I had some power to make him see me differently.

At dinnertime, I sat down with the two of them as usual. But contrary to my usual custom, instead of slumping silently at the far end of the table, I joined in the conversation. I laughed and chattered. Once or twice Madame Montjean looked at me in vague surprise, but she didn't seem to care very much what I did. The energy she had spent on dressing me and cutting my hair had gone, and she had relaxed back into a kind of cocoon of pregnancy. A lot of the time these days she lived inside herself, obviously thinking about the baby and praying that it would be safe and born healthy. I saw her registering a mild relief that I was at last being so friendly to her husband, before her mind drifted back to her own concerns and what was going on inside her.

But she should have minded what I did and how I behaved. I needed her to know what I was up to, to berate me and then forgive me. I needed her to act as a check on me, to confront me, to block me and wrestle with me. I needed her to behave like a mother. But she wasn't my mother; it was unreasonable to expect her to behave so; and anyway I was acting as though I were grownup and didn't need a mother at all.

The more she stared dreamily off into the distance, the more I flirted with Frédéric and the more angry I grew. Don't you realise I could be dangerous, I wanted to shout at

her: don't you realise I could do you harm? She trusted me
but her trust was worth little because it was based on igno-
rance and not caring. Long ago she had cared about how I
behaved but that was over now; it was he who mattered to
her, and now, most of all, the coming baby.

Frédéric found me upstairs that afternoon, when I was
doing the ironing in the attic *lingerie* and she was laid down
asleep on her bed, like a great beached fish. I did not hear
the door open, so well oiled now were the handle and
hinges, but I felt him come in. I felt the change of air, and I
smelled the macassar oil he put on his hair. I had a double
sheet hung on the line between me and the door, and saw
his boots pause underneath it, standing quietly side by
side, just as they did by the bed downstairs.

I wanted to laugh, and also I felt afraid. For a moment
there was silence, and then he made it clear what he wanted
and what I was to do. I could have refused and I did not
know how to refuse and I did not dare refuse and did not
want to. How could I ever have explained that in the con-
fessional? Sin was sin and that was that.

This was to be my newest service to him: to become the
confessor myself; to attend, like a confessor, welcoming and
tolerant and intimate, on the other side of the sheet; to
bend my head and listen to his furious mutter about how
his wife had lost interest and fobbed him off with talk of
headaches and thought only of the baby and how tired she
was and fell asleep so early at night, even before he came to
bed. On and on he went, while I said nothing, and ironed,

and the big sheet of their bed hung between us so that I could not see but only hear how at last his angry sad complaint turned into gasps and then into a groan. Then the boots disappeared, and the door clicked open and shut, and the treads of the stairs creaked, one by one, as he went down.

That was how we went on for some time. Since he never touched me, he swore that he was doing nothing wrong. I understood him to mean I was helping them both, by taking care of him while she was unable to. I was a place where he could put things, a kind of cupboard to contain him. I felt flattered and excited that he needed me so desperately and also I knew that I was wicked. I had imagined taking Madame Montjean's husband away from her and now that fantasy had come true.

The obscenities he recited to me, and the desires he whispered; the things he said he wanted to do to me; frightened and excited me. They aroused my curiosity. My heart dropped to between my legs, where it beat and throbbed, where it swelled, grew big and soft. This frightened me even more. So I would jump a step ahead. I would say: and then? And then? As though I were in control.

The feelings were too powerful. I was too powerful. I longed for Madame Montjean to find out what was going on, so that it would stop; I longed for her to rescue me; I knew I must have totally alienated her affection; I dreaded that she would throw me out of the house.

Once more the summer visitors came exploring along the coast and arrived in the bar asking for food and drink. Once more the harvest season flourished and the workers were out from dawn until very late, past moonrise sometimes, if the moon were bright enough to work by. Sometimes, to get a field finished, before rain threatened to spoil the standing wheat, the harvesters hung lanterns on their carts to give them just enough light to see by. They looked half crazed with tiredness when you met them next day, their eyes glittering in their thin brown faces. They had no choice. The harvest had to be got in and any sort of normal life had to be suspended for the duration.

It might have been logical for Madame Montjean to send me off with the baskets of provisions to the labourers in the fields, while she stayed at home with the baby, but she said she wanted to get out; she had been stranded in the house for six months, because of bad weather and pregnancy; and now she longed to be in the open air and to see her friends again. So that she could feed the child she took him with her. I accompanied her, carting the two baskets of food, while she carried the baby in a wicker affair with handles. She would set him down in the field being harvested, in the shade, under a hedge. He wore a floppy linen bonnet with a deep frill, so that even if a ray of sun crept into his makeshift carry-cot it would not burn him. She would send me back to the house, to get on with my work, and stay out for two or three hours. The baby was always in view, and she could hear him if he cried. She could drop her pitchfork and be at his side in a moment. Then I walked up to fetch her later in the evening, and helped her carry the baskets and baby home. Sometimes I arrived to find her sitting on the ground, leaning against the two empty baskets piled one on top of the other to make a chair back, the baby in her arms, feeding. She talked to him while he sucked, a continuing love song about what a fine splendid fellow he was, what a greedy little pig, oh her darling, king baby, her little duck, her duckling, the sweetest bundle ever seen in the history of the world. He didn't have a name yet. They couldn't agree on one. She called him by a thousand names, nonsense words and endearments she made up like poems.

I no longer spent Sunday afternoons ironing. The sun shone and lured me out to the beach. Sometimes I climbed up the cliff path and lay sprawled, daydreaming, in the soft grass at the top, as near to the crumbling edges as I dared to go. Sometimes, at low tide, I left my sabots behind me on the beach and scrambled my way across the rocks, slithering barefoot over the wet seaweed, curling my toes into crevices to get a good grip while I peered into rock pools and watched tiny crabs dart about. I came home with a pocket full of pebbles and shells, which I arranged on the windowsill of my room, altering the design from week to week, shifting it about as the whim took me. Sometimes I carried the baby down to the sea with me, and showed him the waves and the clouds and the wheeling gulls.

—Thanks, Geneviève, Madame Montjean said when I returned from one of these expeditions: you are a good girl.

Ashamed, I looked away, pretending I was about to sneeze and had to cover my face with my handkerchief.

Goodness in a girl meant chastity. It also meant helpfulness. Goodness in a baby meant not crying too much. Our nights began to be broken and noisy. The child, so quiet and peaceful at the beginning, now woke often, and cried. He cried if he was hungry and needed to be fed, and he cried if he had colic and needed soothing. Perhaps babies dream, and perhaps he also cried if he had bad dreams, and needed comforting. Sometimes he wouldn't go to sleep at all but just carried on with his evening crying and refused to believe it was night. I didn't always hear him, from my room upstairs, every time he started up, but of course his mother and father did, because his cradle was next to their bed. In the mornings they were grumpy and red-eyed with tiredness.

To try and avoid Frédéric being disturbed, Madame Montjean would get up when the baby started to cry, pick him up and carry him into the kitchen, and feed and soothe him there, so that her husband could get back to sleep while she paced up and down and jiggled the bawling child.

—One of us must get some sleep, she told me: and he's got to be up to open the bar. At least I can snatch a nap sometimes in the afternoons when you take the little one out.

In the mornings Frédéric would yawn gustily over his breakfast.

—How long is this going to go on? he would grumble: when am I ever going to get a decent night's sleep?

She had to comfort the baby, and she had to comfort her husband. The strain showed on her face. She looked older, her grey-blue eyes sunk deeper in their sockets, surrounded by creases of worry and tiredness.

One day she snapped back at him.

—I'm tired to death as well. Why don't you think about me?

He snatched up his cup of coffee and stormed off with it to the bar. Madame Montjean burst into tears. Never once had I seen her cry. I scooped up the baby and took him outside to the yard to say hello to the dog, to give her time to recover herself. Really I was escaping, just like Frédéric, because I didn't know what so say. To see her so vulnerable unsettled me. I thought perhaps it wasn't only tiredness that was the problem, but I didn't want to know.

When I came back in she was blowing her nose. I fetched her a hot cup of coffee and made her stay sitting down to drink it while I changed the baby's nappy. Practical things I could do for her, but I couldn't talk to her and listen to her, and help her that way. I had listened to him too often; I had done her too many wrongs and betrayed her too much. I wasn't going to add hypocrisy to my list of sins. I went on thinking only of myself. I told myself she had plenty of women friends among the harvesters. She could tell them what the matter was, get sympathy from them. It was better for me not to be too involved.

That afternoon I coaxed her to lie down on her bed and try to sleep. I abandoned all pretence of housework and made the baby my priority, doing everything in my power to keep him quiet so that he wouldn't cry. Frédéric came through the kitchen and went upstairs. I heard him tramping to and fro overhead in the middle attic, seemingly dragging heavy objects across the floor. It sounded as though he were moving furniture. Later on, when I got the chance to run up and peep in, I saw that he had cleared the storage boxes to one side, dismantled the ironing table, and got out the truckle bed again. He had flung a couple of sheets onto it, from the laundered pile I had left up there and had not yet put away, and he had carried up a pillow and quilt.

Madame Montjean did not go out to the fields that evening. She admitted her exhaustion, in so much as she slumped in her chair by the fire, but she could not allow herself not to work. Her body was like a heavy sigh but her hands moved nimbly, topping and tailing the beans we were going to eat for supper. The baby fretted by her side in his carrycot. He was wailing and querulous, fighting her when she picked him up, turning his head angrily from side to side when she put him to the breast.

—I think he's coming down with something, she said: oh God don't let him fall ill. I couldn't bear it, d'you hear, my precious?

I went outside and milked the cow, then packed the two baskets of provisions and carried them out to the fields. When I got back, she was pacing up and down the kitchen holding the baby to her while he cried.

—I'll sleep upstairs tonight, Frédéric told Madame Montjean at supper: catch up on some rest.

She nodded. He gave a little grunt, like some kind of affectionate word that he was too shy to utter, and then someone shouted from the bar and he got up and went to the hatch.

I shut the poultry into their sheds, let the dog off its chain, locked the back door, fed the stove with wood for the night. I did all these jobs more carefully than usual, as a kind of bargain I was driving with fate. If I fastened the shutters with especial precision, without rattling or banging them; if I made the kitchen rigorously neat and swept up every bulky crumb from the floor; if I saw Madame Montjean comfortably settled into her bed and took her in a cup of hot milk; then perhaps Frédéric would keep the bar open until late; perhaps he would be so drunk when he came up to bed that he would fall fast asleep, and then nothing terrible would happen.

I extinguished my candle and lay wide awake in the dark. I thought of St Geneviève, how she climbed up onto the battlements of the city of Paris to repel the invaders. Singlehandedly she resisted the enemy; she called on God for help; she roused the citizens and made them fight so bravely that the army of evil slunk away defeated. I was not as good and courageous as St Geneviève and therefore could not repel one single man. When his footsteps trod gently up the stairs, along the little corridor, and rested outside my room, I stiffened. I pretended I was a fallen tree-branch in winter, rigid under a quilt of snow. The door handle twisted open with the smallest of squeaks.

He put his hand over my mouth. He breathed into my ear.

—Be a good girl.

After that he did not speak. If he said nothing and if I could not, with his tobacco-smelling fingers clamped against my lips, then he could go on pretending that he was not there; and so I did the same; I began ferociously to tell myself a story about a mermaid; only this time she would not die; she would escape; she would dive into the depths of the sea and hide there; she was not speechless at all she shouted out for Madame Patin Madame Montjean to come and rescue her she shouted sorry sorry sorry and she certainly had nothing between her legs and so she could not be interfered with but swim swim swim.

In the morning I decided I had made it all up. It was untrue. It was a nightmare. Too much daydreaming. Letting my imagination run away with me. I was a wicked girl even to imagine such things. It was all my fault.

The young woman boasted glossy hair so dark it seemed smokier than black, with a shine like that on the wings of blackbirds, that sheen seeming slicked with oil, reflecting blue lights. She lifted off her hat with reverent care and plumped it down on the chair next to her, then put her hands up to the nape of her neck, checking her hairpins.

She had a long neck, which she moved to and fro gracefully, and with her chin tilted up she looked like a wader pecking elegantly along the shore. Her hair was brushed back behind her ears and coiled into a loose knot, so heavy that it looked like slipping undone down her back. Around her slender neck twisted a rope of salmon-pink coral. She wore a red skirt, and a white blouse with a sailor collar, and she unbuttoned the front of her blouse a little way, when she sat down, protesting and exclaiming, because it was so hot.

Refusing to seat herself on the backless beach, she perched on the chair I brought her. She pinched up and forwards the pleats of her blouse, and shook them up and down with exaggerated humourous sighing, like a child showing off. Then she leaned back languidly, with a sigh, and flapped a newspaper in front of her face to cool it.

Everything she did seemed designed to make her companion notice her afresh and admire her prettiness. Her olive skin didn't protest, sweating, at the heat. It stayed fine-grained and smooth. Her eyes were black. Her little mouth pouted. To me it was odd behaviour, to seem so disconsolate with the fine summer weather, whereas of course we were so pleased because it meant all the harvest would be got in before the hot spell broke and it rained.

Her companion sat and looked at her. His brown face was creased with amusement and affection at her antics. His eyes traced her narrow sloping shoulders, her tiny waist, her rounded full lips. He lit a cigar and puffed aromatic smoke-clouds at the ceiling. From his pocket, as though absentminded, he fingered out a sketchbook and pencil. Laying down the cigar, he began drawing her.

While I served them the snack they had ordered, carefully setting down their glasses, pouring the cider, putting out the basket of bread and the plate of pâté, I tried not to look at them too obviously in case they caught me staring and thought me rude. I remembered them from last year. They were the couple who had come in and asked for food when we were not in the habit of serving it, and in that sense they had been my first customers.

I stepped back and hesitated. I twisted my apron corner around my hands. I wished they would look at me. I wanted them to recognise me as I had them. They were so confident, so well dressed, so careless, that it almost hurt to watch them. They were clinking glasses, quite oblivious of me, unrolling their napkins and shaking them out onto their laps.

My voice came out in a croak. I coughed and started again.

—Will that be all? Is there anything else that you would like?

The young woman shot me one impatient glance, as though to say: what's that creature still doing here? She did not deign to reply. But her companion spoke to me pleasantly.

—No, thank you. This is all we require.

I supposed they must be from Le Havre at the very least; they were so fine and spoke in such a distinctive way, without a trace of local accent. I had spoken to them in my good orphanage French, being careful to let no patois creep into my speech, of which they wouldn't have understood a word. Quite possibly they were from even further afield, like so many of the other summer visitors.

—Are you from Paris? I blurted out.

The man lifted an eyebrow but put down his knife and spoke with perfect courtesy.

—We're not Parisians, no. We've driven over from Etretat.

I had wanted to make him speak to me again. I wanted to feel a link, however tenuous, with these strangers; I wanted to believe there was a world outside Blessetot in which there was the chance for people to be happy and good, and these two, I was convinced, lived in it, and so seeing them again I could imagine that I did too and that I still belonged to my days of innocence of a year ago.

—I grew up in Etretat, I said: perhaps you know the place? The orphanage behind the market square?

The man shrugged.

—No, I'm afraid not.

His voice was good natured enough, which encouraged me. I hesitated, thinking of another question to ask, to try and prolong the conversation. But Madame Montjean called for me from the kitchen and so I picked up my tray and went out of the bar. I heard the young woman laugh as I went off, a brief, scornful laugh. She said something I couldn't catch.

I didn't care. She couldn't hurt me. I had plenty of words in my head I could have used against her if I'd wanted to. She and her companion weren't from round here. For us, the word tourist, or foreigner, could carry a certain amount of contempt. Like the word Parisian. A mere bird of passage with more money than sense. Someone from another planet who swanned in then swanned out and knew nothing about the real world. The young woman didn't know that behind our politeness we could regard people like her with indifference, a touch of amusement. So I was well armoured against anything unpleasant she might say or think about me once she had deigned to notice my presence.

I watched them drive off half an hour later. I hovered by the café door, patting their horse's nose, while they climbed up onto the seat of their trap. The woman sat well back, pulling down her veil to swathe her hat and unfurling her parasol against the sun. I untied the horse and threw the bridle back over its head. The man tossed me down a coin, picked up the reins, twirled his whip, and shouted at me to stand clear.

The horse backed obediently, then turned. It strained, then bounded forward under the whip too harshly applied. They went off up the street with a terrific clatter. White dust blew up under the rim of the wheels. I stepped back hastily with stinging eyes. Soon the carriage had vanished over the brow of the steep road out of the village.

Its departure sketched in a line for me, between here and there, a straight line arrowing off into the unknown. They weren't afraid of that road they'd entered and were travelling down, that road I couldn't see from where I stood. They sped off into it. Perhaps they were so confident because they had money. Perhaps because they believed that they were not wicked but good.

The tourist couple gave me a parting gift more precious than any coin. They enabled me to begin believing in the future, that it was possible and real. They allowed me to believe that one day I would leave Blessetot, and begin my life all over again. They handed me a map of escape with the route marked. I could become invisible, as they had done, to any watcher who stood outside the café and shielded his eyes from the sun and looked for me. I could go.

Up until now I had always escaped backwards, into the mirror, into daydreams. Now for the first time in my life I considered the physical reality of going away forwards, letting my legs carry me off into the everyday world I did not know, just seeing what would happen next.

I discovered a new version of time. I was not, after all, stuck for ever, revolving in a nightmare game, like the hands of a mad clock; I was not condemned to repeat the mermaid story from now till eternity. I could grow up; I could move; I could get away.

Back inside the house, later that day, I sat on my bed and counted my money. My wages were low in the extreme, but since I had so little to spend them on, my meagre stock of coins had nonetheless mounted month by month. To me the hoard looked like treasure trove. I thought that if I could somehow hitch a lift to Etretat then I might have enough for the train fare to Le Havre, even to Paris. The further away the better. What would I do when I got there? I would get a job as a maid in someone's house, or I could work in a restaurant kitchen. I could even be a cook or look after babies. I had a moment's unease when I considered that I would need some kind of reference before getting accepted by strangers. Then I reasoned that I could go to visit Sister Pauline in Etretat, give her a carefully edited version of my story, and ask her to write me a letter of introduction. I was not at all sure that she would do it without first kicking up all sorts of fuss and wanting to contact Madame Montjean, but I could think of no better plan. It would have to do. I went downstairs again feeling I had achieved something. Now I had learned that the future existed, all I had to do was wait for the right moment to run away into it.

The annual village feast had once more arrived and gone past. The harvest festival was approaching. This year it was held on the last Sunday in August. A team of villagers decorated the church. Sprigs of corn, tied up in bunches with ribbons, were hung at the ends of the pews, and garlands of corn were put over the heads of the statues of the saints. This year the festivities had an additional meaning, for the Montjean baby was going to be baptised during the mass. His parents had finally decided on a name by the simple expedient of combining their choices. He was to be known as Jean-Louis.

There was a certain urgency in getting him baptised. He was ill, with some ailment that did not get any better. From being a fine, thriving baby he had become a weak, crying infant whose survival was now in question. If he died without being baptised he would not be able to be buried in the churchyard but would find his last home at a crossroads, to signify that he was in limbo, for all eternity, with other good souls, like virtuous pagans, not sinful enough to merit purgatory. But he would never get to heaven, and nor would they, because none of them had been christened first. Not until the very end of the world, when Christ came in majesty and opened up all the graves and summoned out the dead to rise and be resurrected.

Madame Montjean was too distraught about her child's health to think much about the necessary preparations for the day. She paid for all kinds of experts to come and diagnose her poor baby: the doctor, the local midwife, the local sorcerer. Each one in turn prescribed different medicines and spoke out against the other two. The sorcerer made a little ball of herbs, wild garlic and feathers, which he hung over the cot, to chase the evil eye away, for he said there was someone around wishing the baby ill, and this malevolence had to be fought off.

I removed myself from the scene of sorrow in the kitchen and concentrated on practical things. I planned the *vin d'honneur* we would have after the festival mass. I cooked food for the christening lunch. I cleaned and decorated the bar.

This year the dahlias had bloomed in great profusion. They were planted in rows at the end of the garden, tied to stakes to stop them flopping over. A regiment of strictly marching flowers: hot pink curled pom-poms, and raggedy heads of salmon pink, spiked, like little starry explosions; Catherine wheels. In my first summer of helping Madame Montjean in the garden, I had not been sure whether I really liked dahlias or not. I had thought them too perfect, too tightly whorled, somehow unapproachable, but as soon as you picked a few, took them away from the formality of the massed bed, held them in your arms and then put them in a vase, you could see them better, how beautiful they were, so juicy and fresh. Raindrops nestled in the flaring petals, glittering, like beads on a frilly skirt. When you lightly shook each pink frou-frou ball, earwigs dropped out from their hiding-places inside. When you dipped the tip of your little finger into the rolled petals, they felt cool. I liked their smell, which was rough rather than sweet, and I liked their coarse, deeply indented green leaves. I put a bunch on each table in the bar, mixing flowers with buds, and planting a few sprigs of corn, begged from the harvesters, in among the stems.

Madame Montjean came in to inspect my handiwork. She walked from the bar to the kitchen, obviously noting the changes from how she had done things last year. She lifted the lids of pots standing ready on the stove and looked inside. Her face was wan and white with worry and exhaustion but her tone was sharp as she handed out her criticisms.

I held my tongue and said nothing. But I knew I was frowning at her as I bit my lip. I wanted to justify myself and whine: but I was only trying to help, when this is such a difficult and anxious time for you; and it's your fault as well; you taught me to be so capable; is it any surprise I want to test myself against you sometimes? But I thought she probably wasn't complaining about domestic work, and so I kept quiet.

We all duly went to church for the combined harvest and baptism mass. One of the godmothers, a relative of Frédéric's, had not turned up, but the christening ceremony was performed anyway, halfway through, with Monsieur and Madame Montjean walking over to the font at the back of the church, and the other villagers turned round in their pews to watch. I stood nearby. The priest handed out candles, and was busy with chrism and holy water.

A local farmer and his wife stood in as the main godparents. When it came to the moment for them to speak on behalf of the child, to renounce the world and the flesh, in particular to renounce Satan and all his works, they muttered the words in shy voices. The baby began screaming. I couldn't help myself; I stretched my arms out to him; but he only cried harder.

For some reason everyone glanced at me. I could see them thinking this was a bad omen. The priest carried on, splashing the baby with holy water as he baptised him, and the baby struggled weakly in his mother's arms and would not stop crying. I saw people's faces harden as they stared at me, and heard indrawn breaths like hisses, a whisper or two. My status as a villager, as one of them, had slipped away like a shawl falling off. I was the outsider, their looks said, the orphan, the bastard, the odd girl who prowled the beach and the cliffs for hours on her own and had no friends, and per- haps I had brought the family bad luck. Then I convinced myself I had imagined it.

Afterwards people surged into the bar for tumblers of wine, and toasts, and I nipped about serving as I always did, and tried not to notice some of the women's stolid faces come suddenly alive with inquisitiveness and malice.

After the christening lunch the house hushed and emp- tied itself. Madame Montjean retreated to lie down in her bedroom, and watch over the baby in his cot; Frédéric took a gun and went out with a couple of other men to shoot the crows which screamed over a neighbour's fields; and I tackled the washing-up. By the time I had finished it, my half-day holiday was nearly over. A thick drizzle had begun to sprinkle itself against the windows, so that I was disinclined to go for a walk down to the sea. I banged out of the kitchen and into the empty bar, bored and restless and uncertain how to fill up my time.

I rearranged some of the nosegays which stood about. They had begun to wilt already in the atmosphere of heat and tobacco smoke. I found a half-empty bottle of red wine and poured myself a couple of glasses which I drank quickly, wanting to dull how I was feeling. I thought I'd like to get drunk and see what it was like.

Then I found myself sitting on the edge of one of the tables which was drawn up close to the mirror, and gazing at my reflection. Sometimes it felt like having a sister who looked back at me and joined in the discussion about what I should do. Sometimes the mermaid flicked her tail at me and laughed and swam away as I got up, dissatisfied. Sometimes a good girl appeared opposite. More often these days, a bad one scowled back.

Today there was just myself. I was alone. I knew it was my own face peering out, frowning and flushed. There was something I was searching for but I didn't quite know what it was. There was something I couldn't see. Mirrors are supposed to give you back yourself as you are, but my self-portrait was incomplete.

The mermaid had had a mirror. She had been able to hold it between her legs and discover whatever it was she had there, even if that could not be told in the story. I too was curious. So I lifted my skirts, and bunched them about my waist, wriggled my drawers down about my ankles, brought my knees up on either side of me and spread my legs wide. I thought I looked just like a dahlia, so neat and furled and pink.

I'd done it without thinking of danger. But I'd worked the mermaid magic; I'd summoned the man. And this one would capture me; he would hold me up in his net for all the villagers to see; and then he would kill me with his huntsman's knife. I was too panicstricken at being caught to cry out when Frédéric swam up, when he appeared in the mirror behind me and came close; he stepped rapidly round in front of me, standing in between my thighs and blocking out my view, ramming his rain-misted jacket against me and holding me fast in his arms. Then, almost at the same time, it seemed, Madame Montjean was upon us. She shouted. She cursed and cursed.

Millicent

To me the river seems alive, like an animal. Flexing its long back, muscly and rippled, writing across the plain like some great serpent swum in from the sea and now uncoiling itself; thrashing past forests. Swirling wide and deep, it dominates the landscape as far as your eyes can reach. In some places chalk cliffs, white veined with yellow, sweep up from its gravelly shore, while elsewhere they have tumbled and settled, heaps of great boulders with paths cut through them, edged with silvery sand, down to the water's edge.

The river is a clear, pale green, flowing fast, busy with cargo traffic, dotted with the bright sails of ketches tacking to and fro. Some stretches are fringed with willows and poplars, others with marshy shallows pricked by irises and reeds. Wooden landing-stages and quays jut out, rowing boats bobbing alongside, and from my bedroom window I can watch, through a veil of fine rain, the ferry ply back and forth, and the great barges, coming from the direction of Le Havre, shoulder aside all the smaller craft as they make their stately way upstream, loaded with timber and coal, towards Rouen and Paris.

Here, surrounded by water, we seem cut off from the rest of the world. The Seine encloses us on both sides. Monsieur Gérard spread out the map on the dining-room table to show me. The villages of Jumièges is set inside a great dangling loop of river that outlines a teardrop shape; a bag of land whose strings are drawn narrow at the neck; a clutch of fields, gardens and pastures as self-contained as an island. It boasts a ruined abbey, clusters of thatched half-timbered cottages, many apple orchards full of cows peacefully cropping the grass. The Colberts' house is tucked away round the back of the abbey, between its park and the forêt de Jumièges. Monsieur Gérard ran his finger along the dotted line of the boundaries to show me that his garden used to be part of the abbey farm, before the Revolution. He had long brown hands, with very clean and well-manicured nails, but he has inkstains on his shirt cuffs. Shaded by two oak trees, the house is about a hundred years old, low and square, built of contrasting layers of brick and flint, with a blue slate roof, a small neat garden in front and a bigger one behind. Two rows of windows are closed by blue-grey shutters, and a little *oeil-de-boeuf* window projects from the attic. To the side are a yard, a barn and sheds, and a narrow vegetable plot. It's all distressingly primitive: no gas upstairs, for example; I have to go to bed by candlelight.

Monsieur Gérard met me off the boat train in Paris. We had two hours to spare, so he hailed a cab and had us driven around the city. We stopped briefly at a smart café on one of the grand boulevards. I drank a cup of hot chocolate and ate a macaroon stuffed with chestnut purée. Overdressed ladies of strenuous and ostentatious elegance, their eyes flirtatious and their cheeks shamelessly rouged (courtesans, perhaps?), idled in groups at the round marble-topped tables, chattering, fondling their little dogs, their feathered and beribboned hats swaying to and fro like poppies on long stalks. My first encounter with quite a different sort of society to the one I am used to in Surrey!

Policemen stood in twos and threes, discreetly to one side, keeping a sharp eye on all the comings and goings; the air smelled of lime blossom and hot dust; my host lit a cigar. He slumped unapologetically, like an animal, in the warm sunshine. He lifted his chin, pursed his lips, and blew out clouds of smoke, his head tilted back, his legs stretched out and crossed at the ankles. Quite a few raffish-looking men, strolling past, stopped to greet him. Quite a few overdecorated *demi-mondaines* smirked at him as they went by. Then it was time to catch the train. We got out at Rouen and came the rest of the way in a hired carriage.

Monsieur Gérard was very polite. He bowed when we met, looking after my luggage, and handed me in and out of the train as though I were a duchess rather than his niece's new governess. He is rather ugly and quite old; thirty-five or so. He has bushy dark hair which bursts from his head in all directions, a large nose jutting out above the thick moustache which hides most of his mouth, and bright monkey eyes. He smells of tobacco, and of some eau-de-Cologne that's more like a fancy-woman's perfume than a real man's, a mixture of limes and flowers and spice. No Englishman I've ever met smells like that. Arthur certainly does not. Nor did my poor Papa.

JUNE 14TH

Out here my French is not as fluent as it seemed in England. I feel like a dunce. Little Marie-Louise chatters away so fast I have constantly to stop her and ask her to repeat what she's just said. I don't like appearing so ignorant in front of my pupil but it can't be helped. Madame Colbert says not to worry; I shall improve with practice. She is a majestic person, who holds herself very erect. She is short and stout, with frizzy grey hair and brown eyes that turn down at the corners. She speaks with formality, her turns of phrase very precise and polite, and when she addresses me she enunciates extra slowly and clearly. This is both humiliating and embarrassing, though I know she does it to be kind; I can see her graciously trying to set me at my ease; but I seem to blunder more when speaking to her than to anyone else.

The maid Geneviève has a rougher accent than the other three. Her words come out in a singsong rhythm. She's a very simple character. When she hands round the dishes at lunch she starts enumerating the delicacies she has cooked for us as though she's reciting poetry, and meanwhile the food gets cold. The Colberts are not Parisians, after all. I'd assumed they were, because Madame Colbert wrote to me initially from Paris, but it turns out they are Normans, like Geneviève. They were both born here, in this house. Monsieur Gérard has a deep, growling voice, and a rapid, barking delivery. He slows down for me when he remembers. But he doesn't talk to us much. Most of the time he is shut away in his study, working.

I'm disappointed, I must confess. I shan't be living in Paris some of the time, as I'd assumed, but here in Normandy for the whole summer. Monsieur Gérard goes up to town regularly for literary evenings with his friends, but he and his mother want Marie-Louise to spend her childhood in healthy surroundings with plenty of fresh air and good food. They want her to grow up in the country. Her father is working out in Africa. Madame Colbert was talking about him last night. He's performing a service to France, in which she takes great pride. He's doing his duty, showing the natives how things should be run. Making money too. But he sent his daughter home, because the climate was too much for her. Which is why they needed someone to look after her: me. Thanks to the recommendation of that friend of a friend of Mother's I've got this job, and of course I hope I can demonstrate to the Colberts that English teaching methods have something to be said for them!

Geneviève told me the background to the story the day after I arrived, when she was showing me where to put everything away in my room. She was helping me unpack. She was smoothing out my stockings, and rolling them up neatly, two by two, into soft little balls she was lining up in a drawer. I noticed the way her fingers and eyes lingered on the silk, stroking it. Her stockings were grey woollen ones, much darned and baggy round the ankles, so I picked up one of my older pairs, only a bit worn, and tucked it into her apron pocket. So then she began to talk to me about the family. Marie-Louise's mother, Monsieur Gérard's sister, died shortly after giving birth to her, from some complication that led to an infection, and the sad widower went off to Africa to work for a mining company. They are a tight little family, the mother and her son and the small girl. They curve together, click, like jigsaw pieces.

But the real reason we are spending the summer months here, and nowhere else, is because of money.

Geneviève told me this second version of the story yesterday, when she was making my bed and I was sorting out my books and papers on the little table under the window. I shouldn't listen to servants' gossip, but I was curious. Apparently, Monsieur Gérard, being a poet, though a very good one, his faithful maid said with comical emphasis, earns little money, and he and his mother have only tiny incomes of their own from their two farms near Etretat, which is a resort on the coast quite near here. So they have decided to let the apartment in Paris, for the foreseeable future, and live full time in his house, which is much cheaper to run. When Monsieur Gérard goes up to town he stays with friends. He often goes on business to Rouen. Geneviève hinted that his business involves meeting a certain lady friend there. I disapprove of prurient tittle-tattle so I cut her short.

So, anyway, I am having to abandon my dreams of life in Paris and adjust to a far more prosaic reality: a grey-green landscape half blotted out by rain ever since I got here; and a pervading smell of damp. The Colberts seem to receive very few visitors, so far at least, and I foresee that my leisure hours will be dull in the extreme unless I can find some occupation with which to fill them. I can't study French all the time. And for the moment it is too wet to venture outdoors. That is where you come in, dear diary. Keeping a record of my experiences in France will give me something to do.

All that I cannot utter in public, my criticisms particularly, I shall put down there. I'm writing this for myself, after all. Yesterday at *déjeuner* Monsieur Gérard was reading out bits of a newspaper review, to his mother, of a collection of poems by one of his friends I believe; I could not attend properly because I was cutting up Marie-Louise's slice of meat and persuading her to eat the red part in the centre; and he grew very excited, stabbing at sentences with his forefinger and exclaiming that critics were vultures hoping for carrion to carry off in their claws. He slashed at his own helping of underdone lamb as though he had the critic laid out on his plate and was happily dismembering him. He's like his mother when it comes to eating meat: they both like it red; they both like the blood; they get Geneviève to tip the blood from the carving dish into the gravy boat; and then, after the meat course, they keep some gravy back to pour over their salad as well. Rather uncouth, I think.

I had not seen Monsieur Gérard angry before. He offered us more wine on the strength of it. The French may grossly undercook their meat; they sit over their meals far too long; but their wine is really not bad. We drink it at every meal. One small glass, or at the most two, from the corked-up bottle kept in the buffet and ceremoniously produced noontime and night. Marie-Louise has hers mixed with water, just enough drops of wine to tint the water red, but I said I would have mine neat, whereupon Monsieur Gérard pronounced me *une jeune fille sérieuse* and bowed to me as he handed me my glass. You could not possibly get drunk on the tiny amount we have; one bottle lasts two days at least; but I certainly enjoy it, the sweet warmth, drop by drop, down my throat. I try not to empty my glass too fast but in fact I should like to be able to toss back a tumbler at a time to get more of that intense red feeling. The wine livens up our mealtimes which are otherwise rather dull.

Our food is quite plain. I imagined French food would be more exotic. We have a lot of vegetables and soups. The cream, poured over the vegetables and stirred into the soup, is the best thing we eat, and is very cheap, so even in this thrifty household we can eat it several times a week. It comes from the farm down the road. Once the weather improves Marie-Louise and I will walk out to fetch it.

I feel France is making me very greedy. Something inside me is starving and shouting. It's the same feeling that propelled me abroad. Wanting to bite into the world and seize it. I want to drink a lot of wine, eat a lot of cream, go out for long walks despite the rain, run very fast until I'm exhausted, dance until I'm giddy. Oh dear. How badly behaved and childish that sounds!

I'm sure it's not worldly pleasure I want, really, so much as someone to talk to. I miss Mother and I am even beginning to miss Arthur more than I thought I would. He writes to me faithfully every other day and reproaches me for not writing back as often. But I won't think about him too much. I promised myself I would not. Having claimed three months away from him, having asked him to wait while I make up my mind, it seems rather a waste to be hankering after him already, dear as he is.

JUNE 20TH

A sketch of my day.

Geneviève wakes me rudely at seven when she comes clattering in with a can of hot water, opens the catch on the shutters, which squeaks, and bangs them back on either side of the windows. I forgot to mention what Geneviève looks like. She is thin and wiry and nervous. She has a way of standing waiting, poised on her toes like a little pugilist, her feet half rising from her sabots, with her fists clenched at her sides, as though she's ready to hit you at any moment. She's younger than I am; eighteen or so. Her hair is concealed by her cap. She has hazel eyes, a little aquiline nose, and fair, sun-reddened skin. Every day she wears the same clothes: blue skirt, brown bodice, brown chemise and grey apron. She crashes out while I wash, and fetches the hot water for Monsieur Gérard, then stomps back in to help me on with my stays. I finish dressing, put up my hair, and then go and greet my pupil.

Marie-Louise is always awake, waiting for me. She sleeps next door to her grandmother, in a closet-sized space that serves also as Madame Colbert's dressing-room. Her little white iron bed is tucked in between two wardrobes. The walls in here are papered in blue, with a pattern of red trelliswork and green vines, and above the bed hangs a framed oval portrait, done in pastels, of Caroline Colbert as a girl, with waxy brown ringlets dangling onto cramped shoulders. She wears a square-necked white dress and lifts one pearl-encircled wrist.

When I bend over my charge to say good morning she puts her arms around my neck and kisses me. Not so much because she is fond of me; it's too soon for that; we hardly know each other yet; as because it is polite. Morning and night she has to kiss all of us on both cheeks. This French fuss and formality seems hypocritical to me. A hearty English handshake is infinitely preferable!

But I do like the smell of Marie-Louise at this hour. Small warm milky animal. Children smell quite different from adults. Madame Colbert smells of violet soap and the mint lozenges she is fond of sucking. Monsieur Gérard's smell I have already described. Geneviève smell sometimes of eau-de-javel, sometimes of baking, and sometimes of sweat.

We eat a modest breakfast, bread scraped with jam, in the low, square dining-room at the front of the house. The window looks out over the little garden and the road, so you can watch carts going by, and listen to people shouting to each other as they pass. The dining-room walls are painted a deep crimson and hung with mirrors and pictures in ornate gilt frames. On one side of the window is the buffet, in the top of which the plates, bottles of wine and table-cloths are kept, while the lower shelves are laden with precious objects like antique Limoges coffee services and sets of crystal champagne glasses that we never use. Yesterday after lunch Geneviève was kneeling on the floor, under Madame Colbert's hawk-eyed supervision, yawning, dragging these fragile objects out to dust, one by one, then replacing them. Huffing and puffing and generally feeling sorry for herself. She's rather lazy. Opposite the buffet is a set of hanging shelves holding porcelain dishes painted with wreaths of pink flowers and long-tailed exotic birds. The table is oval, with massive legs and feet, filling much of the room. When we're working at it, it's covered by a red felt cloth edged with black bobbles; then for meals we fold this up and put a white one on instead.

We share our breakfast with Monsieur Gérard. He sits hunched inside a battered pink brocade dressing-gown tied with a yellow tasselled belt; he wears red morocco slippers with trodden-down heels and curly toes; he reads the newspaper and doesn't talk to us. Madame Colbert has breakfast in bed, carried up to her on a try by her devoted son. Every morning, whether it's raining or not, he claps on his hat, pulls on his coat over his dressing-gown, darts out in to the garden, picks her a nosegay and arranges it in a little glass, pleats her starched white napkin just so across her plate of hot rolls, fills her cup with coffee, then twirls upstairs as dextrously as any one of those waiters I saw in the café in Paris. Having done his duty, he goes off to his study to smoke a pipe, while Marie-Louise and I help Geneviève clear the table before getting down to our lessons.

After our *déjeuner* at half-past twelve, Marie-Louise is shooed upstairs for a nap while I prepare our work for the following day. When she wakes up, after an hour or so, we are supposed to take a walk, except that it is too wet, so we run across the yard at the side of the house into the big barn and do some skipping and gymnastics. There's a swing in there, and a trapeze, so we can do proper exercises. We also do some marching and drilling, which are so good for deportment and self-discipline. My pupil has much need of both.

More lessons follow, then Marie-Louise's supper. Then she plays a game with Monsieur Gérard such as spillikins, or draughts. Afterwards she sits on his knee and cuddles him. She pretends he is her horse and feeds him sugar lumps; she pats and grooms him; she combs his springy hair; she tugs his moustache quite fearlessly; then she seizes the ends of his cravat and names them reins; she twirls her handkerchief whip; and they are off around the racecourse. Monsieur Gérard bucks and neighs; the old armchair creaks and groans; Marie-Louise whoops with delight and urges on her steed.

At the precise moment when the chequered flag is in view, when they are galloping hard and growing really boisterous, her grandmother lifts up her hands in her lap, the signal to stop, this minute, before over-excitement leads to tears or simply to more noise and hullabaloo. She calls the child over, to calm her down, and now Marie-Louise, sulking a bit, has to practise standing docilely in front of the old lady who is pulling her hair and sash to rights again while the child recites what she has learned that day. We three grownups listen very seriously. She is a sturdy little thing, though small for her age. She has pale blue eyes and brown ringlets, a wide smiling mouth. The performance finished, the demonstration of learning accomplished, she circles the little group, delivering her ritual kisses, and then off she goes to bed.

There is no salon. The house is too small. We females live in the dining-room. So in the evenings, after we've eaten our soup, after the lamp is lit, and the shutters closed, after Monsieur Gérard has gone back into his study to get on with his writing, I sit with Madame Colbert by the stove. Madame Colbert sews. Her son's shirts. Marie-Louise's frocks. Or else she mends the household linen. When she has patched every worn tablecloth in sight, when she has turned every torn sheet sides to middle with a neat double seam, she embroiders florid initials onto pillowcases for Marie-Louise's trousseau. She has offered to teach me these skills, but I declined since I rather despise such mindless pursuits. I read a schoolbook in preparation for the morrow, or I write letters home.

I don't know what Geneviève does in the evenings. Sometimes we hear Monsieur Gérard in the passage, clattering an umbrella out of the stand and then shutting the front door behind him, going off to play chess with his friend the doctor or just for a walk in the rain. When he returns, he stamps and exclaims, shaking the wet off his coat. I think he wants to stir up the atmosphere a bit. He certainly provides a welcome dose of noise. All I hear otherwise is Madame Colbert's calm breathing, the ticking of the clock. At ten, Geneviève brings in the tray set with cups of tisane. When I've drunk my camomile to the last drop I shake hands with my employer and then I come up to bed and write this. Tonight it is still raining.

JUNE 25TH

Liberation. This morning the sun came out. We abandoned lessons after just an hour and went for a walk through the village, to collect the milk, eggs and cream from the farm. We took a detour, so that Marie-Louise could show me everything she thought proper for a guest to see. We briefly inspected the ruins of the Gothic abbey, which are indeed most picturesque, but I didn't experience the awe I expected to feel because Marie-Louise is not in the slightest bit interested in architecture and didn't give me time to get into the right mood. She dragged me off to the farm, where she insisted on introducing me to all the animals. The farmyard was muddy and smelly. The farmer's wife gave Marie-Louise a tumbler of fresh milk and insisted that I try her cider. She served it in a saucerless earthenware cup, with a wide handle. It was dry and sweet at the same time, sparkling like champagne. Not that I have yet tasted champagne. If I ever got to Paris again I might. I daresay those *demi-mondaines* drink champagne regularly.

Behind the farm is the forest of Jumièges, a dense, brooding mass of oaks, chestnut and birch. At the edge of the forest, beyond the ditch, the sun was striking down onto the bright green ferns growing there, splashing them with gold. So vivid they seemed almost transparent, with the green light dancing over them. Further in, under the trees, was deep green darkness your eyes could not penetrate. We stood on the road and looked. A little path led away from us, plunging forwards into the forest's heart. Marie-Louise wanted to run in and play hide-and-seek but I held her back. I didn't want to abandon the sunshine and enter the darkness. I thought we might get lost. So we came home. Immediately, I regretted it and felt I had been foolish and over-protective. However, when Monsieur Gérard heard of the tale of our expedition, recounted to him at great length by Marie-Louise over *déjeuner* and again this evening, he promised that he and his mother would accompany us to the woods for a picnic, some time soon, if it remains fine.

JUNE 26TH

Women's lives, in Madame Colbert's version, are supposed to be unremarkable. If I were truly the person she thinks I am, the person she assumes I'll become, it would be impossible to write this diary because there would be nothing to say. It would be better to be a novelist and make it all up. Or a poet, who can voice the deepest wishes of the human heart. A poet must not keep silent. He must sing. He must fly about the world, create his own world, not get caught in snares and traps, return and give songs to those who can't fly with him or after him. Poetry is made in freedom, and offered as consolation. It wakes you up to the existence of other realities in life besides the round of duty. It expands your soul.

I wish I had brought some of my own books here with me, but they would have weighed down my luggage too much. I should have thrown out the extra pairs of boots and put in some volumes of poetry.

Madame Colbert does not read books, but she enjoys the serials in her illustrated magazines. Geneviève doesn't appreciate poetry either, I asked her to recite me some French poetry, because I wanted to learn some; I was trying to be nice; but she just glared at me and shook her head. She is only a very ordinary sort of girl, of course; she spends her days head down working for the Colberts, and has no time for anything else. Madame Colbert seems quite fond of her, in her gracious way, but keeps her distance.

Yet Monsieur Gérard behaves differently. Tonight I thought he was still out, at the doctor's. I hadn't heard him come in. I suppose I wasn't attending to the sounds in the house, because I was thinking about the walk I'd taken with Marie-Louise this afternoon, down to the river, and how beautiful the water looked in the sunlight. We took off our shoes and stockings and paddled. Tiny waves broke over our feet, stinging and icy cold.

I said goodnight as usual to Madame Colbert, who was nodding over her mending, half asleep in her chair, and went down the passage to the kitchen, to fetch my candle. I paused outside when I heard Genevièves voice; there was no mistaking that forceful and guttural sound. But what surprised me was that she was obviously talking to a friend; she sounded so lively and confident. I didn't know she had any acquaintances who were allowed to visit her at night; that is hardly the kind of thing that Madame Colbert would permit. I rattled the latch, to warn her someone was coming, then went in.

She was sitting at the kitchen table opposite Monsieur Gérard talking eagerly to him. She was turned sideways in her chair, leaning her back against the wall; she was slumped and relaxed, one elbow on the table, her hand raised and gesturing; she had her feet tucked up on the bottom rung of her chair; her eyes were gleaning. The words were pouring out of her. He was bent towards her, attentive, concentrating, his whole body shaped into an attitude of listening, as though he had curved himself into a great ear, a great shell, like one of those fountains surrounded by statues he showed me in the park in Paris, with nymphs and dolphins playing together under arcs of spray, and she was a leaping fish spouting jets of water and tipping herself into him and he a sea-god holding up the twisted cornet iridescent with mother-of-pearl to catch the long white plumes of what she said.

They were so intent on giving and capturing this rushing stream of talk that it took them a few seconds to notice

me. She just glanced at me as though she were simply waiting for me to go away again; she was not going to e hauled
up out of her swimmy trance of telling him whatever it
was. Monsieur Gérard was not in the least embarrassed by
my arrival. He was not in the slightest bit disconcerted to
be found in the kitchen chatting to the servant, as though
they were equals. He jerked his head at me, a sort of hello,
got up, reached down my candle from the mantelpiece
above the fireplace, lit it, and handed it to me with a little
bow. He held the door open for me and shut it again behind
me. I heard Geneviève's voice starting up and flowing on
once more as I went towards the stairs.

Now I am sitting up in bed scribbling this. I had a
queer, violent feeling when I realised with what interest
Monsieur Gérard was listening to Geneviève. I felt myself
blush; I stammered something stupid about needing my
candle. My French deserted me; I could hardly get the
words out.

JUNE 28TH

For three days I have been ill in bed with a feverish cold.
Madame Colbert said I probably caught it walking around
with wet stockings, after our paddling expedition, and not
coming home quickly enough to change them before I took
a chill. She despatched me to bed, observing that I was better off staying away from everyone in case I had something
that was infectious. I feel very stupid, being ill, and that I

am neglecting Marie-Louise. Her uncle is giving her her lessons instead of me. I have nothing to do but drink tisanes and broth, and sleep. How I wish I had something to read. Madame Colbert has lent me some copies of *La Mode Illustrée* which has a serialised story in it, but there are several issues missing in the sequence, so that I cannot follow the serial properly. There are gaps. All I can do is try to amuse myself by filling them in, in my head, while I lie here. I try and work out probable endings.

I wrote to Arthur on the day I caught my cold, telling him I was certain I was the wrong wife for him and that we should not marry. I gave Geneviève the letter to post.

The doctor visited me. He has knobbly hands. His fingers comb his tufted brown beard while he bends over you and talks. Dots of saliva sprayed my face. He says I can get up tomorrow and that I have a very strong constitution; in fact he said the constitution of a horse. He declared that there was not much wrong with me any more. Tonight I agree with him. I want to spring out of bed and get on with my life.

JULY 1ST

The weather continues good. It is warm enough to sit out of doors until about four o'clock, when the sun starts to dip behind the oaks. Monsieur Gérard works with his doors wedged open onto the garden so that the light and air can enter his study through the frame of roses that climb up the back of the house. The doors are long windows, what we call French windows in England, reaching right down to the ground. Outside them he has a tiny balcony with a wrought-iron balustrade, over which clambers and cascades the white rose, and from here three steps lead you down into the garden: an oblong of grass divided by flowerbeds and paths. In the afternoons he goes on taking Marie-Louise for lessons; he does an hour of French with her and another hour of geography or history. I join in these lessons. I am learning quit as much as Marie-Louise.

It came about partly because I was ill, and he discovered in my absence that he enjoyed teaching his niece, and partly because he came into the dining-room on the day I first got up, while his mother was putting Marie-Louise to bed upstairs for her afternoon nap, and glanced at what I was doing. He was looking for spills to light his pipe; he was rummaging on the mantelpiece; and then he wandered over and stood behind my chair, looking over my shoulder. I could smell his eau-de-Cologne. I was drawing pictures for our geography lessons; I was outlining camels and pyramids and sphinxes, because we have been studying the African colonies and now we have got on to Egypt. His hand was on the back of my chair. It shook as he laughed. A sound like a snort.

—You can't draw, he said: these are terrible. Come into the study and I'll show you what camels and sphinxes look like.

I suppose when I stood up my face must have shown I was feeling rather offended. He was still sniggering, turning over my sketches, as though I should not care what he thought of them. He looked quite ugly and whiskery. Like a coal porter or a carpet merchant. At school I was rather good at still life but of course it is much more difficult drawing animals and archaeological features out of your imagination with nothing to copy.

I'll finish writing this tomorrow, because my candle has burnt right down; it's very late; and I do want to record that I had a letter from Arthur and one from Mother too. He is rather hurt, protesting that I'd said I needed three months away to think and I've only been away a few weeks. Mother says I have made the right decision; I should take my time before jumping into marriage; I should grow up a little more first. Dear Mother, she likes to think I am still her little girl.

JULY 2ND

The study walls are painted a pale blue-grey, almost the same colour as the shutters outside. That might seem a cold colour for an interior, but the effect is one of peace and calm. Faded curtains of yellow chintz, patterned with sapphire-blue singing birds and red tulips, hang at either side of the long garden windows, and the second, inner pair of curtains, white films of muslin, are caught back and wrapped around the yellow ones like long twisting tails. Sunlight is held, dark yellow, in the folds of material, breaks free and dances on the sparkling glass. The view out is clear, whether the windows are open or not. You can see the stems of the climbing roses hanging down; they make a thorny green wreath, pierced by light, around the top of the door; and beyond them, the little arbour rears up in the centre of the grass, between the lines of espaliered apples, crowned with a thicket of more white roses.

The garden seems completely different, looked at from this room. Being in the house is completely different when you are in this room. You can walk in and out between house and garden as often as you like and get a new experience of both.

The front end of the study is in shadows, the thick red curtains drawn against the daylight. The desk under the window is piled high with papers and books, a massive cut-glass inkwell on a grey marble tray with a gilt pot full of pens next to it, folders of engravings, loose sheets of maps, squares of pale green blotting paper, a round, loose-lidded blue and white jar of tobacco, cigars boxed in fragrant sandalwood, and various china-bowled pipes. Everything is mixed up in seeming confusion, a jumble of colours and shapes, but it is a pleasing chaos, an intriguing untidiness, precisely because it's personal; it's like the inside of somebody's brain with all their thoughts and ideas for poems flying about.

The top of the cream marble mantelpiece is covered with a runner in yellow Chinese silk, and heaped on this is a clutter of invitation cards and spills; alongside, a group of busts, and a dark blue, gold-rimmed Limoges pot full of flowers. Monsieur Gérard makes nosegays for himself as well as for his mother. He picks tiny bouquets of white daisies, blue pansies and orange nasturtiums. Madame Colbert never comes in here, complaining about the smell of tobacco, for it's the only room in the house in which she allows her son to smoke his beloved pipe and cigars. But it's a good, rich smell. I like it.

Above the fireplace hang a couple of pictures; engravings of sculpture. One is an Eve, from the cathedral at Autun he said it was, lying on her side as though she's swimming, and the other shows some grotesque carvings of skulls and bones from a church called St Maclou in Rouen. In front of the fireplace is a large white bearskin rug, complete with rearing head and spread paws, and Marie-Louise likes to lie on this, clasping her hands around the bear's snout or over its glaring glass eyes, while her uncle takes her through her lessons. His method of teaching is to show us books and pictures and tell us stories. As a young man he travelled in the East with a friend; they made a long voyage taking in Greece and Turkey, Egypt, Algeria and Tunisia. From the Orient he brought back chests of mementoes, and his friend, who was a painter, kept a record in watercolours of all they saw. Leafing through those sketches of exotic places and people, pulling them out one by one to show us, he describes his journey in pithy, expressive phrases.

Some of the paintings he took up and then pushed rapidly aside were of dark-skinned native women wearing veils and baggy trousers and very little else apart from a few necklaces. He smiles at these but whisked them out of sight. I suppose he thought we would be shocked. Or at least he wouldn't want Marie-Louise asking awkward questions later in front of her grandmother. I suppose out in the East he made the acquaintance of innumerable concubines; that's how men get experience and become men of the world, I know. But I wouldn't want black hands touching me. The thought of it repels me.

Marie-Louise asked: who are those ladies?

—Ladies who understand the art of how to please, he told her: plenty of them out there.

Marie-Louise said to me later: in Africa when it is hot you don't have to wear a lot of clothes. I wish it was the same in France. Does my father know those ladies too?

She hardly ever mentions her father. I suppose children forget things easily. I mumbled something; I don't remember what. I helped Monsieur Gérard tidy up and put away the folders and books, after this first lesson all together, while Marie-Louise wandered off through the open French windows into the garden. He keeps all his Eastern mementoes in the three large bottom drawers of his japanned cabinet. I had never seen such a cabinet before and admired it very much. It is a tall, splendid piece in shiny black lacquer decorated with finely painted sprays of cherry blossom, curly gnarled trees and dragons with long twisting tails, all done in delicate gold brushwork. The lower half of the cabinet is broad and deep, squatting on little curly legs. The top part, which slopes gently inwards, consists of many tiny drawers, packed boxlike several to a row, each embellished with a gold knob, and the whole thing is crowned by a pagoda roof. I longed to pull open each tiny drawer and examine the contents but of course I did not.

He saw me looking, though.

—Bits and pieces of poems in the small drawers, he explained: letters and pictures in the big ones.

I imagined him rummaging for words in the little drawers, as a haberdasher rummages in hers, rapidly opening and shutting them, for reels of cotton, to match a particular colour. I wondered how he remembered which bits of poems were where. There were no labels. I imagined him like a grocer, shaking out loose words, tipping them into a bag, mixing them up and so making a poem. But I suppose that would be cheating, to make up poems like that; not enough hard work; too much like playing.

As I was handing Monsieur Gérard the piles of sketches for him to place in the open drawer, one came loose and fluttered to the floor. I bent over and picked it up, of course glancing at it as I did so. It was a pencil sketch, not a watercolour. It wasn't of an Eastern woman but a French one, at least to me she seemed French, with silky dark hair done up with combs, and a curved, pouting mouth. She was wearing what looked like a coral necklace, and an open-necked sailor top.

Monsieur Gérard took the sheet of paper from me quite casually. He grimaced as he studied it.

—I'm as bad at drawing as you are, Mademoiselle Millicent. It doesn't do her justice.

He opened one of the other large cabinet drawers and stuffed the sketch inside. He smiled at me. I felt embarrassed, and went right out into the garden to find Marie-Louise.

JULY 4TH

Long days of golden sweetness, which we spend as much as possible in the open air. As well as carrying a wicker table and two wicker chairs out into the arbour and studying there in the mornings, we also take nature walks in the afternoons. We have been into the forest with Monsieur Gérard and the doctor, though Madame Colbert preferred not to come but to receive the doctor's wife back at home in the garden; she said it was too far for her to walk at her age. The doctor's wife exclaimed what a shame it was that her daughter Yvonne was away visiting relatives and could not come with us. I could see that Madame Colbert did not mind. She considers this Yvonne, whom I haven't yet met because she's been away at school, rather wild and badly behaved, a possible bad influence on Marie-Louise.

The forest is not, as I had feared, the sort of place in which you get lost. It is crisscrossed by a grid of paths, so as long as you have a good sense of direction all is well. Light comes down in golden needles dancing on the ground. You press forwards into the whispering silence. A couple of times we saw the ground suddenly moving just in front of our feet, a ripple of earth: grass-snakes slithering away under the nearest clump of ferns; but I wasn't at all afraid. Apparently they are far more nervous of us than we need to be of them. You just shake your walking-stick at them and they wriggle off. I haven't got a walking-stick of course, but Monsieur Gérard has, so we were all right.

We took a compass with us, to teach Marie-Louise how to use it. We played hide-and-seek. Flattened against the trunk of a great beech, imagining yourself completely alone, nothing around you for miles but bracken and closely massed trees, it is easy to feel rather strange, to visualise the god Pan coming down the great alley that slices through the very centre of the forest, a queer, goatish figure rearing up on his hind legs and playing his pipes. I've seen a picture of him somewhere, yes, I remember now, in one of the books of engravings in the studio.

We had the picnic, as promised. We had our *goûter* of brioche and apricots, cider for us and milk for the child, out of a basket, sitting on a pile of logs, and then Marie-Louise ran about, chasing butterflies, while the two men smoked their pipes and talked, and I listened.

I think the doctor's wife would have liked to come with us. It cannot have been very interesting spending the whole afternoon with Madame Colbert. When we reached the house we expected to find them still in the garden but they had returned inside, because it was so hot, and Madame Polpeau remarked sharply that we had been gone a very long time. It felt oppressive coming out of the golden sunshine into the dark, stuffy dining-room full of thick, heavy material, with the windows firmly closed to keep out the heat. Marie-Louise had wanted to stay in the forest, and I secretly agreed with her. The two men went on smoking their pipes, walking up and down in the garden. When the Polpeaus had gone I took Marie-Louise's hand and promised her that we would go to the forest again.

JULY 7TH

Monsieur Gérard was away overnight two days ago on business. His mother complained about his absence, since she was not feeling very well. He came home late yesterday morning looking tired, a little irritable, just in time to hear his mother fretting over whether Geneviève should cook four slices of liver for *déjeuner* or only three.

—Really Gérard, she approached him: you are working far too hard. Are all these journeys really necessary?

She was giving him a fierce look. He growled something, and brushed past her into his study. At *déjeuner* they hardly spoke to each other. Marie-Louise, picking up on the atmosphere, began to misbehave, whimpering and saying that her slice of liver was too pink in the middle; she didn't want to eat it. It ended with her being sent away from table in disgrace, up to her room. I went with her, feeling in disgrace myself, that I hadn't been able to force her to swallow the undercooked meat which I dislike as much as she does. As I shut the dining-room door and turned to haul the weeping Marie-Louise off along the passage I heard Madame Colbert burst out. Something like: really Gérard, why must you go on seeing that wretched woman, you will bring the family name into disgrace. There was the noise of a chair scraping back, so I picked up Marie-Louise bodily in my arms and started up the stairs with her, just as the dining-room door opened and Monsieur Gérard came hastily out. He took no notice of us but went into his study and banged the door. For supper we had the uneaten pieces of liver minced up and made into rissoles. This time they were cooked through. We ate them *à l'anglaise* with mashed potato and fried onions. Delicious.

JULY 21ST

Calm days. We are making a collection of wild flowers, and I am teaching Marie-Louise to press them We continue with our French, geography and history lessons in the study every afternoon, and it is still warm enough to carry on working outside. Marie-Louise is making good progress, and her grandmother has complimented me. Obviously, she can see that although I allow Marie-Louise plenty of physical freedom and exercise I am simultaneously scrupulous about ensuring she finishes her lessons before having treats and rewards. My English system works!

Monsieur Gérard has not been away again. His mother is tranquil once more. I forgot to mention that he has been lending me books for the last couple of weeks. He encourages me to roam freely through his shelves, take down and borrow whatever I like. My evenings and nights are transformed. Before going to bed I beg stumps of candle from Geneviève, which I smuggle upstairs in my pocket, so that I can go on reading as late as I wish. Novels, poetry, plays, travel, I'm devouring them all. Then the next day we discuss what I've read.

One of the volumes of poetry, *Les Fleurs du mal,* was inscribed on the flyleaf: to my beloved friend Gérard, from Isabelle. I wonder if that is that woman in the pencil sketch? The same one that Madame Colbert so dislikes, or another one? I suppose he must have had a lot of mistresses. It stands to reason that he would. I'm glad that I understand all that. Coming from such a sheltered background, I wouldn't be expected to. But French literature is a great help, I find. Stendhal and Flaubert and so on.

JULY 23RD

My life here is full of happiness. One warm, golden day folds into another. We had another picnic in the forest, without the doctor this time, because he and his wife are away on holiday in Brittany. We played hide-and-seek again and climbed trees. After our *goûter* we lay flat on our backs on the ground and stared up at the sky through the green and gold tracery of the distant treetops. It made you almost dizzy. You felt the world whirling round beneath you; you felt one with earth, trees, rocks and stones, and with the great wheel of the sun. I was dazed with joy. Oh if only I were a poet and could write poems.

I will put it down. I must. I can't bear not to. The most beautiful thing that has ever happened to me.

It has happened. I am in love with Gérard.

It suddenly dawned on me that I loved him. Before today, I didn't know; I just went about my life unthinking; but meanwhile love crept up on me and crack! it was the *coup de foudre*. I am astonished, and rather nervous, but I can't deny it. I am in love with Gérard. Oh the delight of writing those words, of writing his name, in this torment of having to keep my feelings utterly secret and not let anybody know.

It's happened, and there's nothing I can do about it. I feel as though I'm staggering around, shocked, blinking. The air on my skin is different. Inside me an electric current pushes back and forth. I'm changed. I have fallen in love without having the least wish to do so or the least conception it was happening until it was too late. Now I can think of nothing but him. It's an obsession, a fever, a malady. Almost a madness. I'm like a sleepwalker. In my thoughts I'm somewhere else, whatever I'm doing; I'm close to him; I'm with him whether I like it or not.

We were in the forest. The three of us were lying on the ground on a bed of pine needles, gazing up through the treetops. We had our sleeves rolled up to the elbow because it was hot. His bare forearm was very close to mine. Then he moved, and his arm touched mine by accident. I am sure he was unaware of it. My skin burned; the sunlight swam in my eyes. Then I suddenly knew. And when we sat up, and got to our feet, I felt desolation, because his forearm was no longer close to mine.

I can't imagine why I once thought him ugly. Yet, rereading this, I see that at the beginning I did. Now I think him beautiful.

He had been very kind to me. He is charming; he tells funny stories; he discusses with me the books I have read. He makes me feel that I matter to him, just a little bit, that he enjoys my company. This is arrogant and mad. He talks to me only because he's got no one else in the house to talk to. He's got a wealth of friends in Paris. He's got that woman Isabelle to love. What could he possibly see in me? Half the time I think he is laughing at me, anyway. He calls me Meess Meely. He calls me the leetle English meess. I am sure the kind of woman he falls in love with is sophisticated and worldly, like those women with big hats in Paris.

Perhaps he does like me just a tiny little bit. But I must not believe it means anything more than that. I love him and that's got to be enough. I must not ask for anything back.

JULY 25TH

The postman arrived with our letters as usual. Normally he goes around the back and delivers the letters to Geneviève in the kitchen, but seeing the front door open he came towards it. We were all just about to go out. Monsieur Gérard was going to accompany us down to the river, so that we could take Marie-Louise across and back on the passenger ferry, as a treat. Madame Colbert had decided to come with us, because her rheumatism is better, and she said she needed more exercise. I had the feeling she was keeping an eye on me, to make sure I don't become over-familiar with her son. We do, after all, spend quite a lot of time together, even though most of it shared with Marie-Louise. She can't suspect I'm in love, surely; no one can, because I am so discreet; but nonetheless these days I often find her glance on me, swiftly withdrawn as soon as I look up.

Monsieur Gérard had gone upstairs to find his jacket. The postman came up to the open door and spoke to me as I was kneeling on the hallway floor buttoning up Marie-Louise's boots. Madame Colbert was at the back of the hallway, in front of the mirror there, peering at her reflection, tying her veil on over her hat.

The postman said; letters her for Monsieur Colbert, mademoiselle. Monsieur Polpeau is still away and so I can't deliver them to him, as Monsieur Colbert asked, for him to collect later. They've been mounting up. I'm sure he'd like to have them. And there are two for you, mademoiselle, also.

He hadn't seen Madame Colbert at the back of the hall, because she was standing in the shadows. I peeped back at her. I wasn't sure how much she'd heard. She had one long hatpin between her pursed lips and was raising her hand to drive the other into the swathes of black net on top of her head. I sense her stiffen, rather than saw her.

Clearly these were letters whose existence Gérard wished to conceal from his mother. Presumably from that woman Isabelle.

I called out: oh, letters for me, how wonderful.

Swivelling round to face the postman again, I was only half aware of what I was doing; oddly dreamy; everything was happening in slow motion. But quick too. I drove the tip of the buttonhook into the palm of my hand so hard that I yelped with pain as it pierced the skin. Marie-Louise, taken aback, tumbled sideways from her sitting position, fell over, and knocked her head against the metal corner of the base of the umbrella stand. She screamed in shock. Madame Colbert sailed forwards to see what all the fuss was about, but, by the time she reached the two of us, the incriminating package of letters had vanished into my pocket and I was blocking her further progress by remaining sprawled across the hall floor with my arms around the sobbing Marie-Louise, trying to comfort her. She was frightened by the knock on the head and by the blood on my hand.

All Madame Colbert saw, as the postman apologetically retreated, were the two letters with foreign stamps which were indeed for me. Madame Colbert turned back to the mirror. She took her second long pin and drove it into her hat like a javelin.

After we had collected ourselves up, washed bruised forehead and stanched bleeding hand and applied iodine, we set forth. Marie-Louise was delighted with the red stain on the side of her head, where the iodine had been dabbed on. She seemed to think it was a badge of courage. She rather enjoyed having a wound. I felt the same about the red mark in the centre of my palm. It throbbed and stung, just like love does.

As we left the house, Gérard stood holding open the door to let us pass. I came out last. Madame Colbert was busy smoothing her gloves and telling Marie-Louise to wrap her scarf more tightly around her throat in case it was chilly down by the river. I hovered next to him, for just a second. I felt his hand come up and pat my shoulder; I did not dare look at him; and then the door was shut and he was ahead of me on the path, tucking his mother's hand into his arm.

We took the ferry, exactly as we had planned. The wind got up, gusty and fresh, as we stepped aboard; it whipped our cheeks and we held on tightly to our hats. As we reached the centre of the river the sun suddenly came out from behind a large grey cloud and dazzled on the surface of the water. I felt as though it had broken out inside me too, rays of golden joy; the whole word was shining fiercely inside me and out; the river seemed to be pouring through me; I was flying into the light like a seagull. All I could think of was that Gérard had touched me. Now he has touched me twice. Of course I shake hands with him morning and night but that's a mere conventional courtesy in public; it doesn't count.

Madame Colbert had moved away to the other side of the ferry, to speak to an acquaintance she had spotted there, and Marie-Louise went with her. Gérard stayed standing next to me for a while. He leaned idly on the rail, drumming on it with the fingers of his left hand, whistling, looking straight ahead as though he were simply admiring the view of the forêt de Brotonne rising up on the opposite shore. But I was certain he stayed because he wanted to be close to me. In case I had anything to tell him. Or to give to him. Then he moved casually off across the deck and went to talk to his mother and her friend.

JULY 27TH

The Polpeaus are back from Brittany. They came to *déjeuner* on Sunday, but without their daughter Yvonne, who was spending the day in her room as a punishment for being rude to her mother. Marie-Louise, hearing this, looked rather wide-eyed, and behaved impeccably throughout all five courses. The Polpeaus described their trip at great length.

They made a little detour before coming home; they returned via the coast of upper Normandy. They visited Etretat, which they described as very pretty and picturesque, and then drove all the way up to St-Valery-en-Caux, via Blessetot, Yport, Fécamp, and Veulettes-sur-Mer. Geneviève seemed agitated, her mind elsewhere. She dropped a plate onto the floor where it broke. Luckily the plate was empty. Gérard got up and patted her arm and told her not to worry. He helped her pick up the shards of china and insisted it was his fault, the he had jogged her elbow by accident. How kind that man is. How many other men would bother about a servant's feelings, as he does? She's just a clumping girl from the country but he treats her as though she's one of us.

With our coffee we drank tiny glasses of Bénédictine, a present brought back by the Polpeaus from Fécamp. It was sweetish; green and oily; delicious. I wanted a second glass but of course could not ask for one. In the evening Gérard did not go out. He played chess with me instead. He taught me, since I hardly know the game at all. We played under the eyes of his mother. Marie-Louise sat with us and tried to help me win. She urged me on and held the captured pieces very tightly between her hands.

AUGUST 1ST

Madame Colbert has proposed that we are to have a holiday, since Marie-Louise has been working so well and so hard and deserves a treat. If we are to make a little voyage, my employer declares, then we should make it very soon, before the weather changes. Sea-bathing is good for the health and the sea air will do us all good. Monsieur Gérard will of course accompany us, to escort his mother.

She is taking a leaf out of the Polpeaus' book. She has decided we are to go to Etretat. This may be one way of putting paid to Madame Polpeau's long-winded descriptions of all she and the doctor did and saw while they were there. When she comes to call in the afternoons she regales her hostess with detailed accounts of cliff walks and fish suppers to which Madame Colbert is bound to listen politely while having nothing of her own with which to fight back and stun her guest. When Madame Polpeau opens her mouth a stream of twittering banalities gushes out; her voice sandpapers your ears; after only a couple of minutes in her company I want to scream with irritation and boredom. Gérard feels exactly the same as I do. When he sees her coming he vanishes into his study, or he claps on his hat and escapes into the garden.

Artists must be free, and unshackled by the normal petty conventions of domestic life. I know this because I have the passionate soul of an artist myself. Gérard suffers terribly from the restrictions imposed on him by the need to live with his mother and take care of her. It seems it would be unthinkable for him to set up his own separate establishment. She is his widowed mother and he is her devoted son and that is that. She is the heartiest, sturdiest widow that I ever saw. Why should she not be? She is the luckiest of women: she lives with Gérard, she depends upon him for all her amusement and interests in life; he will never leave her as long as she lives.

At the seaside he will feel much freer. No wonder he has needed to escape to Paris from time to time. Or to that woman.

She turned up yesterday afternoon. She pursued him into his own house. I would never do such a thing. So forward and unfeminine.

We had finished our lessons. It was very hot again. I took Marie-Louise upstairs to look for her hat so that she could put it on before going out; Madame Colbert is very nervous of the effects of sunshine on the unprotected head and never goes out herself without quantities of veils and parasols. The hat had been left in the wrong place and we were searching for it in the wardrobes. I went into my room and found it in the cupboard there. Just as I was about to call Marie-Louise from across the landing I heard the noise of a carriage outside. It stopped; it was clearly at our gate. I ran over to the window and peeped out.

A veiled woman descended from the open carriage, holding her pale blue skirts scooped to the side, a meringue puff bunched up in one hand. Her slender ankles showed, a gleam of gauzy grey stocking, small feet shod in pale blue. She flowed rather than simply got down, swiftly and nimbly. The elegant cut and hang of her clothes, the flimsiness of her little boots, marked her out as a city-dweller, one to whom fashion would mean far more than protection from rain and mud. Over her dress she wore a thin silky-looking coat, also in pale blue, trimmed with black lace, and she carried a furled parasol and a small handbag. She paused by the garden gate shaking out the creases from her skirts, inspecting her gloves and tugging them straight. She threw back her veil, revealing the little straw hat perched on her gleaming black air, which was done up behind her head in a chignon.

The curve of her cheekbones, the pout of her small mouth, her large dark eyes: all seemed familiar, yet I could not imagine where we could have met. I watched her square her shoulders, draw a deep breath, and smooth the material of her dress down over her stomach in what seemed an oddly nervous gesture for one so beautiful. Then she put up her parasol like a little flag, turned and faced the house, opened the gate, and marched into the garden and up the path. She walked with that slightly bow-legged gait of women who wear high heels, with clenched knees. Your feet on tiptoe can't take the weight of your body, so your thighs arch and grip and you lurch a bit. Slightly crab-like.

She had not noticed me studying her out of my window. I drew my head back inside as I heard the bell peal downstairs, once, twice, then once again. I hesitated for a few seconds, wondering what to do. Geneviève, hanging out the washing at the far end of the back garden, might not have heard the summons, and Madame Colbert, woken abruptly from her nap, and not expecting a visitor, as far as I knew, might feel flustered and in disarray. Gérard was in his study, not to be interrupted. I decided to run down and open the door myself. If the woman in blue had come to the wrong house by mistake it would take only a minute to set her right, and then Madame Colbert need not be disturbed at all.

As I slithered down the stairs I realised that of course I knew who the woman was. So did my employer. She had got to the door just as I started up the hallway, and was holding it open. Her neck poked forward, as though she were listening momentarily to something squawking below her, a chick fallen out of a nest, perhaps, floppy and broken-boned. Then she straightened herself. Her back was magnificent. It was the back of a general with his besieged city behind him and his troops drawn up in readiness to repel the invader, addressing the raggle-taggle regiment of the insolent army who dares to believe there is a skirmish to be fought. Over my dead body, said that fierce and indomitable back: will you ever enter my house. And the wrinkled hand gripping the doorknob added its translation and apostrophe: you impudent baggage no better than you should be; you little cheapskate strumper; how dare you turn up uninvited and expect me to welcome you in; I'd like to slap your falsely smiling face.

Beyond that small, iron-moulded back, that bulwark against the fretting sea, there was an agitation of pale blue, a flutter of white, as though the visitor had drawn herself back and up, all her courage gathered into one gesture, a small wave trying to become a massive tidal one, willing herself to be powerful, determined to break on our shore. You felt her trying to surge forwards through the doorway with a force born of desperation.

Madame Colbert did not flinch. She held her post. She said in a soft, calm voice as though she were addressing a wilful child: there has been some mistake. I am afraid you cannot see my son, madame. He is unable to receive visitors because he is not here. He is away, and I have no idea whatsoever when he will return.

I skipped backwards, onto the bottom rung of the stairs. I leaned over the banisters to hear what happened next.

—Goodbye, madame, said the stern old woman, and shut the door.

I tiptoed back upstairs and fetched Marie-Louise's hat. From my window I watched the carriage drive away again.

When the others came in Madame Colbert was seated in her little armchair, yawning, as though she had dozed off and had only just woken up. She put up her hands and patted her hair, making sure it was tidy. She pulled Marie-Louise to her and gave her a kiss. Over supper she suggested that we all have a little holiday and set off for Etretat.

AUGUST 9TH

We have taken rooms in a hotel on the front. All of our windows face the sea. Gérard is on the second floor and the rest of us on the first. Geneviève has come too. Madame Colbert says she is feeling her age, and dreads the return of her rheumatism. So Geneviève is to look after her, while I look after Marie-Louise. Geneviève and Marie-Louise are sharing a room in between Madame Colbert's and mine.

My bedroom is square, with a high ceiling. Last night, as I got into bed, it felt sculpted and mysterious, a new place to discover, like an underwater cave. This morning, full of sunshine, it suggests magic and enchantment eve more strongly, the haunts of those talking seals in Marie-Louise's collection of fairy tales. The walls are washed greeny-blue; a kind of turquoise; almost exactly the colour of the sea this morning with the sun gleaming on it from the unclouded sky; and the gilt-framed mirrors on either side of the open window bring in the bright light, which sparkles on the brass bed-rail, on the polished wooden backs of chairs, on the creamy marble top of the washstand which is streaked and flecked, white on grey, like one of the pebbles on the beach just outside.

Lying in bed, propped on my huge square pillow and fat bolster, I pretend I'm swimming underwater. Through the open window I can see blue sky, and below it, seemingly just outside my windowsill, a gently descending slope of pebbles, then an expanse of wet shingle, drawn up on whose ridge are three fishing boats, their hulls glistening and black. Dropped beyond them is the blue-green sea dazzling with light. Gulls cry and swoop, and the long white muslin curtains flutter like gulls' wings. The air blows in onto my face, salty and fresh. I'm floating between sea and sky; I'm surfacing into a dream from which I don't want to wake; the quilt lies lightly across my knees like a fat white cloud. I want to stay here for ever, caught in this moment of purest happiness, suspended, idling in the brilliant light. But now I must get up and dress and go next door to see to Marie-Louise.

LATER

It turned out that Geneviève had got up early and gone out, forbidding Marie-Louise to accompany her, bidding her wait for me. She said to Marie-Louise that she couldn't help it, she just had to got outside and look at the sea. I can understand that. I fell asleep last night to the repeated soft crash of water onto the beach, and I believe I heard it all night long, waking up into it, as though the waves were surging into my room and wanted to take me away with them. Geneviève came back just in time to help Madame Colbert do her hair. We breakfasted hastily then went out to make a cursory exploration of the little town.

The valley opens out like a mouth, for the sea to rush into, and Etretat sits in it, wedged between the steep chalk cliffs rising on either side. It's a small town, triangular shaped, a maze of narrow streets tight with old houses and cottages, some half-timbered and some built of flint, with back alleys leading to tiny gardens tucked in between. Wherever you go you hear the gulls crying overhead and you smell the sea. We saw the sights which tourists are obliged to visit: the Romanesque church, the old market-place, several ancient and picturesque café-restaurants. Gérard turns out to know the town well and squired us about. Geneviève stayed behind in the hotel to organise finding a washerwoman and getting our laundry done.

Déjeuner was a big bowl of *moules à la marinière* followed by grilled mackerel with sorrel and butter sauce. The fish is caught in the morning, sold on the stalls at the top of the beach, cooked a moment later then whisked onto our plates, as fresh as can be. After *déjeuner,* Gérard vanished outside to smoke a cigar and to talk to a couple of old acquaintances he had met who were also staying at the hotel; painters, he said, who come here every year to paint the changing light. Marie-Louise pleaded to be allowed to forgo her nap, to go out again immediately and walk beside the sea. Madame Colbert did not argue. She was drowsy with food and wanted her own doze. She settled herself in a wicker chair behind the glass wall of the hotel sun-porch, which gives onto the broad esplanade running between the two sheltering wings of the cliffs. We left Geneviève on duty beside Madame Colbert, ready to chat to her when she woke up, and we ran off like children given a day out of school, down the broad flight of steps onto the beach.

Once there, you're in a new element. You jump down onto the damp stones; you smell fish and the sharp salt breeze; you become transformed; another creature. Freer. More daring. Not caring about how you look or what other people think. Marie-Louise felt it too. She grabbed my hand and shouted aloud with pleasure.

We slipped and slithered down the steep shelf of pebbles, digging our heels in, leaning backwards. Then we reached flat shingle. The tide was now going out, leaving behind a fringe of seaweed, broken shells, dead starfish, bits of cuttle-fish. We crunched to the sea's edge and bent down to dip our fingers into transparent water. It was so cold our hands felt gloved in ice, but nonetheless we took off our shoes and stockings and paddled in the shallows, letting the spent waves ripple over our feet, enjoying the shock of the chilliness. Quite quickly we were warm again, standing in the sun, covered all over by it; like a coat. You could feel the power of the tide under your soles, the grit sliding around your toes as the sea tugged against them.

We wandered back and forth, looking at the views, the great arches of cliff that dive out at either end of the beach and plunge into violet-shadowed sea. Then, still barefoot, we picked our way slowly over the stones as far as we could go to the left, past the start of the cliff path and down towards the flat black expanse of rock. We teetered over heaps of floppy brown seaweed and peered into pools like tiny steep pockets of water among the crevasses, floored with fine sand, with cushions of feathery green moss so vividly bright you blinked, swarming with tiny white crabs, so pale they were translucent. Of course at this point

I had to carry Marie-Louise's shoes and stockings so that she could have her hands free, first for waving in the air to help her balance on the slippery surface of the rocks, and then for scooping down into the rock pools, trying to catch crabs, to prise off stubborn limpets. If you caught these unawares, you could shift them a fraction, just for a second, before they took fright and hunkered back down, leaving no jellied gap between fluted shell skirt and rock. While Marie-Louise hunted, I picked up pebbles. I liked their coldness and smoothness inside my clasp. Soon my pockets were weighed down, bumping against my knees, and my fingers, when I licked them, tasted strongly of salt.

Next time I looked round, there was Gérard standing on a boulder, quite close to us, hands in his pockets, staring out to sea.

I didn't move, or wave. I just waited. I was content simply to be near him. His presence made me happy. Nothing else had to happen. We were together, by the sea; we shared the rocks and the green waves and the sky; that was enough. I wanted the moment to last. Then, somewhere behind us, a dog barked, and Gérard glanced up, saw me, and came towards us.

We trod out further over the platform of rocks. The tide was now so low that you could walk through the great archway cutting under the cliff, towards the next bay, picking your way over yellow boulders already scoured dry by sun and win. Right in the centre of this tunnel-like path, the cliff wall gaped to reveal an opening. Bending over, we crept into a cave that reached back into darkness. Under our feet was wet sand shaped into ripples by the departing sea. Difficult to walk over. So we sat down near the mouth of the cave and rested, out of the sharp breeze, and Marie-Louise and I put our shoes and stockings back on. I wore my stocking strolled down around my ankles like socks. I couldn't very well do otherwise, with Gérard there. I didn't want to waste these precious minutes of his company finding a boulder to retire behind. I didn't want to be coy and have him laugh at me.

Apparently the sea lends you a cave like this just for a short time, before the tide turns and the waves come racing back. These are dangerous places, Gérard told us, these caverns along this stretch of coast, that rise into chimneys reaching right up through the cliffs; people have perished here, coming out to explore but then forgetting the hour of the turning tide, becoming cut off and trapped by the rising waters, unable to get back to the safety of the main beach.

Marie-Louise loved feeling a little frightened by Gérard's tales. She wanted to stay on in the cave and play houses, but we were cold and wanted to get back into the heat of the sun, so we coaxed her out.

We were too tired, suddenly, to talk the walk we had planned, up the cliff path and down again. I promised we'd take it tomorrow. We sat on Gérard's coat on the ridge above the tideline, instead, and skated stones down the beach towards the far-off water. Marie-Louise, who had missed her usual nap, suddenly dropped, worn out by sun and fresh air, felled by the salt breeze. She curled up between us and fell asleep.

—We'll be her windbreaks, Gérard said to me: her sentries. You're not desperate to go back yet, are you?

—No, I said; I'd rather stay here.

At first we sat propped against the steep slope of stones at our back, looking out to sea, knees drawn up, chins resting on folded arms, and then we turned to face each other, reclining on our elbows, so that we were looking at one another as we talked. I don't know how I managed this. He was so close to me that I felt I was trembling. I wanted to touch him so much I had to concentrate fiercely on keeping still. I could scarcely speak. I could hardly form an opinion let alone shape it into words; I felt tongue-tied and stammering. When I said anything I thought how stupid I must sound. This intimacy was what I desired more than anything in the world and yet it unnerved me. Something powerful, a tide of wanting, was drawing me towards him and pushing me back, forward and back, like the rhythm of the sea itself, the waves falling urgently onto the beach. My insides leaped about in a mad ballet; I lay there a hand's touch away from him, but not quite touching him; I thought I might turn to water.

I'd emptied my pockets of my collection of pebbles when we sat down, and now his hand kept picking them up, one by one, and caressing them, examining them one by one in his palm, then stroking them slowly with his forefinger. I can't remember all we talked about. It's his nearness I was conscious of, that I was reclining on his rough old coat, next to him on the damp stones, as though we were on a bed. We talked a little about our childhoods, and he told me about his life in Paris, before his father died and his mother came to live with him. He has been to London twice. He said he'll never forget the smell of the London fog which crept under the window sash and swirled about in his rented rooms, gritty, smelling of soot.

Marie-Louise began to stir, and it was clearly time to go. Gérard leaned forward and kissed me on the cheek. He looked at me for a second then made to do it again. I quickly turned my face so that the kiss half landed on my mouth.

Then we scrambled to our feet, and lifted Marie-Louise by her elbows, and took her back to the hotel for her tea. All evening I have been restless, in a fever of not wanting to sit still, which I have tried to hide. All I want to do is talk with him, stay close to him, and of course I can't; I mustn't. It is a relief to have come up to bed early, pleading tired-ness, and to be sitting beside the open window scribbling this. After supper Gérard went out for a stroll. My soul has flown out with him to walk beside him, invisible in the fragrant salty night. I imagine I can smell the scent of his cigar and see its red tip winking in the darkness. Like a bea-con marking the harbour and I'm the ship making for the shore.

AUGUST 10TH

I am writing this down as though I believe it but I can't. Gérard is not going to stay with us in Etretat after all. He is going away. He accompanied us here simply to settle us in and will depart early tomorrow morning.

I don't know where he is going because Madame Colbert did not say. She gave me this news idly, as though it were not important, as I was helping Marie-Louise sort out the bucket of shells and stones she had brought back from the beach. She spoke quite casually but her little eyes were sharper than buttonhooks. That woman is my enemy. She does not want me to be happy; she wants me to suffer. And I am suffering; my entire body feels as though it is being torn slowly in two and I feel sick and couldn't eat any supper. All the time Madame Colbert watched me speculatively as though I were a spider she had found in the bath and she was wondering whether or not to scoop me out or simply squash me.

Marie-Louise was distraught at the news, and comforting her helped me to pretend that I wasn't.

—Of course Uncle Gérard is going away, the hateful woman informed Marie-Louise; we can't expect him to spend all day doing nothing, merely keeping us company by the seaside; he has work to do; he can't hang around here indefinitely wasting his precious time.

I was pleased with myself. She wanted to hurt me; she stabbed me to the heart with her cool words, which she flung out as though they were meaningless and ordinary, like the florets of seaweed Marie-Louise was arranging in patterns on the tray; but I did not let her see her words' effect; I refused to grant her that satisfaction. The victory is mine. I glanced at her as though what she had said was not very interesting, far too banal to bother with over-much, and I murmured: oh, really, yes of course. And then I watched my fingers pick up a fragment of mussel shell and fit it neatly into place in the child's mosaic. Her words ripped me open; I began to bleed; but I felt my mouth stretch into the grimace of a smile and heard my voice say, quite unconcerned: it's time to tidy up, *chérie*, it will soon be lunchtime.

I don't know what else happened today. Gérard did not reappear. I have not seen him since breakfast when he sat behind the paper in silence. I have crawled through the day. I had the sensation of pinning my lips together so that I would not cry out; my mouth could not spring open and release a scream of anguish. Now I'm upstairs, in my night-clothes. I heard everybody come up to bed, their doors close, their bedsprings squeak once, twice, as they sank down on their mattresses. I am waiting until she, my enemy, his mother, is fast asleep. I am waiting for the entire hotel to settle down. Then I am going to creep upstairs and find Gérard. I have got to know when I shall be able to see him again. He must tell me. I don't understand what is happening and he must explain. I must go upstairs and find him and be with him. He will talk to me and he will tell me everything will be all right. I'm sitting here crying and shivering, crying very quietly so no one will hear. I must dry my eyes, wash my face and brush my hair. I must go upstairs.

AUGUST 11TH

Gérard departed this morning, immediately after breakfast. He shook my hand and said goodbye.

Geneviève

The only thing to do was to get out of there as fast as possible. I fled from Madame Montjean's house, from Madame Montjean's husband, from Madame Montjean's sick child. I escaped what the curé would have called the future or possible occasion of sin, by putting distance between myself and it, but I took with me the memory of Madame Montjean's face, of Madame Montjean's voice. Etched into my flesh like acid, a burn of shame.

Frédéric had backed off, stood leaning against the wall. Now he shouldered forwards. Perhaps he was going to hit me. I hauled up my disarranged clothes then flung myself at the door. My legs were shaking but I managed to get out. Somebody was howling but you couldn't hear the noise.

The air seemed full of collisions and cries. Then came a long moment of silence. I avoided whatever happened next. Leaving the two of them facing each other in the bar, I darted out into the kitchen and upstairs into my room. On the top shelf of my cupboard reposed my neatly folded woollen cloak, and, on the one below, my leather purse, swollen with coins. I grabbed these, then slunk downstairs again, out of the back door, across the yard, and into the street.

The village drowsed in its afternoon hush. I saw no one as I blundered through it with my belongings scrambled under my arm. My breath heaved and sawed painfully in my lungs as I ran; tears and snot flowed down my cheeks; all my bones scraped. Moments later I had got past the outlying cottages and was heading away from Blessetot, up the steep chalk road that led inland. When I met the main coast road, I turned right into it and began to make my way towards Etretat.

I trudged along with my apron pulled up over my head, a makeshift veil, so that my head and shoulders were screened from the hot sun of early afternoon. Behind this shelter I could cry in private, with no one to see me. With luck no one would be able to say which way I had gone.

Arrived in Etretat, I made for the orphanage, not knowing what else to do. I was dull and stupid from so much weeping, from walking through the hot afternoon. My feet led me to the pointed gate in the high wall, and my hand, of its own volition, stretched up and tugged the iron bellpull. I had no idea what I was going to say to Sister Pauline. Words were something I seemed to have left behind. But convent rules saved me from having to dig for language. The nuns' routine was not to be broken by chance visitors arriving as supplicants. The portress who peered at me through the tiny barred window that flew open in the gate was a young sister whose bony face, framed in the well-remembered white coif and black bonnet, I did not recognise. Her hand, resting on the catch of the casement, was looped with a rosary of black beads. I had interrupted her prayers. She moved her thin lips impatiently but said nothing.

I mumbled Sister Pauline's name.

The nun lifted her sandy eyebrows. Forced to speak, she sighed. She said in her pinched voice that Sister Pauline was of course in chapel, singing the Divine Office, and could not be disturbed. She glared at me as she spoke. Clearly I was an idiot heathen not to know at what times the nuns sang the Hours in choir. Worse, I was probably a prowler up to no good; perhaps she would have me driven away. I did not dare ask if I could leave a message. I stuck my hands in my pockets and stared at the nun's chin. She had a mole on it, wrinkled and brown as a currant. I had forgotten how much time the nuns had to spend in church. I felt sorry for Sister Pauline. I couldn't imagine how she survived all those hours on her knees. But I felt envious too. She might be bored but at least she was safe. She was not in trouble. I realised I couldn't possibly explain to her what had happened to me. It was a blessing, really, that I wasn't given the chance to soil her ears with an account of my wickedness. I could protect her. Her innocence could survive intact. For a nun that was important.

—Come back on Monday, said the portress: that's our day for giving alms. I will see to you then. But for now, be off with you.

The little window in the door slammed shut. I sat down on the kerb and wondered what to do. The late afternoon felt fidgety and hot, full of edges that rubbed and cut. The street was my only house now, but it was too shaky a place to shelter in. The market hall was hut. I could not creep inside and take refuge there. All the houses had turned themselves inside out and thrown me out; the roofs had all blown off; the walls were of straw; the wolf as prowling near. If I curled up and escaped the difficult afternoon by going to sleep, as I longed to do, my back would feel too exposed; I'd be too vulnerable; someone might come and attack me. Only bad people loitered in the streets of bars and cafés behind the market-place, that was clear. Good people had homes to go to. A passing woman frowned distantly in my direction and twitched her skirts aside. I suddenly felt afraid that the police would appear and haul me off to a cell.

Male passers-by, drifting along in twos and threes, glanced at me speculatively. Their glances assessed my flesh; livestock at market. A couple of these men, bolder than the rest, approached me and suggested I accompany them to a nearby café. They mimed to each other, laughing, what we might do next. I was trapped in dreamy panic. My limbs were sandbags, too heavy to lift. The only thing to do was to hide inside this passivity. The only way I could defend myself was to anticipate what they'd do next and act before they did, get in first, as though I were not at all afraid. Forestall being gobbled up by the wolf by throwing myself into the wolf's jaws. Appear willing; offer to go with them; do whatever they wanted; while the real me hid safely somewhere else altogether.

One of them put out his hand and touched my breast, while the other nudged and jostled me from the side. Contact was a shock, awoke me and made me jump, goaded me out of lethargy into action. I shouted at them to leave me alone.

Their faces went blank with surprise, their ingratiating smiles wiped away.

—Stupid little tart. We were only trying to be friendly. Ugly little whore, who'd want to bother with you?

They took themselves off, red-faced and muttering, and I stumbled around the corner into a quiet side-street. I sat on a low wall to recover, wiping the sweat from my face with my handkerchief, waiting for my knees to stop shaking.

The only thing to do was to get out of town altogether. Start again somewhere else. Take a train to Rouen or Le Havre or even Paris, depending on how expensive the journey might be. At least I had money. But when I clapped my hand to my pocket I discovered that it was empty. The two men must have filched my purse, and I'd been too scared of them to notice what they were up to.

Not knowing what else to do. I made my way to the beach. The esplanade was thronged with people in their summer best taking the early evening air. Arm in arm with each other, little dogs on leads looping about their feet. I edged through them and slipped down the wide flight of stone steps onto the pebbles. Here I stood still for a while, bending over and wrapping my arms around my waist to stop myself from crying, heaving in gulps of fresh salt air laden with wetness. Then I straightened up and stared at the sea. It swelled and sank, calm under golden milky light. The ride was up, and the fishing boats were preparing to put out. Men and boys were lined up on either side of the black hulls, ready to shoulder them down into the waves.

I slid past these intent groups and went left, towards the great cliff arch which reared up and out and plunged its foot deep into the sea, at the far end of the beach. Here there was just a strip of pebbles to walk on. No rocks showed. The water lapped just beyond my sabots. I was at the top of a ridge which began to shelve where the rippling breakers met it. I remembered this beach well from those rare outings in childhood. It dropped down sharply here into steep depths, a strong current. It would be like jumping off the cliff. Anyone who could not swim would find her clothes gathering water, ballooning then soaking; the weight of saturated cloth would drag her down, so heavy; the sea would rush into her open mouth and she would swallow the sea and drown.

I wondered how cold the water was, and thought I should find out. I slid and scrambled down the wet hill of stones, plunging through fine spray, into the waves. Chill and glassy green they broke over my skirts, wrapping the thick material around my knees, clogging them. I staggered, then began to flounder forwards.

Through the splashing of the waves and the shrill calls of seagulls I heard voices shouting behind me. I plunged onwards, throwing myself under a crest of foam; my feet sucked up from under me as I was snatched, spun round and thrown up again; the sea a great mouth spitting me out; then whirled forwards again, gulped down with choking salt streams, gasping, inside a green-veined tunnel; then cruel hands clamped to my waist and took me away; I fought and kicked but they were hauling me, pebbles bumping my face; my back being thumped; and retching, retching, while harsh voices cried above me like birds pecking at prey.

I was lying on the beach, vomitting seawater, face scoured by the cold wind, flesh chilled to the bone, my sodden skirt lying on me like a stone shroud, while fishermen bent over me and scolded me and I flopped like a caught mackerel in the net of their arms. For some reason the beautiful black-haired woman swam up too; her white face glimmered above me and I thought she was going to have me tied up in a net and laugh; but no; her mouth was a wide red o of astonishment. I shut my eyes which were leaking salt streams because I had not managed to drown.

Two of the fishermen made a chair with their linked hands and carried me up to the top of the beach. They laid me on something softer than stones. Hairy. Somebody's coat, perhaps, or a heap of nets. They tapped my cheeks to make me wake up and look at them and prove I was not dead. Above us was the esplanade. People's hatted heads hung over it; their faces, eager and greedy for corpses, stared down at me. Propping me against the side of the esplanade wall my rescuers produced a bottle, uncorked it, thrust its neck between my teeth and tipped a fiery liquid down my throat. I spluttered and dribbled as raw heat hit my stomach. Somebody seized my hand and chafed them. The beautiful black-haired woman reappeared with her male companion. They collected me up, stomach, face, hands; they insisted I was not just a mess of loose bits but a person they recognised and pretended they knew. I was floating and weak; they had me lifted, taken up the steps to the esplanade, carried indoors somewhere warm, undressed and put into a bed whose shelter I embraced as though I were a loaf going gladly into the oven's fire not caring whether I lived or died so long as I could be warm. I pulled the covers over my head and felt sleep knock me out, a soft hammer blow that sent me happily down, down, down to depths where there were no dreams, only all-enveloping blackness.

I slept, apparently, for a day and two nights. I woke up finally empty of cold and of seawater and very hungry. Smooth pillowcase against my cheek. Morning sunlight eased around the iron bedposts. The room was unfamiliar. It smelled of eau-de-Cologne and soap. On the bamboo table by the bed lay a pipe, brownish-gold, and I stared at this for some time, unable to comprehend why it was there. I knew it wasn't Frédéric's, but that was as far as I could get.

The door rattled, opened. An elderly woman in apron and sabots came in. She explained that she was the landlady, that I was in Monsieur Colbert's lodgings, yes, in Etretat, that he was gone away for a couple of days to escort his friends back to Rouen, and that on his return he would decide what was to become of me. She folded her lips over at this point, like the crimped edges of pastry on a pie, to indicate that he had forbidden her to ask me any questions. Her fluted lips reminded me of those apple tarts I had made long ago with Madame Montjean in the kitchen at Blessetot, how carefully we had pinched the dough into patterns, and I felt tears begin to roll down my cheeks.

—Come now, don't cry, my hostess said: whatever you've done, it's over now; nobody's going to hurt you here.

I got out of bed, to show her in return for this forbearance that I could look after myself and not be any more of a nuisance, and she brought me some hot water so that I could wash, and my clothes, which she had dried. She took me into her kitchen and gave me a bowl of potato soup and stood over me to make sure I drank it. She disapproved of me strongly, yet she was kind. When Monsieur Colbert returned from Rouen he was kind too. He told me he and his companion had recognised me when I lay as one dead on the beach, knew me from the café in Blessetot. They'd fobbed off suggestions of fetching the police, certain I wouldn't want them to interfere. Monsieur Colbert spoke to me as though it were quite normal that I should have been fished out of the sea; the merest of accidents that I nearly drowned. He saw how humiliated I felt and chatted away pretending not to notice. He fiddled with his pipe, tamping the tobacco with one finger, throwing spent matches on the floor, while I got used to him.

I had not wanted to be rescued. He had helped drag me back to life, and I would far rather have been lying curled up on the sand at the bottom of the sea. I had already been back down to the beach and thanked the fishermen. They were as gruff and shy as I was; they nodded and grunted then began making jokes about their extraordinary catch of slippery girl. Nor did Monsieur Colbert want to listen to my blurted and angry thanks. Instead he found me a job. He took me back to Jumièges with him, introduced me to his mother, whose cook-housekeeper had just left to get married, and insisted she employ me.

Nine months later Marie-Louise arrived, and then, in June, Miss Millicent to be her governess. The house took me in, and in return I swept and dusted it and cared for its inhabitants.

Madame Colbert was as different from Madame Montjean as she could be. She knew nothing about me save that I needed a job, had come from the orphanage, and had already been in service. Her son's recommendation was all she required. She demanded no other references and asked me no questions. When she spoke to me she sounded courteous and kind but as though she were leaning down from a balcony. I could not love her, which was a relief. To love someone you have to get close up. You can't love someone from a distance; you can only revere them or worship them; I knew the difference.

Not that Madame Colbert required to be loved by her maid. She would have felt surprised, even insulted, if she had been made aware that I had personal feelings about our relationship. We were *bonne* and *maîtresse* and that was that. In return for the wages she paid me she expected nothing but prompt, dutiful service, which I gave her.

Nothing involved her except her family, which she held as sacred as any curé did that of Mary, Joseph, and Jesus. People like me might come from orphanages; people like her never. People like me lost their relations and possessions along the way. People like her kept hold of private incomes, inheritances of money and property, heirlooms passed down from one generation to the next, attics full of furniture. People like her lived their family lives behind a wall of inviolable privacy. People like me lived under the surveillance of our betters.

But Madame Colbert did not bother me. Now that rheumatism and heart disease had shrunk her interest in the outside world, her immediate family was more important and holy than ever. Her son was her fixed star, around whom she revolved adoringly. A calmer, quieter affection was lavished on her granddaughter Marie-Louise. Her indifference to me suited me, gave me a breathing space. I soon settled into the ways of her household. I kept my head down and got on with my work.

For the moment I simply observed them all out of the corner of my eye. I witnessed the English governess begin to weave her life into a shining love story like a cobweb spangled with rain. I saw her swivel her eyes, rapt and eager, after Monsieur Colbert, alert to his least gesture and word, twitching and turning pink whenever he spoke to her. I watched Madame Colbert reach her own conclusions about this. She was the fiercest of guard dogs, seeing off any woman suspected of threatening her peace, of loosening her son from her love's grip. She had her teeth firmly sunk in him, because she had nothing and no one else to live for. She was too infirm to go out performing good works; travel did not interest her; she disliked reading. She attended mass on Sundays; she sewed; she sparred with Madame Polpeau; she glanced at magazines; and she fussed over Monsieur Colbert. She threaded her needle with the umbilical cord; she tried to stitch him back onto her, to pink their two skins edge to edge and run a seam along; she wanted him to wear her like a new coat fresh from the tailor.

All he cared about was his work, and the hours when he could get away from the household and shut himself up in his study to write. Over and over again he ripped himself away from her: he got up and left the room, or he went out and caught the train to Paris; and her careful sewing tore into holes; the layers of fine cotton were rent apart and bloodied and could not be mended. Patiently, proudly, the most affectionate of maternal spiders, she pretended not to notice, and cast out her lasso again, her looping stitches, to catch him and rope him in once more. Docile, appeased by his moment of freedom, he would return, until he began to fidget again under the pressure of so much attention, and had to break free for the hundredth time of the embroideries she cast round him like nets.

I despised her for the unrequited love which made her so vulnerable to hurt. I thought she was a fool to love him so much. At her age she should have known better. He had to live with her; he had to care for her; I am sure that he did love her as the good mother she was; but she wanted an extra ration of love and would never get it. When she stabbed her needle into the work she cradled in her lap I thought she was stabbing him and herself. He would never love her as much as she desired. Her love frightened me; it was so violent; it laid her open to such sorrow and such despair.

His work, in any case, was where he lived; poetry was his lover and family; words dancing and making love on paper were the most real life he could imagine. The other, the one that Madame Colbert called real, was something of a shadow by comparison.

I understood this because he used to come and talk to me sometimes. The kitchen was a peaceful place: bare and plain, with just a stove, a table and chairs, two shelves of pots and pans. It was behind the dining-room, at the back of the house, whitewashed and cool, with a tiled floor and a window onto the garden. I kept the windows open whenever it wasn't raining, the muslin curtains looped back, so that I could see out as I peeled vegetables or cut up meat, and feel the air on my face. Flies buzzed in, but I didn't mind them; no point trying to catch them on strips of sticky paper; they simply circled my head and then buzzed out again.

Marie-Louise would have liked to be my regular visitor but she was not allowed to hobnob with me in my domain; she was not to hang around the servant in case I infected her with some menial's disease of talking or thinking badly. Since the child was not to disturb my cooking and scrubbing, no one else in the family except Monsieur Colbert interrupted my labours. I was a safe audience; someone to bounce words off. I wouldn't fall in love with him or ask him to love me. He had his friends in Paris and elsewhere, but while he was at home in Jumièges his only true friend was the doctor, and the doctor was not always available because after all he was married and had a wife and a family. He had to attend to them. He could not spend time talking as though he were still a bachelor with hours to spare; he could no longer sit up half the night over bottles of wine or go off on a walking tour on a whim or simply not bother returning home for supper. Now there was a wife waiting for him, jealously wanting to wean him off his old loves, making her own claims. Monsieur Colbert used to grumble that his friends' marriages robbed him of the closeness and comradeship he esteemed so highly. A man got married and that was it; he vanished and his oldest dearest friends saw him no more.

Inside myself I thought: and what about their wives? It's just the same for them, but no one even imagines for a moment that women need friends too just like men do.

I could have said this openly to Monsieur Gérard. In one sense I didn't need to care what he thought of me; after all, it was not he who paid my wages but his mother; and I knew that he was an honourable man; he would never tell her, even if he was cross with me, that he had brought a would-be suicide, sinful and unstable, into her house. But also I needed to maintain my distance from him; I was always struggling not to resent him for having helped to stop me drowning in the sea. This made me angry with him, rather than as cool as I wished. At the same time I wanted him to like me enough so that I could go on living in his house. So when I was annoyed with him I didn't show it, just got on with cleaning the lamps or whatever else I was supposed to be doing. Set my face into a calm expression and concentrated on trimming the wicks and wiping soot off the glass shades.

Sometimes he tried to get me to talk about myself. When he prodded me with the fingers of his questions about my past life I clamped tight shut and said nothing. I did want to give him something back, however, to make sure there was nothing too condescending about his visits, no being kind to the poor orphan who nearly died. Eventually I admitted to myself that I enjoyed his visits to the kitchen, our odd, one-sided conversations; I was lured into being pleased that a human voice resounded in the space between the stove and the table; I ended up wishing to join in, to reciprocate in some way.

So I told him some of the stories Madame Montjean had told me. He swallowed them with gusto, tipping them down his throat like oysters, relishing all the patois phrases I taught him. I served him up further helpings of tales; and I told him the story of the mermaid; her sad end.

He went on being kind to me. Seeing how lonely I was in the evenings, he brought me the newspaper to read, magazines, books from his library he thought that I would like. I hid these in the woodshed so that no one should know. So the summer went on.

During the family's trip to Etretat I mostly stayed away from the beach. I went down to it just once or twice. The sea swarmed with creatures who were dangerous, monsters whose names I knew, to whom I'd given birth, abortions I'd scraped out of my innards then drowned secretly in the waves when no one was watching. Night after night these poor deformed creatures rose from the sea to confront me, holding out their cold white arms and crying to be rescued. Night after night I woke up sweating and panting in my bed in the hotel, Marie-Louise waking too to ask in a frightened voice what was the matter? When she crept into my bed for comfort I was ashamed to have alarmed her and at the same time relieved. Protecting and caressing someone else helps haul you out of the nightmare, stops you being quite so afraid. Wrapping my arms around her, rocking and cradling her, I soothed myself at the same time. I told both of us not to worry; there was nothing terrible waiting for us out there, no sea-beast trying to get in; nothing could harm us here; we were safe; we were surrounded by friends.

Poor little mite. She had no mother, and her father was gone away; she was a kind of orphan too; and there was I, supposedly in charge of her at night, scaring her with my anxieties. I was not behaving like a good nursemaid should; I was not looking after her in a responsible way. I wanted to promise her I would keep her from all harm and grief; I would never abandon her, never betray her, never let her down. I wasn't quite such a liar and a hypocrite. I kept my mouth shut and clasped her close to me, so warm and soft, and it was she who comforted me, she who gave me renewed strength as she snuggled her head between my breasts and my chin, she who consoled me with her trusting embrace, falling asleep in my arms as though I was a good person who loved her and would not hurt her, someone for whom there might yet be hope.

It was on our third night at the hotel, when I had settled Marie-Louise back to sleep in her own bed, after I'd woken both of us up crying out in a bad dream, that I heard Miss Millicent get up and creep out of her room. Her bed creaked, the door handle opened and shut with a springy rattle, her footsteps pressed along the uneven boards of the corridor and up the stairs. I decided to follow her and see what she was up to. I knew this was spying, but I could not restrain my curiosity. I knew, of course, who slept on the second floor. I wanted to know whether it was his room she was visiting. My excuse to myself was that if she was walking in her sleep then she might come to some harm and so it was my duty to follow her. I didn't believe this for a minute.

She glided up ahead of me, trying to tiptoe in her loose slippers that thumped on the carpet, her dressing-gown clutched about her, her hair in a plait down her back, a lit candle in one hand. I kept well back, in the shadows.

Straight to his door she went. Paused, leaned forward to listen, tapped very softly, once, twice. Turned the handle gently, slid in. Light was extinguished. I hovered in chilly darkness. Outside somewhere a dog yapped, thought better of it, quieted again. Here inside the hotel everyone seemed asleep in the hush of midnight.

Eavesdropping is wrong but that is what I did. Pressing my ear to the door I caught their two voices, his deep and abrupt, hers high and protesting. Then silence. Then a loud creak of bedsprings, as though someone were getting out. Or in. Then silence again.

I shifted from foot to foot and shivered, feverish and guilty, trying to imagine what was happening inside that room. I wanted the door to dissolve and let me pass through it insubstantial as a ghost; I wanted to creep close to the bed; to touch their hot skins and watch their mouths meet, their hands play; I wanted to know how people behaved when they desired each other and chose freely to make love. I was so ignorant. I wanted to learn from a safe distance; I wanted to watch passion enacted while remaining securely separated from it. They couldn't see me but I'd see them.

Another creak inside the room. Footsteps. Like a warning. Turning me back.

Now I suddenly felt ashamed of myself. Miss Milly was in love. At least she had had the courage to do something about it. She had made a decision and acted on it. She might not get very far, but at least she had tried. I envied her that bravery and simplicity. I had no business behaving in this disgusting way. I ran downstairs and into my own room. Five minutes later I heard Miss Milly fumble open then shut her door, sink into her bed. I heard her move restlessly around. She cried for a bit and then was quiet.

Next morning Monsieur Gérard went away on business. We stayed at Etretat another week. Then, her three months' governessing cut short, and in a state of great upset, Miss Milly left, to go to Paris and thence return to England.

Madame Colbert and I settled back into our old routines at Jumièges. Her health was increasingly bad, which worried Monsieur Gérard. He spent more time with her in the evenings, and the doctor was frequently called. Monsieur Polpeau told us bluntly that he did not expect the old lady to live long. We would be lucky if she survived the coming winter and made it to spring.

Isabelle

Gérard liked to describe to me the baths he had visited in north Africa, room after pillared room dense with billowing clouds of hot steam, the alcove where he lay on a stone bed and the attendant rubbed him with aromatic soap and oils then scraped him down with a wooden strigil, the curls of dead skin dropping to the wet marble floor like shavings of wood in a carpenter's shop. In that hotel room behind the place du Saint Esprit where we used to meet we played a similar game, taking it in turns to massage and be massaged. Or we washed each other in the bath, rinsing and caressing, then fell into bed damp and smelling of carnation soap. To this day the scent of carnations brings him back. That powerful, almost choking combination that hits your throat: cinnamon sticks mixed with the rough sweetness of pears. He loved a particular eau-de-Cologne too, a fusion of lavender and limes, and I used to buy him bottles of it from the perfumier round the corner from my shop. Glass-stoppered flasks fastened with a blue paper seal, and an oval label printed with a branch of green limes. The sharp fragrance mingled with the smell of tobacco which clung to him; *essence de poète* I used to call it. I wanted to give him presents all the time, and had to restrain myself. I wanted to give him all my best things. I wanted to cook for him. To give him myself over and over again. I kept these desires a secret, so as not to embarrass him.

After my husband Armand died, Gérard altered. As a married woman I had been safe, our adventure perfectly understood on both sides, to both our tastes, a liaison conducted with humour and gaiety, but as a widow I was dangerous. Potentially fully available. Too serious. Our time together now shrank like woollens washed in over-hot water and became just as unsatisfactory and intractable. I couldn't pull it back into a shape which pleased me. As a lover Gérard constricted himself: fewer scribbled notes spilling words of affection, fewer bunches of violets tied up with silver string, an end to the boxes of nougat and Turkish delight he used to bring me, whipping them out with a flourish from his coat pocket, leaves of waxed paper flying open, powdered with icing sugar, a hint of vanilla.

Before Armand's death, Gérard would meet me once a month or so. Now, I hardly saw him. He rationed himself more meanly than the jellied fruits and sherbet drops that you dole out to a child on Sundays, a reward for good behaviour, no bawling or whining; he locked himself away like a fine Médoc that you keep in the cellar for weddings and christenings. People should not, I suppose, be viewed as edible; it sounds disrespectful; but nonetheless he brought those hungers alive in me. Only at the moment he started to back off did I clearly realise how necessary he had become to me; how truly I loved him.

I'd read those poems of his stating that love is admiring and generous, like the worship of a troubadour for his lady; wishing only the best for the beloved. All very well, very lofty and fine; but now I discovered love's greedy side too; its need and desperation. Now I starved, wanting him; desire twisted and knocked about in my empty belly, and I had to find a way of feeding myself, filling myself up with loss, provoking and tempting my appetite with memory, gorging on fantasies of shared future. In his absence I feasted on the thought of him, what he had said and how he had looked last time I was in his company; playing with those morsels of our skimpy joint history; rolling them over my tongue where they tasted of sadness and were insubstantial and soon melted away.

Our love affair had lasted sixteen months. I met Gérard for the first time when I was twenty-five, and became his mistress at the age of twenty-six. I fell in love with him comfortably and quickly: I wanted someone to love, and there he was, clever and funny and kind. Ugly too, but that didn't matter; he could be so charming. On the second occasion I went to bed with him, when we were in less of a hurry, I discovered I could come. Before that, I'd thought only men did. I'd been a lonely child, strictly brought up, no brothers and sisters, no little playmates, not a cousin even, for me to experiment with. No secret games in the long grass at the end of the garden, such as my schoolmates described, while the adults slept off their Sunday lunch. Now, when I doubted it existed, just a figure of speech invented by poets, I began to experience sexual pleasure.

Gérard and I were good lovers together; we were sensual and inventive and we made each other laugh. He was as attentive to me as I was to him; we were equals who enjoyed finding out what we liked in bed; responding to each other. Sex was like writing poetry, he informed me: you didn't expect to get it right first time but took it through many drafts; you had to listen to your lover/muse; practise; discover and refine the techniques that produced your artless, spontaneous effect. What a pedant you are, I told him. But since this theory described such happiness, I agreed with it. I added my own understanding: how desire fitted bodies with each other like well-cut clothes. Without desire you couldn't cut or stitch. Then he told me I was as much of a pedant as he. No, said I: merely a poet.

I believed I was a lighthearted and sophisticated mistress. I dressed for the part as for a role in the theatre, swathing my hat with a black spotted veil so that I could arrive at our assignations without being recognised. A couple of hours with Gérard in our little pink-washed hotel room, and I would glide away again, down the unpolished stairs, gripping the banister as though it were Gérard's hand, and back out into the street. I was home five minutes later.

My alibi concerned an old lady whose existence I made up, called Madame Flaubert as a salute to our city's eminent novelist, a demanding and exacting client, whose fittings took a long time. I discovered the fine art of lying; I developed my talent for inventing stories as neatly as I tucked and draped sleeves; I pinched the truth into finicky pleats of my own fastidious design.

My hunger for food diminished. Dinner interested me less than the illicit Communion wafer I ate in private: my insubstantial fantasy that Gérard loved me as I loved him. I lost weight. Regular customers exclaimed, coming into the shop, and said that business must be good; clearly I was dashing about delivering innumerable frocks; the kilos were dropping off me. I smiled at them silently, turned, stretched up and reached down the rolls of cloth they wanted to inspect. Armand tweaked my waist and grunted and enquired whether I were ill? Oh no, I replied: I've never felt better in my life. Passers-by in the street, when I went out shopping or delivering orders, glanced at me appraisingly. I had enjoyed eating well and becoming plump and now I enjoyed the reverse process. *Aussi mince qu'une Parisienne.* In my line of business a trim figure is an asset, anyway. A dressmaker who's a good clothes-horse is going to attract more customers. It's obvious. This is not merely a question of frivolity and vanity but good business sense.

That's what I used to tell Armand's sister Marie when she came for lunch and supper on Sundays and frowned disparagingly at my new lace collar or ribbon bow or whatever it was. She noticed every little addition to my clothes, every little gift from Gérard that I could not resist wearing. Waving these flags under Armand's unsuspecting nose. Flaunting my bad behaviour. Marie was fifteen years older than I was, ten years Armand's senior, and wore black, not just because she was a widow but because it did not show the dirt. I enjoyed people taking a second glance at me in the street, their eyes catching mine telling me I looked stylish and well dressed, and so I informed Marie in a moment of misjudged candour one day. I suppose I wanted to provoke her. Our tiffs were usually my fault. I could not stop myself from goading her. I was bored and she provided sport. She was the bull and I danced round her, planting darts in her heavy flesh.

She was standing on the table in the dining-room while I adjusted the hem of the serge skirt, black of course, that I was letting down for her. I had pinned it in place; we had agreed on the length; and now I was going to tack it. Marie's feet, in cotton stockings, were damp, stained dark brown at the toes with the dye off the inside of her canvas boots where the rain had soaked through. Though it was early summer, it was pouring outside, good Normandy rain sheeting finely down, and Marie had brought the warm steaminess of the day inside with her. That unsettled me, made me remember those tales of Algerian bath-houses, summoned imaged of Gérard, naked, excited by someone else.

Once or twice he had boasted to me, in bed, of his youthful exploits with whores; his prowess and their exotic sensuality. I used to snap at him that he was paying them and that therefore of course they faked it well; that was their profession. He seemed to have thought, in those days, that all Eastern women were whores by nature. I told him that as a good Rouennaise going about our city and port on business I had encountered plenty of prostitutes; they were simply working women. He didn't know a thing about their lives. I didn't like the side of Gérard that gloated over his adventures with these women; I preferred not to hear of his with them. He would call me a prude; the conversation would end with a pillow-fight.

I wanted to throw the windows wide and let in the scent of the climbing rose flowering outside in the yard, its long branches, laden with curled white blooms, trained to scramble up a trellis under the sill. Gérard had given me this rose in the November of the first year I met him, before we began our affair, a cutting from his own bush in Jumièges, a vigorous plant that grew rapidly. Of course I saw this as an emblem of our friendship. In return I gave him a book of poetry. I couldn't open the window, however, because my sister-in-law was afraid of draughts. These crept up, stealthy and maleficent, on the back of your neck, smote you like mysterious visitors breaking and entering to steal your goods, caused you to drop down with untreatable wind-induced illnesses. The workroom was airless and close and Marie smelled strongly of perspiration after her brisk walk through the wet weather to my shop. I had sewn dress guards into all her clothes for her, little triangular bags of lavender that hid in her armpits and were supposed to sweeten their hairy depths, but they rotted quickly; they spoiled under the onslaught of her sweat, musky and pungent.

Gérard's sweat, now, I liked, because he was my lover, but Marie's, raw and harsh, made me wrinkle my nose. Disgust, I started thinking, was a relative matter of strangeness and intimacy. When you loved someone and shared their bed, you liked everything about their physical being, even the smell of their shit; you didn't mind it, anyway; what came from them was good. But a person you disliked had a body that repulsed you and made smells you considered noxious. A person you had once desired, and no longer did, produced the same effect. Disgust was only the other side of desire, after all. The one slipped easily into the other. Disgust protected you from feeling desire, perhaps; the wrong sort, anyway. My God, did that mean I desired Marie?

As a dressmaker I'd met many women I considered attractive and desirable. I enjoyed helping them to choose new clothes whose cut and flow would make them even more so. I helped them off and on with their clothes and admired their bodies, so varied, so differently shaped. I liked the way women were made: the little swell of flesh at the tops of their arms, their breasts which were either pointed or round, the long ovals of buttocks and hips. In order to fit them properly I was trained to look at women this way, dispassionately, assessing their good points and bad, and it doesn't sound kind, but I looked with affection; I felt tenderness for all that soft flesh that clothes often merely squeezed and confined.

It wasn't only men who could appreciate women's beauty. A woman, I thought, could look at a member of her own sex and pay her homage. I began to wonder why, if that were the case, I had never been aware of wanting to go to bed with another woman. Lack of opportunity, I concluded. Marriage had cut me off from the women friends I had as a girl, and I worked so hard I had no time to make new ones. The only woman I was really intimate with was Marie, whom I saw every day, and I was sure I didn't desire her. I couldn't imagine going to bed with her. I could never imagine her going to bed with her husband either, however often I tried. But perhaps one day I would find myself in bed with another woman.

I realised that Marie was talking to me. Responding to what I'd said before my mind flew off onto questions of sexual philosophy. Her opinion was of course that now I was married I should have settled down, adopted a *convenable* style of dress and given up on fripperies, and not be wasting Armand's hard-earned housekeeping allowance on decking myself out like someone seeking to attract male attention, therefore no better than she should be.

—You see, Isabelle, she droned: Armand won't tell you but I will; your hair style, for example, it's much too young for you; it makes you look as though you want to be thought still a girl. It's quite unsuitable in your station of life.

My hair was drawn up and back in one thick, glossy plait which flopped over my shoulder, nestling there like some friendly animal, a cat or a tame rabbit, that carried about with me. I liked my plait. It was a new style for me. I liked doing it up rapidly in the mornings, my fingers darting between the three silky strands, flipping them one over the others into a slippery coil, a sequence of fat knots, and I liked shaking it out at night, my head bent and my hand shrugging through the loose weave to unravel its slick length down my back. Gérard liked my hair. He would gather it in his hands and bury his face in it, kiss it, wrap it around both our throats, tying us together. To Armand it was just hair.

Marie tried my patience when she lectured me in this pompous and ridiculous way, even though I'd invited it with my badly timed confidences. I couldn't answer her back immediately as my mouth was full of pins. I swore to myself instead, one of the good sturdy oaths Gérard had taught me, and I reminded myself for the umpteenth time that Marie was a broken-hearted widow who had not to be teased but treated with special consideration. That was why she had come on honeymoon with us, and why she took so many of her meals with us, because she needed company and cheering up. She had accompanied us on all our walks around Etretat, on our wedding journey, several of our jaunts along the coast, and now that we were ensconced in our flat and shop in Rouen she dropped in to visit us every day. I was an excellent cook, with the knack of stretching money and provisions a long way, and Armand felt it was our duty to let his sister share in the good things I served up. Also, since I was so gifted at sewing I made many of Marie's outfits for her, charging her practically nothing. She saved a lot of money, having me as a sister-in-law, and she was not as grateful as I thought she should be. Armand, when I put this to him, pointed out that Marie, having no children, would leave all her money to us when she died and that this was yet another reason for being kind to her.

I wanted to run outside, into the rain, whirl around in it, dance, get soaked. I straightened up, spat the pins into the palm of my hand and burst out: I earn the housekeeping money myself, out of the income from the shop; it's quite distinct from my clothing allowance which I also earn myself; and you may be Armand's sister but really it's none of your business.

She couldn't flounce out and find Armand to complain to because she was captive: she had no blouse on, so that I could better fiddle with the waistband I was letting out for her; she'd taken off her boots to mount onto the table; and I had the gathers of her nasty dark skirt fast in one hand.

She said in her squeaky voice; you misunderstand me, Isabelle; nothing is dearer to me than your and Armand's welfare; you are part of the family now; I was only trying to give you some helpful advice.

—My advice to you, I returned: is to stand still so that I can check this hem level.

The temptation, of course, was to turn bullfighter again, let my hand slip and accidentally prick her thick ankles with a pin, but I managed to desist. Later on we went upstairs to the little flat, and I made us a cup of coffee. As a way of apologising for my rudeness. I served her with my favourite cup, the pale green one with the gilt rim, and offered her a thick slice of buttered *pain d'epice,* crusted with dark honey and crystals of sugar, which I knew she loved. Not good enough. As soon as Armand came up, from his bit of the shop, the tailoring workroom on the other side of the passage from mine, she said to him, with the corners of her mouth turned down and the words slipping meanly out as though they were greased: I won't stay for supper tonight, dear. Isabelle's had enough of me by now. She looks so tired.

—Of course you must stay, he insisted: and then we'll all go out to the café for a glass of something. I promised you, and you know I like to keep my promises.

The kitchen was shaped like a shoebox, with a high ceiling, and a tall window at one end overlooking the street. I was ricocheting back and forth in the narrow space between the tiled walls doing too many things at once: washing spinach and picking it over, making a béchamel, heating water to poach eggs, cutting bread. Marie leaned back, the loose back of her wooden chair creaking complainingly, at the oilcloth-covered table in the corner, tinkling her coffee spoon in her saucer, watching me. Armand sat down opposite her, bending forwards, face reddening, to remove his shoes. There was really only room for two chairs, but I had fetched a third chair from next door and set it down in between them so that they would remember there were three of us needing seats. Waging my silent war against pieces of bulky furniture which didn't know their place I spent a lot of time carrying this chair back and forth between kitchen and dining-room, but that was better than allowing it to claim permanent residence.

—You must let me help you, Isabelle, Marie said: you mustn't always insist on doing everything yourself.

I decided to take her at her word.

—Thank you, I replied: then could you take over cleaning the spinach? That will let me get on with finishing this sauce.

It was a test to see whether she really wanted to help or was just trying to look good in front of her doting brother. I couldn't trust her to stir the sauce. She had no feel for cooking and would have let it burn. What happened was exactly what I had predicted to myself. While I grated nutmeg and Armand eased his feet out of his shoes, sat up straight again and smiled approvingly at her, she began to plunge the spinach clumsily in and out of the water, splashing her dress and the floor with a shower of drops, clattering the tin bowl against the sink so that it scraped and screeched on the porcelain. Then as soon as he had gone next door into the dining-room to find his slippers she slowed right down. After a couple of minutes she took her hands out of the dirty water and hastily dried them on the towel that hung by the sink. She was in too much of a hurry to rinse her hands properly and so the clean towel I had put out only this morning was now covered in muddy streaks and would have to go into the wash. I objected to her creating extra work for me to do, and at the same time I felt depressed that I had such a petty mind. But nonetheless it was I who had to do the washing and not Marie; it was a major labour and I didn't need it increased.

—I shan't be a moment, Isabelle dear, Marie exclaimed: I've just remembered, there's something I must ask Armand before he gets stuck into the newspaper.

She vanished next door.

—Wash your hands in the sink, not on the towel, I recited to the empty air.

I sounded exactly like my mother , who had often ticked me off for the same crime. Thinking of her reduced me, as though a weight on my head pushed me down, like a plate pressing on a pâté. When I am unhappy I feel short, as though my legs have been trimmed above my ankles. I watched my mother bulge out sideways with grief, like an overstuffed sandwich. I assume my mother loved me in her own silent way, but I got away from her as fast as I could. Now here I was, living a life remarkably like hers, when I had sworn to myself I was going to be free and only do what I liked.

I carried on with making the supper. When I ran in to lay the cloth and announced I was ready to serve, I roused the two of them from their murmured tête-à-tête, broke through their fond glances, their discussion of investments, of share prices and interest.

—The spinach can't wait, I informed them: or the eggs will go hard.

They glanced up, frowning at my insensitivity. A nice woman would have hovered, apologised for disturbing them, waited placidly for them to finish talking, but I was not nice. The sooner we'd finished eating the sooner I could put on my new straw hat with a white velvet daisy stitched into the band, and the sooner we could go out to the café and I would have other people to look at. Having flung the cloth onto the table and jerked it straight I darted back to the kitchen and fetched my load of food, cutlery and serving utensils. I whisked back in with it, bumping past Armand's chair just as he began lumbering to his feet, so that the supper nearly went flying.

Marie roused herself in a bustle. She smoothed her damp skirt, smiling to show she forgave me for not having offered her an apron, and said, reproachfully: oh, Isabelle, why ever didn't you call me? I told you I wanted to give you a hand.

I slammed down my heavy tray, unloaded the knives and forks. The plates, and the dish of *oeufs florentine.* I'd forgotten the bread so had to go back for it. Then I had to make a final journey to fetch the third chair. I ate my meal in silence. They thought I was sulking, and I was.

I hadn't expected marriage to be like this. I hadn't expected to feel so much bitterness and resentment so much of the time, nor to have landed a husband who was apparently more in love with his sister than with his wife. Why didn't they just get on with it, I wondered, move in with each other, live together and share a bed and all the rest? It was obviously all either of them wanted. They had grown up together and were each other's best friends. They were physically alike, heavily built, with very white flesh, pale blue eyes, faded reddish hair. Even their sweat smelled the same. They were a pair of twins, really, who should never have been parted.

I felt justified in taking a lover. I did think Armand should have told me before we married that he was not particularly interested in making love, that it would only happen on Saturday nights, if then, and last ten grunting minutes or so, before he rolled over and fell asleep. It wasn't something we discussed, at any rate. It wasn't a subject to be mentioned. My mother was not happy in her marriage and I felt rather than knew this, without her telling me. You saw it in the way she moved and gestured, the hunch of her shoulders, the droop of her head, the shuffle of her feet.

I had not let myself love her too much because I was terri-
fied of becoming like her, trapped with a husband I could
not esteem. She took herself off to church, and my father
went silently to the bar, and I plotted how to get away from
that stifling little house filled with their pain.

Armand was fresh-faced, robust. Our parents talked
about how well suited we were, he being a tailor and I a
dressmaker, and we smirked at each other across the Sunday
slices of pale cake. Perhaps I should have guessed then, during our brief engagement, when I noticed he bolted his
food without savouring it, that he was not a particularly
sensual man. I wasn't paying sufficient attention to my own
feelings, to my own desires for happiness. I wanted to leave
home, and so I wanted to get married, and so I took the first
man who came along, without realising that I was taking
Marie too, and a bucket of resentment. Armand was steady
and obliging, a hard worker. He wouldn't let me down. But
he had. He did.

It wasn't only his fault. I was to blame too because I had
married him in haste without loving him. I had assumed I
loved him, but I had loved only what he represented: the
chance to set up house away from home. Love wasn't supposed to matter, anyway. People like us were not expected
to be romantic. What counted were the realities of working, earning a living. Armand had chosen well, picking me,
because I was a gifted dressmaker as well as a thrifty housekeeper. In due course we would produce children, and I

would pour my excess nervous energy into caring for them. That's what he must have thought.

I suppose his clumsiness in bed was due to nervousness and inexperience but I was unable to help him with it, to turn it into a game that could amuse us both. He resented my whispered suggestions as though I were ordering him about. Worse, these made me seem unchaste, as though I'd done this before. I hadn't, but I had an idea of what would please me: someone stroking my skin as a dressmaker strokes her velvets and silks. Someone who talked to me, in bed and out. After six months of being poked and shoved, I felt nothing but furious recoil.

A commonplace story of sexual misery. Uninteresting and boring to anyone but me. But it was my life and I was determined to do something about it. I wasn't going to waste my youth suffering and whining, watching myself wither while pleasure passed me by. I wasn't going to give up and resign myself like my poor mother had. Divorce might be impossible but I wasn't going to act crazily like one of those heroines in books, either, who ended up ruined, in disgrace, and killed themselves. I had read *Madame Bovary,* that forbidden text, under the desk at school, a copy, veiled in brown paper, smuggled from one pupil to the next, and I had decided on a better fate for myself. I chose a happy ending, not a tragic one.

I met Gérard on honeymoon. He was staying at the same hotel as we were in Etretat. I watched him come into the dining-room the fourth night that we were there. Armand and Marie, napkins tied around their necks, had their heads down over their steaming plates, big spoons cramming in their fish soup. I was very hungry, but I was waiting for mine to cool a little, because it tastes better then. I looked up and saw Gérard. He had a brown, creased face, very alive, and humorous blue eyes. I thought involuntarily: I like your body; I bet you're beautiful with your clothes off. I knew straight away I would like his penis. I already knew I didn't like Armand's.

Things progressed easily: exchange of speaking glances, apparently coincidental meetings, introductions, conversations. Armand felt flattered that I had made friends with a poet; it reflected well on him; afforded him a cosmopolitan shine. That Monsieur Colbert is no snob, he exclaimed: fancy him wanting to take up with people like us. Marie said: what's he got to be a snob about? We're just as good as him. Armand had no interest in going on too many energetic expeditions and was relieved I had found a companion to squire me about. He was quite content to sit on a rug on the beach with Marie, gossiping gently with her, while Gérard took me for drives and for walks along the cliffs.

The following summer we all met at Etretat again, and this time Gérard and I became lovers. We occupied the corner of each other's lives; we were the initials on each other's pocket handkerchief; and we were content. Mostly we met in Rouen, in the discreet backstreet hotel. Once, when

Armand and Marie had gone to visit their mother in Lisieux, and I pretended at the last minute to fall ill, so that I could stay behind, Gérard and I snatched a couple of nights in Paris together. We went to visit some painter friends of his who had become enthusiastic photographers and bought a camera, and we each sat for our picture. We slept the night in the studio, on a bed of cushions, and in the morning, once the light had poked through the blinds, Gérard took some more photographs of me, secret and intimate, which no one but ourselves would ever be shown. I had copies of the two portraits. I kept them under a piece of lace in the bottom of the drawer where I stored my best handkerchiefs, turned face to face, so that our mouths were touching.

Loving Gérard, who represented my hope for something better, even something beautiful, I could face my life. I didn't have to feel let down by Armand any more, because I trusted in my image of Gérard. Armand could be unsatisfactory because Gérard wasn't. Was it merely childish and immoral, to think like that? It did seem easier to have two men, not just one, the second more delightful than the first. I couldn't believe I was doing wrong because love seemed to be improving my character. Pleasure in bed fuelled me, gave me more willing energy for the hard daily round; happiness made me kinder. Also, I had an ideal now, that I discovered I needed, and I believed in it ardently. Perhaps it could flourish all the more strongly because it was outside my marriage and so less bruised by everyday life. That distance kept it safe. At the same time it was an ideal of marriage and helped keep my marriage intact. It shone secretly in my mind, like a silver statue hidden in a cave, that only I knew was there.

It wasn't that I worshipped Gérard as a god, or thought him perfect, or anything so absurd; it was that loving him enabled me to believe people could be humorous, ardent, not simply ground down by existence, playful, full of good things, generous, giving. I didn't mind if, like anybody else, he also picked his nose or farted or lost his temper sometimes. He represented my desire; I wanted to find out all about him; he awakened my curiosity; and I began to understand love as a voyage, travelling constantly towards the other, departing from the beloved in order to turn round and come back, to arrive again.

I fitted the image of Gérard around the shape of my husband, a kind of shining but invisible crust or cloak. It was of him I thought constantly, to him I chattered and told jokes and silly stories, for him that I kept myself well groomed and well dressed. It was to him I wrote frequent letters in my head, and it was his arm I took on Sunday afternoon strolls in front of the cathedral. My marriage benefited, of course. I could be less scratchy to Armand, share pleasant moments with him, not grit my teeth so much in bed. I even began to enjoy myself with him there, since now I wanted lovemaking, and ten minutes a week was better than none. I learned how to adapt, to make love at speed, to come sometimes. I complained less. I could sense Armand feeling relieved I had calmed down.

Thus a million adulterers defend themselves. How banal. How hypocritical. I did no harm, they plead; my love affair made me sweeter and nicer to my spouse. It's just that in my case I was convinced it was true.

As well as writing long, imaginary letters to Gérard every day, that were a substitute for being in his presence, and endless conversation with which I indulged myself, I wrote him real letters too. Billets-doux. Hasty messages. Suggestions for rendezvous. I kept them scanty, short, because how could I write adequately to a poet, a master of language? I could dress well on a small income; I could cook; I could manipulate scissors, cloth and thread to perfection; but my prose had no style or elegance; my grammar was weak; my spelling merely inventive. And yet loving Gérard has turned me into a writer, and this is my love letter to him; the real one, the one in which I indulge myself and allow myself to acknowledge my passion for him; the one I don't dare send; language that can flow and does not have to stop, a long cry uttered in silence.

I posted my letters to the address of Gérard's friend, the doctor in Jumièges, so that his mother should not suspect what was up. He did not always reply.

Once I went to his house and tried to see him but his mother told me he was not at home. His castle was well defended with female troops. All in love with him. His

mother glared at me from the front door, repelling my entry
with the force of her icy politeness. The servant. Geneviève,
peered at me through the back garden fence, ready to fight
me off with a pitchfork or a frying pan. I'd been kind to her
when she nearly drowned at Etretat; I'd helped to rescue her,
yelling at the fishermen to hurry and pull her out; she owed
me a favour or two, you'd have thought; surely she could
have let me slip in round the back of the house; but no, she
didn't want me going near her blessed master. And Miss
Milly, whom Gérard had described to me as the English
dragoness who guarded his niece: I glimpsed her peeking at
me out of the upstairs window, and rather young and pretty
she looked too, not at all the gaunt spinster I had been led to
expect. No help to be hoped for from that quarter, either.

Between them they routed me. I decided to admit a
temporary defeat. I turned tail and went back to Rouen. I
dreamed of coming by water next time, of swimming quietly along the river from Rouen to Jumièges, disguised as
an eel or a carp or some such, slipping ashore, gliding from
puddle to puddle, wriggling under Gérard's study door and
landing flop! on his carpet. Then he'd have had to take
notice. Scoop me up and put me in the bath and wonder
what to do next.

Daydreaming prevented me from noticing my husband's state of health. Armand died the following winter. I
didn't know that he had a weak heart. I hadn't bothered to
find out. He might have had warning pains, some inkling
of illness, but I didn't ask him how he was and he didn't tell

me. He probably felt I wouldn't be interested. He had a way of peering at me reproachfully over his spectacles, pouting a bit, that used to make me feel both guilty and angry. It was too late to mend things. The tear in our fabric was too long and jagged. Our affection for each other had not strengthened but worn out. When you've got a bed sheet in that state you don't waste time trying to patch it just one more time; you rip it into squares for dusters and that's that. It's only in marriage that you're not allowed to admit defeat. But I was defeated and I knew it.

He dropped down dead one day in his workroom, after a heart attack severe enough to fell him in minutes. I heard the scrape then crash of a chair falling over and ran in. I was too late. I told myself afterwards that at least I had tried; my instinct had been good; that I had rushed in wanting to save him from whatever it was.

Marie had no need for such self-justification. She collapsed, weeping as though she, not I, were the widow. She was a most faithful sister; she cried for two; she sat, red-faced and red-eyed, snorting and sobbing, in my workroom, while I coldly and hastily stitched my black dresses and sewed lengths of black crape onto all my hats. I hated the clothes that custom forced widows to wear, that made you look like a walking sarcophagus; as though you yourself were the corpse; to be hidden under layers of black draperies. People were ghouls, peering at me to see how I was coping. To give the gossips something meaty to chew on I made myself one lovely hat: a black velvet cap with a silky black tassel. Marie squelched into black-rimmed handkerchiefs. I had to respect her grief though I couldn't share it. On the other hand it annoyed me, because it was such a reproach.

Gérard kept away from me. Not out of delicacy, respect for my supposed state of mourning, but out of nervousness, I was sure. I knew him well enough to be clear about this. He feared I'd want him to marry me.

Then Madame Colbert died too, in the spring. I sent Gérard a brief note of condolence, hoping that politeness would force him to reply. But of course he was not polite. He was a poet, and poets spoke the truth. If they couldn't speak it, then they simply fell silent.

I was forced into dumbness. I kept quiet. I waited, to see what he'd do. I went on with my life, about my business. I needed something to live on, after all. Armand was a young man still when he died; we had saved nothing. Shutting my ears to Marie's gloomy predictions of failure and ruin, refusing her offer to come and live with me so that we could pool resources, I set myself to combat poverty. We had rented the shop, and the landlord declared himself quite happy for me to take over the lease on my own. I shut up Armand's side of the business, and cleared out his workroom. I thought I might turn it into a space I could rent to a tenant, and so I bought an old iron bed from a junk shop, scrubbed and painted it and put a mattress on it, and hung some curtains.

I got up earlier in the morning, to pack more working hours into the day, as I went to bed later. I stopped advertising myself solely as a dressmaker and expanded my services to include labour I had previously disliked when I had the luxury of choice. Now I took in all kinds of mending and alterations. I cut and sold paper patterns for women wanting to stitch their own chemises and nightgowns at home. I operated a discreet sideline selling second-hand clothes, and I rented out frocks by the week or by the evening. I started making hats; very simple ones, that I could manage; hats for women not wanting too many frills. I decided that I would do better to engage a sewing-woman to help me out, and began to look around for someone suitable.

I made ends meet. Just about. There was little time for being in love. After the first weeks of my widowhood, passionate thoughts of Gérard receded to the back of my mind, like previous objects you store deep in a cupboard and take out to look at on high days and holy days. At night, before falling exhaustedly asleep, I gazed fondly at his image. It floated behind my closed eyes. The fact that he wasn't with me no longer caused me unbearable pain. I had discovered a way to cure myself, temporarily at least, and I would reflect on this as I laid my cheek on the cool pillow.

I could blame the weather. It happened one unexpectedly fine afternoon in May. Even in Normandy we sometimes have cloudless blue skies. I had been out, delivering a frock, and was dawdling home, not wanting to hurry, because it was so warm, and even through my black mufflings I could feel the sun. Pinned to my hat I wore a black spotted veil, that I had thrown back so that the spring warmth could caress my skin. It was the fine net veil I had first bought for my assignations with Gérard. Pity to waste it, I'd thought earlier, finding it on the wardrobe shelf, and had fixed it in place before coming out. It cheered me up to wear this veil; to me, at least, it declared that a real human heart beat under these swathes of black; and I could feel myself beginning to smile as I wandered along, glancing into shop windows and feeling the heat pressing on my shoulders like hands.

Then I caught a man's eye. Well-dressed, youngish, reasonably attractive; not repulsive, at least. He was sauntering like me, but he slowed down and took a second look. I looked boldly back. He was a *flâneur,* and I was—a street-walker. He hesitated, then approached me. I thought: why not? I liked his face, his swagger.

It was simple. I let down my veil, took his arm, conducted him to the hotel in the rue du Saint-Esprit, and spent an hour with him there. He couldn't believe his luck that it wasn't money that I wanted, that I even paid for the room. He was excited by my being in mourning, so to please both of us I kept the veil on.

I was performing an experiment. I wanted to discover whether it was Gérard I had to have, at all costs, or whether someone else would do just as well; whether it was simple pleasure I was after, or love and romance also. I didn't discover the answer to my question, but I found out that the adventure of going to bed with a stranger carried its own erotic charge, flavoured with danger, and thus served not only as a stimulant but also as a palliative for a broken heart. Perhaps I should say: wounded vanity. At any rate, the dose was easily available whenever I felt the need of it.

As a result, perhaps, of this new experience, my beloved Gérard shifted in significance in my mind. He was no longer the hero, the prince who would ride up to rescue me; he was my dear, my difficult friend, who needed to shut himself away in order to write. He had once said to me: for some, art is a parallel life and for some it's a substitute one, and for me it's both. I began, at last, to understand this mechanism, or to think I did.

He kept a woman—me, or someone else—at a distance, so that her absence could provoke him to desire her, to write a love poem. If the woman had been there with him all the time he wouldn't have needed to write to her. The poems would have been lost. He couldn't imagine that others might have come in their place: poems of presence, of enjoying, of possessing. He only believed in loss, in not having. In not being allowed to have. I thought that was the wall he put up against his mother. Who valued him so much, because he was a boy, and her husband was dead, and with whom he had decided to live, I suppose wanting her and rejecting her all mixed up, and, after all, he must not have wanted to be reminded of once being a tiny infant and needing her so much; that might have been the comfort that whores gave him, that love didn't come into it, and he was the one with the power to say what she should do.

Oh, I passed many lonely evenings developing such insights, during those first weeks, when things changed between us, when I reflected on all this, sewing, and cursing him for being so tricky; I had plenty of time in which to refine my new theory of sex, all about absence and not having. All about his power, and my having to agree with him, either to go along with him or lose him.

He liked sexual pleasure, I concluded, but he also liked doing without it for the sake of his work. I wasn't sure that I had chosen to renounce sex in the same way, but there was no doubt that my love of him could learn to feed on not having him. I learned to become like him in that way. Perhaps he had corrupted me and perhaps he had also liberated me. I didn't know. In his absence I had a picture of him that I could love. His absence inspired and provoked my love. Should I give up loving him? Could I? Was I harming myself by continuing to love him? I wasn't sure what the answer was to all this or whether I needed one.

I did know that the last thing he wanted was for me to claim to understand him. He despised all such speculation on a lover's part as idiocy and presumption. At this point in my musings I would yawn, ask for God's blessing, and fall asleep. And then the following day I would refresh myself with a trip into town and perhaps a visit to the hotel.

Another of my afternoon sorties in early May brought me a different kind of encounter. Walking home one day from a dull business visit delivering a parcel of altered clothes to a customer, I ran into Miss Milly. I didn't know who she was at first, this rather pretty, fair-haired young women in a badly cut navy blue coat and skirt. She was waving to attract my attention. Slowly I realised. I'd glanced at her peeping face, framed in an upstairs window, for five seconds, months ago, when my mind was on other things: how to get in through the front door, past the spear-wielding, lion-taming mother, and find Gérard. I hadn't really remembered this girl, apart from vaguely noting that she seemed to have that perfect skin of youth.

Our meeting occurred on a Tuesday. I was walking under the Gros Horloge when she called to me, came across the street, introduced herself and shook my hand. She stood close to me, eager as a puppy dog waving its tail.

I didn't want to like her. She had rather a naive priggish look and she was some sort of a rival, wasn't she? She'd lived in the same house as Gérard, which I'd certainly never achieved. Here she was in Rouen, when Gérard had told me she'd been sacked by his mother months ago, last year, and been sent back to England. Against my will I was intrigued.

Also I could not help myself; my mind rushed on so rapidly I was scarcely conscious of thinking at all; speaking to her would allow me the pleasure, eventually, of referring to Gérard, of pronouncing his name; a pleasure normally denied to me; and that felt very sweet. For the sake of prolonging and repeating this pleasure I embraced the jealousy that was mixed up with it; salt on my strawberries.

Milly's face was flushed pink like a ripe gooseberry. Her fair hair bunched under her hat which had slipped to one side. This was a lumpy affair in dark blue felt that my fingers itched to alter and improve. To give them something else to think about I inspected my black lace gloves, tugging the gathered wrists straight. People were surging past on either side of us. The sun fell hotly on our backs. We were joined together, sharing this cloak of sunlight. So when Milly asked shyly if she could walk a little way along with me I said yes.

Geneviève

Madame Colbert's funeral was held after Easter. A cold Easter, as it so often is, the spring like an egg unsure whether or not to crack open just yet. Patches of blue sky showed now and then as the wind tore through the grey clouds above the river, tossing its waters, and rain showers alternating with hailstorms. Bursts of sunshine coaxed the flowers out, bluebells fringing the forest paths, clumps of primroses and cowslips studding the hedgerow banks. Daffodils and narcissi shook out their chilly ruffles in the orchard's long grass. All around the village the pear and plum trees exploded into clouds of blossom, the promise of a good harvest of fruit in summer if the frost didn't get the flowers first, nip them in the night with its icy fingers and spoil their perfection. Blight them and kill them stone dead like girls in fairy tails.

My favourite fruit tree in the Colberts' garden was the cherry, because its blossom was the finest. I used to wake with the first light in the morning, leap up, run outside and check that the tree was all right. This far north, cherries don't always flourish. Ours was protected by stone walls and hedges but still I felt obliged to keep an eye on it.

The cherry tree was a tall cone of white flowers, snowy and fragile. If I was up early enough, before I was needed by the household, I used to sit on the orchard gate for half an hour or so and just gaze at the knobbled black branches which wove together to make a sieve of white foam; I lost myself in a dream of shivery whiteness. I couldn't tell whether I'd ever see such powerful beauty in my life again so I'd better spend time with it now, learn it well so that I could remember it always, the way it was, delicate and miraculous, before the wind ripped the flowers from the branches and the bunched leaves thickened out and showed jagged green against the blue sky while the white petals showered down upon the ground.

Jumièges was all *en fête,* transformed to laciness and froth, an island floating in a sea of white. People drove out from Rouen on Sundays to admire the scene, the yellow and black half-timbered thatched cottages set in the meadows whose green was sharp and new, encircled by hawthorn hedges tipped with white, and the airy blossom shaking its creamy drifts overhead. Later, towards May, the apple trees would come into bloom. Now, there was a sweetness like hunger in the air, an anticipation, the sense of something beginning, forcing its way up out of the earth; it could not be stopped; it was something that had been buried and pronounced dead coming alive again and searching desperately for the light. For me this was my belief in resurrection. Not that of Jesus but my own. The spring cracked me open, broke me apart; I had no choice but to rise up too, like the wobbly-legged calves in the pastures, like the daisies in the grass; and obey it.

It was the season for weddings as well as for funerals, thought I didn't let myself think of that; I preferred to remain as mindless and ignorant as the sticky buds unfurling on the horse chestnut trees. It's in the nature of chestnut buds to stop being tightly wound plump spindles, merely promising, and to release themselves, to unclose like fists and thrust out floppy young leaves, so new and tentative they look wet. I was like that. I don't say this in my own defence. I could have seen what was likely to happen, but I did nothing to prevent it; I even helped it on its way. I was too taken with the coming of spring to bother about right and wrong. Spring was like the mermaid; she summoned you; she made her own demands. The dead nettles lifting their pearly blooms in the shelter of the orchard hedge did not consider morality and neither did I.

I got on with my work. I thanked heaven that since I was not family it was not my job to nurse Madame Colbert. I cleaned the room in which she lay, brought in the fresh linen, removed slop pails, and that was that. The doctor's wife came in to look after the dying woman, who had been her good neighbour and friend.

You could see Madame Polpeau relished having something different to do out of her usual routine, something new she could talk to her husband about every night when she went home. Something different to put in her letters to her daughter Yvonne away at school in Le Havre. While she cared for the old lady calmly and patiently, coping uncomplainingly with all the stink and mess of illness, she did not change her personality. She kept to her normal behaviour. With a captive audience in her hands she gave her tongue free rein, and chatted away in her soft, twittering voice about her favourite subjects: her travels along the coast the previous summer, how hard her husband the doctor had to work for such low rewards, her corns, her tendency to acid indigestion, the lack of manners of the village children. Or she recounted at great length how a corner of wallpaper in her salon was torn and curling up, what the postman had said to her last Tuesday about the Final Coming, how the herrings she had ordered for lunch tomorrow might not stretch far enough, how large the holes in the doctor's stockings were.

A dying person requires a certain amount of peace and quiet, to get her soul into shape. Madame Colbert was allowed no such chance. She lay mumbling and dribbling in her bed, poor lady, too polite to tell her friend to shut up. If I had been forced to listen hour after hour to Madame Polpeau rambling on I should have died of desperation or of boredom. Madame Colbert just stared at the ceiling or at the wall.

But quite soon she was past minding. Passing the half-open door one day, my arms loaded with a heavy stack of clean sheets, folded and pressed, I glanced into the gilt-framed mirror, suspended above the little grey marble mantelpiece, tipping forwards like a single stern eye looking down at a miscreant child, and caught sight of the sick woman's reflection as she lay with her profile turned towards me. In twenty-four hours her life had ebbed low, had sunk almost out of sight. I glimpsed her death mask: wasted flesh, beaky nose in cavernous face, hooded eyes half open and seeming to stare at me, dropped jaw. I smelled her imminent death. The stench of bodily decay, under a layer of eucalyptus, lavender water and eau-de-javel, forced itself up my nose and into my mouth.

I tried to blot it out, dipped my head and crammed the fragrant sheets against my face, fled from the harsh rattle of her breath. You couldn't just listen to that sound; it got inside your throat and rasped you raw, made you want the poor woman to die as quickly as possible so that the noise, like a blunt saw inexorably worked to and fro, would stop. After that morning I tried to keep well away from my employer's room. I didn't want to catch her looking at me again. I wanted to hide from her severe, considering gaze, which seemed to say she knew what I might get up to and condemned it in advance.

In the evenings the doctor's wife went home. While his mother was dying, and after she died, Monsieur Gérard sat with her at night and kept her company. You have to sit with the dead for three days and three nights; that's the custom in the countryside. The body is dressed in its best clothes, the hands crossed on the breast. People come in and out to pay their respects and say goodbye.

Monsieur Gérard arranged sprays of white spiraea blossoms, which he went out and cut from the bush in the garden, in two vases, one on either side of the bed. On the chest of drawers he put a pot of white crocuses. He parked himself on the armless chair covered in yellow velvet that stood on the far side of the room from the corpse under her white counterpane, opened the window a little way and smoked his pipe.

The doctor's wife suggested that smoking in the presence of the dead showed disrespect. It made her uneasy. Madame Colbert had disliked the smell of cigar and pipe smoke while she was alive, and had banned smoking, and surely one should wait a little after her death before beginning to flout her wishes.

Monsieur Gérard was quite unconcerned about what his mother would have thought. Or else he was only too well aware, and was taking a certain pleasure in being able to disobey one of her edicts at long last. He sat opposite her and corrected the proofs of his new book through those three long nights. That upset the doctor's wife too, that he wasn't reading the New Testament or some such religious work. Monsieur Gérard didn't care about that, either. He sat opposite his dead mother in a rich, fragrant fug, unshaven, wearing his old Turkish dressing-grown and red leather slippers, drinking coffee, puffing on his pipe and reading poetry, the long galleys slipping and slithering over his lap like so many serpents. Then, on the day of the funeral, he had a thorough wash and brush up, put on his black suit, and followed on foot as Madame Colbert was carried to the church.

Boyng . . . boyng . . . boyng . . . The church bells began to ring. They were ringing for Madame Colbert. Just for her. They tolled loudly, a long, slow, regular pounding of iron upon iron that rolled through the village and into the surrounding fields. It was an awe-inspiring and mournful sound, reaching deep into your heart, filling your entire being, as impersonal and majestic and mysterious as death itself. It signified the end of Madame Colbert on earth and the start of her last journey through the village. It was the summons to the grave.

The coffin had been carried out of the house by four farm labourers, specially recruited for the purpose, and loaded onto a cart draped with black crape. We had been waiting, standing in the road just outside our gate, for the signal. As the bells began their thunderous music we started off. The Polpeaus walked three paces behind Monsieur Gérard, and

I followed at the tail. The cart lurched over the dried ruts of mud in the road and the coffin slid back and forth inside it. People stared from their doorways as we passed; children stuck their thumbs in their mouths and didn't know what to make of our small, slow procession. When we reached the church, the four labourers heaved the coffin out of the cart, carried it up the aisle and deposited it on the waiting bier. The curé lit the tall candles flanking it on two sides, and Monsieur Gérard sat down alone in the front pew, clutching his hat, while the Polpeaus settled themselves just behind.

There didn't seem to be any other Colbert relatives. With Marie-Louise parked in her boarding-school, considered by her uncle too young and impressionable to attend a funeral, and her father still in Africa, the family was shrunk down to one man in a shiny black suit, his head bowed. His shoulder-blades looked lonely. I hung about at the back of the church, not liking to go too near the Polpeaus, who would have thought it was not my place. I loitered in the cool darkness, drawing in that holy smell of damp stone, incense, smoking wicks and brass polish. I whiled away the wait by looking at the statues of saints that stood about, perched in niches, like a bunch of friends gossiping at market. Saint Geneviève was not among them. I recognised St Joan of Arc, clad in armour, sword upraised as though to slay dragons or any other monsters bothering her friends' peace. I was thinking of poor Marie-Louise, of the plaintive letters she wrote home from her exile in Rouen. It was clear to me, when Gérard read these letters to me, grimacing and guilty, that she was not happy. He'd said she'd become too upset if she attended the funeral; it could not be allowed; but it was his own upset, I thought, from which he was protecting himself.

Eventually the church bells ceased their slow tolling and began to ring the summons that you heard before every mass. A different voice, faster, more urgent, a peal tumbling out telling you to hurry up, make haste, mass was about to start and you should not be late.

All of Jumièges turned out for the requiem, as was the custom when anyone in the village died; whether they had known Madame Colbert well or not, people tied on their black armbands or black ribbons and trooped along to see her well prayed for then duly buried in the cemetery. Many neighbours came back to the house afterwards for a glass of cider or of wine. They showed their sympathy and respect by taking these previous hours off work, which they could ill spare. Monsieur Gérard showed his appreciation by serving them with something good to eat. He asked me to make brioches, told me not to stint on the butter and eggs; thrift was not the issue for once. The night before the funeral he sat with his mother and I stood at the kitchen table kneading the dough for batch after batch of brioches. At the *vin d'honneur* I darted around with a tray of these, cut into yellow wedges, making sure everybody got a slice.

It was an awkward occasion. People wiped their boots anxiously as they came in, then stood in little groups, tongue-tied and shy, the men twiddling their caps, the women huddled together in the corners. No one had any small-talk. Nobody wept or looked sad. That would have been considered bad manners; drawing attention to yourself in public. I moved through an uneasy silence with my big jug. Acting as waitress reminded me of my days in the café at Blessetot with Madame Montjean, made me uncomfortable and clumsy; I knocked people with my elbows as I went past them, and tripped on the frayed edge of the carpet. I recovered myself by hiding briefly in the kitchen and downing a glass of cognac Madame Colbert had kept for visiting tradesmen. Out there, where nobody could see me, I felt better.

The guests departed into the chilly outdoors. A light, cold rain sprinkled the garden. It was early afternoon. The house was empty, an emptiness that was not a simple lack but charged with something positive, almost palpable. The atmosphere was uncertain and strange, as though the walls were wondering what would happen next. The rooms seemed echoing, as though all the furniture had gone, leaving just bare floors the wind whistled over. But of course what had gone was not chairs and beds but the corpse. The dead presence of the mistress of the house.

When I had finished washing up all the glasses we had borrowed from the doctor and the curé, and had packed them into baskets ready to be returned the following day, I felt suddenly clammy and depressed, and sat as close to the kitchen stove as I could get. Imaginary portraits of my missing parents whom I had never seen swam up, solemn and unsmiling, two strangers dressed in their best clothes. They hovered just in front of me, twin photographs edged in black, like the *faire-parts* Monsieur Gérard had had posted throughout Jumièges, as the custom was, to let everyone know his mother had died. I pulled my sleeves over my hands and wound them together in my lap. Hours passed. I was numb; in suspension; I couldn't feel or think. Yet deep down, underneath, like a creature gliding over the seabed, something stirred, and a decision got made.

After a long while I realised that I was hungry, and then I remembered Monsieur Gérard and thought that he too might be glad of something to eat. In the food cupboard I found some slices of cold roast mutton left over from yesterday, and some gravy, and some cooked white beans, and so I put these all together into a saucepan and left it to heat up on the side of the stove, and went to find Monsieur Gérard.

He was sitting in his study, slumped over a meagre fire, pretending to read a book. His eyes were red as the velvet cushions of his armchair. How odd to see him broken out of his usual routine; no pen in his hand; not working. That made him defenceless against the exhausting day just passed, wide open to its curious and exacting freight: boredom combined with grief; long, formal rituals performed under the public eye; and the same tiny conversation repeated a hundred times about what a fine woman Madame Colbert had been, what an excellent mother. He was the chief mourner and so he had had to look after everyone else.

He had had to console Madame Polpeau whose sadness made her twitter worse than ever. His own tears had had to wait.

He would feel more cheerful, I thought, when he got back to his writing. He hadn't been able to do any properly for weeks. His study felt very empty because he wasn't sitting at his desk. As though he himself had been ill.

He had taken off his jacket, collar and tie and put on his shabby old dressing-gown. A signal that he was back in the private domain again, with no one observing him, his doors closed against the village and all well-wishers. I wasn't the public, so I felt able to disturb him. I'd had enough time by myself in the echoing kitchen, in any case, and wanted some company. Offering him food was a way of not staying out there all alone, locked into silence, feeling too noisy when I moved, as though I must keep very still and not bruise the air. I think he felt something similar because he looked up and smiled at me when I coughed to remind him I was there.

—All right, all right, he said: I'll eat something as long as you agree to share it with me. It will be an act of kindness on your part to have supper with me in the dining-room and talk to me.

—I can't possibly sit down with you there, I objected.

He shrugged and came into the kitchen. My territory. It was the warmest place, after all, being so small, and the table being near the stove.

Having come to my decision, I acted on it. I spread a white cloth and put a tumbler of daisies in the centre. I took down from the buffet shelves next door the fine porcelain plates painted with red flowers that Madame Colbert had used on Sundays, rather than the everyday white china ones with blue rims, as a sign of respect to mark the significance of this day. Monsieur Gérard lit candles rather than the lamp, so that we kept a kind of vigil. He went into the cellar and brought out a bottle of red burgundy, opened it, and poured some into two glasses. I was used to being offered a glass of rough red wine mixed with water, on special occasions, every now and then, the sort Madame Colbert had kept for the servant, but tonight, the wine being such a good one, I drank it neat. It tasted of cherries and blackcurrants, of tannin and earth. I remembered the burgundy I had drunk with the Montjeans, to toast their child. Now I'd had burgundy twice, and could compare the tastes.

We talked. We'd always been able to do that. We had been friends, in our own quiet way, for a long time. After we had eaten, and finished the wine, I saw him suddenly perceive what he wanted, what was possible. He got up and pushed back his chair, came round the table, stroked my cheek, then kissed me. That set a seal on the evening. It flowed from the sorrow and strangeness of the day, from our conversations over the last months, and from the need we both had to stare death in the face and spit at her. When he blew out one branch of candles, picked up the other, took my hand and led me upstairs to his room, I went with him willingly and death slunk off.

The walls of his bedroom were washed a faded blue like seawater. The shutters were closed against the rainy night. The bed stood in one corner, mahogany, with curled-over ends, like a boat. Candlelight shone golden over us swimming between the smooth linen sheets. I felt glad I had washed all over so carefully for the funeral, that my hair was clean, and that I wearing my best Sunday chemise. I didn't feel ashamed taking my cap off, stepping out of my clothes; of what he'd see. How warm he was, when I slid under the quilt into his arms and he held me, how warm and vigorous and alive. That almost did for me. It was very alarming, being so close, and I felt rigid, like rusted clockwork, dry as a bucket of sand, with huge, unwieldy limbs. The fear was my bridge to him. Over the mountain of my fear I climbed to him. Telling him how afraid I was made the fear fall off me like a shirt, and then I was perched on the edge then diving in; we were nosing and jostling each other like two dolphins playing in the deep, bumping and leaping; his bed was as inviting as the salt ocean; welcoming; he made plenty of room in it for me. I forgot that there had ever been a death in the house, a funeral. I forgot all about his mother.

We lived together like that for a couple of weeks. I don't know what anyone in the village thought, whether they thought anything at all. The doctor's wife dropped in from time to time, and the doctor. They witnessed me getting on with all my usual jobs just as though nothing had happened. Neither of them said anything to me, so presumably they noticed nothing amiss. Not then, anyway. Not immediately. To them I was just a pair of hands that kept the house running; hard work was what I was for; this didn't need to be commented on; it was a part of life, useful, dependable and wholly unremarkable, like a hinge on a door. On the other hand their dear friend was a poet, a sensitive creature; he was in mourning and in need of solitude, not to be interrupted too often by tactfully shown sympathy. People brought him little gifts, a bunch of chives, a few eggs, a pot of pâté, which they left on the doorstep, acknowledging his wish for privacy. Then they went away and we remained alone.

I knew, of course, since he'd told me, that Monsieur Gérard had previously been involved with the Rouennaise lady whom I'd met two summers running, Madame Isabelle, and that they were currently estranged. This made him feel safe, I thought: able to embark on sleeping with me; because this other woman existed, with a prior claim on him. She was a kind of chaperone who protected him and allowed him to keep a certain distance. And for the moment I too felt safe. I could abandon myself in bed but inside myself I held back; my soul remained my own and did not stretch out of me, fly to embrace a soulmate like it had done before; it stayed tidy and tucked in.

These days, anyhow, I wasn't quite such a fool as I'd been before. By now I knew perfectly well that men slept with their housekeepers and maids without it meaning anything. It was the employer's privilege. They took advantage of female servants if they were so inclined and the woman got the blame and your best chance was to keep well out of their way.

I did not keep out of Monsieur Gérard's way. He was not exploiting me. I had made a free decision to go to bed with him; I had helped set the whole thing in motion; we were equals. No one would have believed that, of course. But as it was, for the moment we both existed in a simple-minded, comforting cocoon, and somewhere outside it was Madame Isabelle. Gérard was probably relying on her, I thought, to draw the line for him; at some point she would return; something would happen; everything would be all right.

The proof corrections were all finished and done. He decided to take the parcel up to his publishers in Paris himself, rather than trust the post. The tenants who had been renting the family flat were due to move out, and had to be visited. The family lawyer had to be consulted and the terms of Madame Colbert's will discussed. These pieces of business were urgent enough in themselves. The trip would give him, also, the chance to get back in touch with his writer and poet friends, go to the literary salon in the rue de Rome that he liked to frequent when he could, catch up on a couple of plays at the theatre. All his friends had written to him to condole with him on his bereavement. The letters lay in a heap on his study table, unanswered. He had decided it would be easier to reply in person to most of them than in writing.

—I'll be away for four or five days, he said: perhaps a week. I'll let you know when I'll be coming back. I'll send you a telegram.

He was sitting on the edge of his bed, buttoning his shirt. I hadn't even got up yet. I lay luxuriously in the warm space he had just vacated. Nine o'clock in the morning, and our shutters were still closed. Passers-by would draw their own conclusions; the village would start to talk. Gérard was quite oblivious to this.

I yawned and stretched. I reached out my hand and stroked his back.

—Fine, I replied.

I wondered whether he would try to see Madame Isabelle while he was away. I didn't ask him and he didn't tell me. I bade him a calm goodbye. I was pleased at the idea of having some time to myself in the house, to do as I liked. He clattered off, with the doctor, in the latter's carriage, to catch the train in Rouen. I set to and got on with the spring-cleaning.

It was the season for it. All over Jumièges women were doing the same thing, performing a rite every bit as important as the Easter vigil. It demonstrated that the long, cold winter was past: you renewed your life as you scoured and scrubbed and polished, just as you discarded worn and rotted feelings by throwing out the rubbish and dust. Now that the weather had grown warmer, the winds and rain lessened, doors and windows could stand open, letting in sunlight and fresh air. The village smelled of soap and bleach. Curtains were taken down and washed, hung in the orchard to dry, rugs and carpets shaken then beaten mercilessly. The glass in the windowpanes sparkled, cleaned with vinegar and hot water, dried with crumpled newspaper. I rubbed beeswax into the furniture.

All this work of restoration and renewal shored me up, provided me with peace and contentment. I missed Monsieur Gérard in one way, and felt his absence, but in another way he had not departed at all: he was in my mind all the time, for I was preparing the house against his return, creating a surprise and a welcome. I let myself forget that this was not my house. I rejoiced in it as though it were. Alone in the house, I possessed it. I was not pretending. Madame Colbert had gone, and Marie-Louise, and Madame Isabelle, and Miss Millicent. I was the only woman left. I was like a child playing with her dolls, dropping them off the doll's-house roof one by one. But in my mind this scenario was not a game but real.

The only room I did not spring-clean was the one upstairs in which Madame Colbert had died. It stayed closed and undusted; the key reposed quietly in the lock; and I left well alone.

The housework completed, I tackled the garden, giving the orchard grass its first scything of the year and shearing the hedges. Weeds were showing their heads in all directions, unfurling their rolled leaves in a tremendous hurry. I pulled up fistfuls of dandelions, buttercups and speedwell from the flowerbeds and from around the base of shrubs. An abundance of pretty weeds grew at the boundaries of the lawn, where it met the gravel of the path. Here there was space for them to flourish, not drowned out by grass. Wild clematis sprouted here, and crane's-bill, columbine, violets, early vetch, daisies, herb Robert. To me these were not weeds but wild flowers, beautiful in their own right, not bad but good; I couldn't bear to pull them up; I decided they had staked their claim to exist there on the edge; they had arrived by accident and I would make room for them. Some of the wild forget-me-nots I even dug up and transplanted into the formal beds. I sowed proper flowers, too: sweet peas, marigolds, morning glory and nasturtiums, using the seeds, I had saved from last year. In the *potager* I planted peas and beans, set onions, sowed parsley and chives. When I put my fingers into the earth I got a shock from how it clung to them moist as a mouth, warm as the flesh of an animal. It made me know the earth was alive.

From time to time various neighbours dropped in, to see how I was getting along, to bring me gifts of plants for the garden, to ask for a hand with their own spring-cleaning. We all ran in and out of each other's houses all day long, and so during those hours you couldn't hide anything. There wasn't much happening in the daytime that everyone didn't know about. The nights were another matter. People bolted their doors and closed their shutters and retired inside their privacy. At night you could do what you pleased, beat your wife, rape your daughter, as long as there was no evidence of it visible next morning. Monsieur Gérard and I had not been as discreet as we should, but nobody asked me any awkward questions, during his absence in Paris, or gave me any meaningful looks. They were biding their time, like spectators at the theatre, waiting to see what would happen next. They behaved like friendly neighbours to my face and kept their speculations to themselves.

The doctor's wife, who had constituted herself the guardian of my health and morals, was another matter. She believed herself bound to pry into my life and came poking around a couple of times, like a chicken scratching for food in the dust.

First of all she inspected the garden.

—It's much too early to have planted your peas, she scolded me: May's when you want to do it. You wait and see: they won't come up; they'll all rot in the wet, a complete waste of time and money.

Her eyes swivelled about, piercing and uprooting.

—You want to get rid of all those weeds. They're an absolute disgrace.

Next, she was bustling upstairs, under the pretext of collecting her rosary which she declared she had left by Madame Colbert's *table de nuit*. I heard her creaking from room to room, opening and shutting doors, trying to work out who was sleeping where. I had taken care to disarrange my bedclothes every morning, just in case, and when she came downstairs again I gave her the demurest of smiles and bobs. She was beaten back. So far she couldn't catch me out.

Over and over I imagined Gérard's return. I told it to myself like a story, repeating it, refining the details, getting it just right.

He warned me by telegram, as he'd said he would, when to expect him. The doctor and his wife drove into Rouen to fetch him from the station, and dropped him outside the house. I watched from behind the curtain and saw Madame Polpeau lean down from the carriage and speak to him earnestly. They drove off again, and he waved. Then he came in. He greeted me calmly, and went upstairs to change out of his travelling clothes.

I laid two places at the table in the dining-room, putting out the best crystal glasses and the red-flowered plates, the big starched napkins normally kept for Sunday guests, the silver salt cellar. I sat down with him there and shared his *déjeuner*. This was an act of disobedience and disrespect towards the house and the rules that had always prevailed in it, as forbidden and daring as going up to the high altar in church, opening the sanctuary gates, pushing through them and past the little red light flickering its warning and telling you to keep back, not even to imagine entering that sacred space. Only the priest was allowed to approach the altar, where the Real Presence of Jesus Christ reposed hidden in the brocade-covered tabernacle. For anyone else to come close was desecration. Here was I sitting in Madame Colbert's old place, in her straw-seated chair with curved wooden arms, shaking out my napkin from her silver ring and wielding the silver fork bearing her monogram. This was behaviour demonstrating the utmost insolence. My hand shook a little as I picked up my wineglass and sipped at it.

We at the early asparagus he had brought back with him from Paris, with hollandaise sauce, and potatoes from the sack in the shed. After lunch we took a turn around the garden. The sun came out and shone brilliantly from behind the scudding grey and white clouds. The gravel in front of the house glittered, each sharp point distinct, newly washed. Raindrops trembled on the fleshy leaves poking out of the pots of tulips lined up along the path, on the lilac bushes, on the vivid green grass, a flung net of watery jewels glinting in rainbow colours when the light caught it. The cherry blossom snowed down and lay, almost translucent, on the turf underneath.

—You've made the garden look lovely, Gérard said.

He put his arm round my waist.

—Poor girl, but it's too much work for you, all by yourself. The doctor's wife was saying so, on the way back from Rouen. She thinks you're much too young to have so much responsibility. She says I should engage another servant, to give you a hand. That would be much more *convenable,* she says.

—I can manage, I said.

I knew what Madame Polpeau had been hinting to him. He knew I understood, without him having to put it into words. I could catch his meaning from his blue eye stealthily glancing sideways at me, his hand tugging his moustache.

By now I knew how much he disliked fuss, how little of a ladies' man he really was despite his occasional swaggering talk, how much he had relied on his mother to run his domestic life and how lost he felt without her. He had begun to rely on me instead, but he had also begun to realise that things could not go on as they were.

I could see him wondering about the next step. Whether he should consider marrying me. I looked after him well; I made no demands; and being from a lower social class I wouldn't expect to be taken to Paris and introduced to all his fine friends. In the country he could live with me the quiet hermit's life he liked, which was crucial to his writing, and then, whenever he fancied a change, he could run up to Paris and jaunt about, knowing that back at home things were ticking over nicely.

—But perhaps you think I should leave? I asked.

We went to bed. I exerted myself to please him to the height of my powers, employing every sensual trick I could think of, every gesture and caress I knew he especially liked. I stroked licked sucked ate drank fucked him. Afterwards we lay collapsed. We talked in low voices, addressing each other's pillows as though, big and solemn in their frilled white cases, they were bewigged judges able impartially to decide our fate.

—Men don't marry their housekeepers, I objected: it isn't done.

I had given myself a promotion. Housekeeper sounded a lot better, more possible, than servant. And I had constituted myself counsel for the prosecution so that I could enjoy hearing Gérard speak up for the defence.

—The poet Mallarmé married a governess, Gérard returned: a working woman; it's not so unusual.

—If we were married, I pointed out: you wouldn't have to pay me. You'd save on my wages.

The verdict was given. It was decided. We fell asleep.

But it didn't happen like that. No, it didn't happen like that at all. I had told myself the false story, which annoyed the true one, and so the true one burst out and took over, a torrent which could not be stopped.

It began as soon as Gérard had left for Paris.

The house became filled with icy draughts. However carefully I closed the doors, they jerked open again once I'd gone past, all by themselves, then banged shut and opened again. The wind whistled past my ears and tugged my ear-lobes. It was sly. It was spiteful.

The atmosphere of that death chamber upstairs was leaking out through the keyhole and poisoning the entire house. I tiptoed past the door on my way to bed in my own room, at night, making no sound, but nonetheless something inside had become disturbed; something had been roused up and made angry and wanted to attack me.

Downstairs, in the daytime, I felt a presence, a damp, chilly web of fear that lurked in the corners of the dining-room then draped itself across my shoulder-blades and clung to the nape of my neck whenever I turned my back.

Unease like a cold slime hovered in the air, waiting for me whenever I came in from outdoors. Objects moved about when they had no right to. In front of my eyes a plate lifted itself off the buffet, hovered sideways, fell on to the floor. Towels that I had left in a low white pile at one end of the kitchen table reappeared, tumbled and disarranged, at the other. The sewing scissors simply vanished and I never found them again.

At night I couldn't sleep. I shivered in the darkness, clutching the edge of the sheet, listening to the noises downstairs: doors slamming shut then opening again, saucepan lids rolling clattering across the kitchen floor. Some fierce energy rattled the shutters, knocked back and forth inside the chimney-breasts as though it were trapped and wanted to break free. I shut my eyes, put my head under the bedclothes and prayed to God for help. The fear waited implacably, leaping in to clutch my throat in between the words of my gabbled invocations.

When the dawn came I would jump out of bed, grateful for the light. I went at my cleaning and gardening tasks ferociously, as though determination were a virtue that would drive my demons away. But by the time afternoon arrived, I would be as frightened as ever all over again, watching the shadows thicken, starting and jumping when a cart creaked by outside. By now I knew there was no escape from whatever it was. Something was waiting for me. Getting gradually closer. Enjoying my terror and wanting to make it worse.

I didn't dare tell Madame Polpeau when she came prowling round. When she asked me if I was managing all right I held my tongue and just grunted.

On the third night the disturbance moved upstairs. Around midnight something crashed to the ground in the room along the corridor that had been Madame Colbert's. In the morning I bullied myself to go in and check. I twisted the frilled oval top of the iron key in the lock, felt the tongue of the latch click and slither aside, grasped the cold china egg of the doorknob in my reluctant fingers, turned it slowly sideways, pushed the door open.

Inside all was chaos and destruction. At first I thought there had been a flood, then that I was looking at ice and glaciers. The gilt-wreathed mirror that had hung, tilting and sloping forwards, over the grey marble fireplace now lay shattered on the tiled floor in front of the empty grate, a crazy spread of great glittering fragments like spikes of a frozen waterfall. These jagged shards were widely scattered around, as though the glass had been wrenched off its hook with great force and flung down contemptuously by someone who hated it.

I was forced to remember the last time I had looked in that mirror, which so acutely reflected what lay on the bed. How on the morning after Madame Colbert's death the door of her room had been left open by stupid, careless Madame Polpeau, so that running past with a can of hot water for Monsieur Gérard to wash in I had caught a fleeting glimpse of the corpse.

Once there had been a live person here, a real presence, but she had gone. She had vanished overnight and would never be seen again. In her place was this imposter, this fake, a doll of greenish wax who had arrived in the house secretly, by some unknown means, who had been parked on Madame Colbert's bed, her flesh seeming stiff but no more solid than blancmange, threatening to yield to the probing finger like a rotting cheese. Her eyelids were drawn down like blinds, over empty globes cold like marbles. She was all shut up and sealed off.

She was playing a game, pretending to be Madame Colbert, who had gone away, but she was a replica. She was a model in porcelain, a dummy to frighten the children with, smuggled into my employer's bed as a sadistic surprise. I told myself: don't be stupid, this is a dead person. Not a person at all. A dead body. But how did I know? The horror was that she might be playing a joke and not be dead at all; she might open her sightless eyes, sit up, stretch out her clammy arms. I edged away.

I have heard people say that corpses are not frightening, that once the spirit has left the dead body is just clay, peaceful, not threatening, not like the person at all. They should try living with a corpse for three nights and three days, as I had to. There she lay, Madame Colbert's exact double, her mysterious and terrifying other self, with her hooded eyes and curved nose and jaw, her complete stillness. As though she were stifling her breathing, willing herself not to move. Any minute now she would break the spell, jump up and laugh. Who was she and what was she? What was she up to? She was dead; she was inanimate matter; she was now just rubbish, because her soul had flown off; she wasn't even a she any more but just stuff, and she should have been got out of the house and put somewhere else, at a good distance, while we waited to bury her. But oh, to have to share a house with her, strange and uncanny uninvited guest: that made me feel she was very much alive, too much so, gleefully hiding under her carnival mask of green skin, and simply biding her time.

She was as gruesome as the mermaid washed up on the beach then slaughtered. She was that bruised, bloated body that would not drown but kept on resurfacing, shrouded in rags and seaweed, however often the sea dragged her back. She was the wicked girl who did not deserve a mother's love, who deserved to die, and so the ghost was coming for her and would get her and would not let go.

Now the dead woman came alive in the grave of the bed and sat up. She wanted her revenge. She wanted to punish me. And so night after night she slunk in through the front door and pattered up the stairs, looking for me. Mind the stairs, someone's voice sang: they're steep and narrow; it's easy to slip and fall. Mind the stairs.

The stair treads creaked. The floorboards along the corridor uttered their oak warning as she inched along, searching for me.

She was my angry mother, determined to exact vengeance, and sooner or later she would find me and I would have to be killed and hung up in a net in the church porch while everybody laughed.

I couldn't stay in that house and let myself imagine I could love Gérard. That was much too dangerous. I had to protect him from my wicked self and from the cold mother who was hunting for me to kill me.

I left the day before he was due back. I crept out of Jumièges very early in the morning, before anyone else in the village was up. The sky was pink. The house yawned and relaxed as I abandoned it. The evil spirits went off somewhere else. I headed towards the river.

Marie-Louise

This effort of trying to discover and collect my earliest memories of my uncle reminds me of one of my pleasures on wet days in summer. While the drenching August rain tapped on the windows and the roof and chilled the house, I would vanish into the curtained space underneath the stairs. My grandmother's maid, Geneviève, employed this dark, windowless cubbyhole as a cupboard, in which she kept stacks of old newspapers tied up with string, brooms and mops, the wicker baskets with sturdy handles that she carried to market, and so on. The charm of this place was double: I was hidden inside it; and also it represented the unknown. Squatting in here on the floor, with the flowered chintz curtain pulled across to block out the dim light of the kitchen passage, I had crossed over into a place which was the other side of all that was familiar: I saw the underneath of the stairs above my head, curving up, up, up and round, precise as the steps in a story leading to the denouement. I was below that narrative, in a world both enclosed and limitless, my eyes and fingers exploring the outlines of the coal box, with its sharp handles, and the sewing-machine like a small coffin, sitting still under its wooden shroud. My cave tapered away to a point in the blackness into which I couldn't squeeze, beyond which I couldn't go, but I sent my imagination on ahead of me into that new country; I dreamed up what was there.

This section of my memoir of my uncle which touches on my childhood would not be complete if I did not add to all these memories of the times I was privileged to spend with him a quick account of the day my childhood in Jumièges ended, in which tragedy (to my small mind, at least) he was crucially involved.

That summer, when I was seven years old, I had an English governess, whose duties were to oversee my studies and to teach me her own language. We spent two months in my grandmothers' house in Jumièges, now the Musée Colbert (where I sit writing this), and we also all stayed in Etretat for a while.

The entire household shifted to a hotel on the front. With Miss Milly and Uncle Gérard I played on the beach. To a child's eyes this was a magical landscape prodigal with riches: hills of sea-washed pebbles down which to slide, sand-floored caves to explore, tunnels leading up through the inside of the cliffs, small bays hidden beyond the cliff arches, expanses of tumbled boulders and rock pools, all kinds of shells, dead starfish and cuttlefish to collect. Nowadays, if you go to Etretat, the beach is often most unfortunately clotted with patches of sticky tar. But in those far-off times it was very clean; you could step barefoot over the stones, and spread out your picnic without fear of soiling your clothes.

Invalids, and semi-invalids like my grandmother, sat, well wrapped up in shawls and blankets, on the promenade outside the hotel, to breathe good fresh breezes for the sake of their health. It is true; they were invigorating, those damp, salty winds, impregnated with the liberating idea of the sea, with the taste and smell of the sea itself. There was plenty to look at, a constantly changing spectacle of strolling passers-by, the antics of dogs and children, the cries and gestures of the men on the boules pitch nearby, the deft movements of the fishermen putting out to sea with their boats or bringing in their catch, the play of the bright sunlight dancing on the blue-green water, the little wooden canoes, for tourists to rent, drawn up in gaily coloured rows at the top of the beach. My grandmother had plenty to amuse her; she had begun making acquaintances among the other ladies staying at the hotel with whom she could chat and play cards; she was quite happy to see me go off down to the sea. Once I had solemnly sworn I would

238 — THE LOOKING GLASS

not remove my sun-bonnet and that I would not sit about on wet stones with wet feet, she gave me a kiss and waved me off.

Miss Milly had always been a kind governess who could enter wholeheartedly into a child's games. Uncle Gérard was very similar. With the two of them I spent a happy afternoon, that first day in Etretat, pottering about at the water's edge, scrambling over rocks, examining quartz-filled pebbles and filling my pockets with them. There was something going on between the two adults, though I was not exactly sure what. I observed them while pretending to be wholly absorbed with my shrimping net and pail. They, of course, assumed that a small girl was necessarily oblivi-ous of grownup emotions. I was a little policeman, suspi-cious, dogging their steps, wearing my detective's disguise of childish skipping and shouting.

Miss Milly was certainly strongly impressed by my uncle; whenever he spoke to her she turned pink as a boiled prawn. To me this affection seemed reasonable: he was great fun when he was in a holiday mood; he could be playful and kind; it was normal to love him. Miss Milly gazed at Uncle Gérard with an enraptured look like someone in church coming back from Holy Communion; her face blurred to dreaminess; she sat next to him on the beach, listening to him talk, with her hands clasped as though she were pray-ing. I lay curled up between them, supposedly taking my nap, but it was too interesting, what was going on just next to me, to let myself drift away into unconsciousness. I peeped through my half-closed eyelashes, when they thought I was asleep, and saw them kissing each other. A kiss which linked up with the softness of my uncle's coat padding the pebbles underneath me, and the heat of the sun on my cheek. The two of them were my windbreak, a sheltering pavilion of bodies. They arched over me, joined by their mouths.

Almost immediately after that, Uncle Gérard went to Paris, and Miss Milly disappeared. My grandmother explained that she had returned home to England, to see her mother who had suddenly been taken ill. Geneviève said that she was sure Miss Milly had been sacked. Why? I demanded. Oh, she said vaguely: your grandmother was displeased with her; she didn't do her job properly; something like that.

That must be my fault, I was sure. I hadn't worked hard enough, and I hadn't learned enough English. Guilt was a blow that made me stagger. Change whirled upon me, a thundercloud out of a blue sky. A change in the weather. My two suns had departed and left me exposed and alone on the chilly beach, shivering. Uncle Gérard might return, but Miss Milly never. I felt so lonely one night that I took my collection of stones and shells to bed with me and slept with them under my pillow. In the morning the pillowcase was stained with salt water and the chambermaid complained and I was made to throw my treasures away. Geneviève helped me collect some more and lent me a handkerchief to keep them in. The knotted bag hung from the bedpost so that I could see it if I woke up and be certain it was still there.

Sometimes at night Geneviève cried, but she wouldn't tell me what about. Sometimes she took me into her bed. Her arms stretched out and encircled me as the cliffs did the beach, arching out like wings to catch and hold me. I lay against her like a sea lulled after the tempest, breathing in and out on the shore. She was soft, despite being so thin. She wore a thick linen nightdress, and being in her embrace reminded me of the afternoon I lay on the beach on Uncle Gérard's coat. I loved falling asleep with her in her bed, melded to her side like a limpet to a rock. I made her promise not to tell my grandmother or she'd be sacked as well.

Back in Jumièges, the summer drew towards its close. I took chilly walks along the river bank in the fine rain, picked sopping bunches of wild flowers to present to my grandmother on my return. The house felt empty, fidgety.

Uncle Gérard was now back from visiting his friends in Paris. He continued to give me a daily lesson, and the rest of the time I worked at my books under the eye of my grandmother. I am afraid I was not easy to teach; I was a sullen and grumpy child at this time, only too prone to bursting into tears when reproved. My grandmother would cast up her hands at these tantrums and exclaim: what are we going to do with you! To cry in her presence was a sign of great weakness. Often I compounded my disgrace by not being able to stop crying and had to be sent to my room.

One weekend in early September Uncle Gérard took me to Le Havre for an overnight visit. We stayed in a dim, gloomy hotel in a cobbled backstreet. We were invited by the Polpeaus to go with them, riding in their carriage as far as Rouen and then taking the train. While they were settling their daughter Yvonne back into her school before the start of the new term, for special coaching after failing her end of year exams in June, my uncle took me to the sea.

The beach did not shelve steeply, as at Etretat, but seemed completely flat, a wide expanse of grey under uncertain sunshine and racing clouds. No pebbles here, either, but sand, which children are supposed to prefer. You can run across it barefoot, build castles with it, and so on. I didn't like the sand. It blew into our eyes, into our *goûter* of bread and chocolate; it gritted inside my socks when I put them back on; it dried on my legs and scratched.

I felt it was only polite to reassure my uncle, who was looking after me on his own because my grandmother had business in Rouen and could not accompany us, that I was enjoying this treat. But Le Havre felt foreign, and too big. There was too much town crowding up onto the promenade, and too little sea. It was low tide, the water's edge a long way out, the waves almost invisible, a grey wrinkle on the horizon. To get to the sea you had to walk over what seemed kilometers of grey sludge, leaving everything familiar far behind. I dutifully marched down the beach a little way, past the seaweed-draped breakwaters, until I reached the tideline, where dry sand was replaced by wet, and by coarse shingle. I kept turning round to check that my uncle was still there, lying, propped on one elbow, further up the beach, looking bored and smoking a cigar. He had dwindled to the size of a doll. I didn't want him to get any smaller, and disappear, so I stopped, and chose my digging place.

I dug a hole in a wet patch of sand and poured seawater into it from my little red and white tin pail, plodding to the far-off low breakers to fill this. I made several journeys but the level of water at the bottom of my hole got no higher. I couldn't hold the sea in my hands. It vanished every time, seeping away through the grey squidgy walls of what was not even a puddle. I don't know why I bothered doing this. I suppose I hadn't the energy to raise a castle; I retreated from such an assertive act; I chose concave over convex.

I returned to my uncle and outlined the problem of the water not being willing to stay. He grimaced and said I was a philosopher seeking to understand infinity; an impossibility; he couldn't help me. Then, as I gaped at him, he snorted and added that surely I knew that water leaked through sand; I was old enough, surely, for heaven's sake; I was seven years old.

I remember that day so clearly, perhaps because we were both edgy and discontented, showing each other how we felt but unable to cheer each other up. Also because it was almost my last day of freedom. Soon afterwards I understood the reason for the visit to Le Havre. It was a special treat, a kind of farewell to the summer holidays, and an introduction to the wider world outside Jumièges which I scarcely knew at all. My grandmother's trip to Rouen had been in order to arrange for me to become a termly boarder at the junior school attached to the *lycée* there. With Miss Milly gone, my grandmother naturally wished to assure herself that I would be properly cared for and educated. Her health was too shaky for her to go on teaching me my lessons herself, and my uncle was really too busy to continue his part of the business. My father had written from Africa to say that he was making plenty of money out there among the black people; the fees would be no problem. So off I was to go to school.

The prospect frightened me. School sounded like a punishment. I believed that if I was sent there I should become lost, like a parcel, and never find my way home again. I plucked up my courage and visited my uncle in his study to tell him this. Unfortunately I chose a bad moment, when he was in the middle of writing something. A poem, I suppose. We were not meant to interrupt him in his study, and his face, as he turned it to me where I stood hovering at the door, was at first absent and then irritable.

I pleaded with him not to send me away; I promised to reform and become an angel of virtue if only he would allow me to stay at home. It made him quite angry to have to say to me that it was not his decision; it was not he who had charge of children; my grandmother ran the household and we must respect her wishes. She was doing it for the best, etc., etc. I saw how ashamed he felt, and that even he could feel as powerless as a child. Immediately I felt I must protect him and so said no more. I duly departed for school.

I was as unhappy there as it is possible to be, even more unhappy than I had expected. I thought I would die, in those first weeks, of the strangeness and loneliness. The nights were the worst, since, being the youngest boarder, I was sent upstairs before the others. The stairs up to the dormitory, polished and carpetless, loomed like scree on a mountainside. I hauled myself up over their menacing edges, rising higher and higher into blackness, towards whatever presence waited for me there. The corridor at the top was lit only by a single lamp at the far end. Walking through this hall of shadows felt like approaching hell; I was convinced that demons lurked in the darkness, eager to clutch hold of me. At night I frequently wet the bed since I was too frightened to get up and walk what seemed a kilometre to the lavatory. I would lie in my cold and stinking sheets, waiting wretchedly for the morning, the humiliation of having my shameful state discovered, and being made to strip the bed and carry the sheets past all my fellow pupils down to the laundry. I should not dwell on that period in my life, however, since this is not my story but Gérard's.

It's just that, years later, when I was grown up and could properly appreciate my uncle's poems, I read his chef-d'oeuvre *Men and Mermaids* (written while he was still a young man) for the first time, that long, astonishing sequence of jagged, dissonant lines whose uneven music you can fancy represents the crashing of the waves onto the shore; that complex meditation with its interwoven themes of sea serpents and monsters and mermaids, one seductive image metamorphosing into another in the same way that the sea is described as shimmering with layers of constantly changing colours. I was intrigued to discover what seemed to me such clear references to the unforgettable and dramatic landscape of Etretat, which meant so much to me during the short time I was there and was so bound up with people I loved.

The poem mimics a landscape of the heart, certainly, a landscape of the imagination, but, to this reader at least, paints a vivid picture of the real. As I turned the pages, there it was, the eager sea, its surface tint altering subtly with the light, from green to turquoise to violet and back again, the rough, white-capped waves pounding the beach and sending up walls of spray, the powerful salt-laden wind, the caves hidden inside the arching cliffs, the heaps of black nets, the fishermen's thatched black huts, their piled lobster pots. I was very proud to think that I could share a memory of all that with my uncle, that I'd actually been there with him.

That was all, of course, many years ago. Looking back from the vantage point of the present, I struggle to understand exactly how the present changes into the past, how what seems utterly modern, now, subsequently becomes charmingly old-fashioned and quaint. The present can appear so brash—Etretat full of motor cars, noisy with blaring music, the old shopfronts marred by lurid advertising posters—that it's easy to look back at the Etretat of the past and see it as far more beautiful, more unspoiled. Yet as a child visiting Etretat I saw it as utterly modern and up to date: the hotel newly decorated; the women in the latest fashions. It was the present, the epitome of progress.

Deeper than this, my nostalgia points me towards something I've lost; some treasure of goodness and beauty that belongs in the remote past. Some golden age of happiness, some paradise land of long ago. I used to think I was some kind of reactionary, always moping for what was gone, insisting things were better then. Now I think that that yearning back has to do with mourning my mother, whom of course I never knew. In my imagination death has preserved her incorrupt; eternally beautiful and young; she can't be bruised or spoiled by age and time. And in my imagination my beloved uncle, also, lives on unharmed, fixed for ever as handsome and smiling, as though in a studio portrait. Is that what the imagination does for us, then, preserves for ever what we most love? So imagination and memory are one. And to remember is to become an archaeologist, discovering images of the past whole and undamaged. Or, at least, knowing how to fit the remains together again; to mend what was destroyed; to make something new out of it.

My uncle's work gives me back my mother. His poems heal and repair the wounds of my childhood. What more could he have done for me?

None of this is explicit in *Men and Mermaids,* naturally. I have brought my own musings to the poems. Yet, reading them again, I'm intrigued to rediscover how the figure of a pensive young woman drifts through them, an insubstantial wraith who seems only half flesh and blood, half created from foam and seawater. The Muse? She doesn't speak in human language, the poet tells us: but in an unknown tongue that he translates for the reader. She is never named, and we don't know who she was.

What enchants me, reading and re-reading this group of poems, is my discovery of how art has the power, so realistically and convincingly, to summon and recreate the past, to find and invent it; how it hasn't gone away and vanished for ever as we might suppose. The past can come back, like a spirit from the dead. The poems' metaphors allow the past and the present constantly to blur into one another, like watercolours. *Men and Mermaids* presents me with a childhood world whose colours and shapes are as fresh and bright as those in a picture book.

Perhaps poetry in itself is a metaphor, a metaphor of presence, beginning with absence and then making something alive out of it, revealing that emptiness can be inhabited by fullness. Space on the blank white page suddenly leaping with the black squiggles of words. Yes, conception and birth. So to remember and to write seems to mean to be haunted, and simultaneously, to feel fertile. Did Uncle Gérard feel like this? I imagine not! These are my own images, for my own writing: this memoir that sprawls and dashes about all over the place, that wants to be given its head and won't stay tidy, within the bounds of some logical narrative of what happened next, but which is as fanciful as any fairy story. Writing this, I'm a bareback rider standing astride two galloping steeds: memory and desire.

Ah, that armchair, and that uncle, that prancing delight on which I rode, night after night, excitement mounting to fever pitch—no wonder my grandmother always stopped the game at a certain point of overheatedness and sent me off to bed.

Was I in love with my uncle, then? Yes. Can a child of seven be in love with a man of thirty-five? Most certainly, yes. Miss Milly and I were both in love with him, and we were both punished for it by being sent away. That, to my childish mind, was irrefutably logical. That I can acknowledge it at all, now, so many years later, is because help and rescue arrived just as I had given up hope.

Geneviève

I had thought I would have to walk all the way from Jumièges to Rouen, but a passing sailboat took me up and gave me a lift along the tightly winding S of the river. Its owner came alongside one of the numerous little wooden quays which jutted out over the milky green water and invited me to hop on board. He was a ferryman, he told me, who made a living transporting people, and sometimes their poultry too, trussed by the feet and squawking loudly, up and down the great waterway which was our main road. Having taken a couple of tourists, laden with folding easels and camp-stools, downstream to their early

morning destination, a popular sketching spot in our particular loop of the Seine, he was returning to his boatyard
and was happy to have a passenger to keep him company.

He was a grizzled old man with faded blue eyes in his
brown, weatherbeaten face. He was bent and shaped by
work in the way that thorn trees get blunted by the wind.
Seeing the basket over my arm he assumed I was on my way
to the market in Rouen, and I assented, glad that my flight
could appear such a normal journey.

Once we were away from the shallows and out in mid-
stream, our sails felt the fresh breeze knocking against them,
filling them, and we fairly scudded along. The river, buoy-
antly rocking us up and down, seemed enormous, and our
craft so tiny it might easily capsize. We were skimming the
surface of what felt like unknown depths; you could imagine
them swelling underneath you, like blown walls of liquid
glass; we tilted along precariously on top, ready at any
moment to plunge and topple down. Grey-green water
raced past on either side; my face was level with the distant
willows lining the shore. Everything but the surrounding
river seemed very far away. I sat in the bows, watching the
pilot's skill, the tiller leaping in his hand like a live thing as
the wind drove us along and the sails cracked and whipped
like taut sheets drying on the line. Then Rouen rose up, and
I said goodbye to the kind ferryman as he put me ashore. He
had not bothered me *en route* with curious questions about
where I came from and what household I worked for, and
now he wouldn't take any money for the trip. He grunted

his refusal, handed me out, and pointed me in the direction I should go, to steer clear of the port and into town.

Rouen was waking up, stretching, yawning, as I walked into it. Shutters above my head squeaked as they were pushed open from within then creaked apart, wooden lips ready to announce the start of the day, releasing quilts, like fat tongues, sent flopping over windowsills to air. Voices called out abruptly from inside, staccato, harsh, and the rhythm of a child's crying interlaced itself with the soothing murmurs of a woman, the one tone leaning into the other, a counterpoint. Shop doors gaped wide; awnings were lowered screechily down; buckets of soapy water sluiced across the pavements onto the cobbles, scummy and frothing, so that I had to scuttle out of the way as I passed. My boots made a loud clattering noise in my ears, uncontrollable, though I told my feet to keep quiet; I was a surprise who surprised myself; I was afraid I was creating a disturbance, whereas I wanted to pass through these fresh morning streets invisibly, unnoticed by anybody, like a cat-burglar slithering in and out of casements, tiptoeing over eaves, in the middle of the night.

I had been following the sun, but now I felt less sure of what road to take. At a junction I hesitation, not knowing which way to go, yet reluctant to draw attention to myself by asking someone. In the end I headed in the same direction as a couple of women in front of me. They looked, with their bags over their arms, as though they were going shopping, and so I followed them. They walked at a good pace,

springily; their backs were energetic. They talked and ges-
ticulated, their free arms flying up and their hands tapping
the air. Their sabots rapped on the cobbles.

As we went along the sun increased in strength and the
streets got busier. Now there were plenty of people in country clothes about, laden with heavy baskets and pushing
barrows, obviously making for the market. I mingled with
them, slipped along in their wake.

The fruit and vegetable stalls were setting up on a *place*
not far from the cathedral, connected to it by an ancient
street dominated by an enormous clock. I walked up and
down this thoroughfare a couple of times, liking the view,
then turned back into the market. Tightly packed rows of
curly cabbages and lettuces glistened with water, and
behind them, beyond the rooftops, the enormous holy
building reared up like a monster snail happily anticipat-
ing grazing on this abundance of salad. I lingered, relieved
to be anonymous amidst the bustle of people and animals,
the stallholders yelling jokes and cheerful abuse at each
other as they hauled their wooden handcarts, piled high
with bunches of green-topped carrots and whiskery onions,
creaking over the rough *pavé*. Ducks, chickens and rabbits
occupied their own special section, with crates of chirrup-
ing ducklings and chicks to one side. The *charcuterie* stalls
came next, hung with *saucissons* and displaying earthenware
terrines of glossily crusted pâtés rimmed with rich grease,
dishes of galantine gleaming with chopped jelly, bowls of
solid mayonnaise packed in ice, on the counters. Tubs of

mussels, wheels of herrings and mackerel, shone nearby. Next I inspected cheeses, baskets of eggs laid on straw, and buckets of cream, and then a rack of men's work-shirts in rich Rouennais indigo.

I knew I was just putting off the moment of doing what I had come to do, and then the succeeding moment of knocking on Madame Isabelle's door. I told myself that my delay was because I did not want to disturb her too early, but that wasn't true. I was nervous. My heart thumped and banged in my chest like a dog jumping against the wire walls of its run. Passing a baker's shop and smelling newly baked bread, that powerful scent of yeast and sweetness gushing out and enveloping me, I was suddenly faint with hunger, punched in the belly; if I didn't eat something quickly my knees would give way and I would collapse.

Why was it so difficult to enter a shop and buy myself some food? In this place I didn't know it seemed an aggressive act, to require all the courage I possessed. I wasn't sure of the etiquette of shopping in a town; people might laugh at my accent, stare at me and snigger. I looked down at my boots. Wooden-soled, hob-nailed, canvas bound with leather strips, stoutly laced. I plaited my hands together over my coarse brown apron and glanced at them, red from years of immersion in hot soapy water, the nails chipped and black-rimmed with earth from gardening. I remembered Madame Isabelle's dismissive glance in Blessetot all that time ago. No point dwelling on that. Either she'd let me in or she wouldn't.

I drove myself forward. I pushed open the tinkling door of the *boulangerie,* entered the warm, bread-lined interior and bought myself a large roll. Not wanting to arrive empty-handed at Madame Isabelle's house, I bought a whole loaf as well, a nice round one, and dropped it into my basket. I had brought away from Jumièges the housekeeping money for the week, in lieu of the wages Monsieur Gérard owed me, stowed deep in my pocket. I could afford to eat, for the moment anyway.

The woman behind the counter served me calmly and without fuss. She waited patiently while I managed not to get into a fluster, to count out the correct number of sous without blushing or dropping coins on the floor. She had floury forearms, like white gloves. When I asked her for directions to the junior school of the *lycée* in the rue des Pénitents she glanced at me without surprise and indicated that it was quite close by, a turning off the far end of the rue Martainville which led away from the church of Saint Maclou behind the cathedral. I thanked her and went out tearing at my heartening breakfast, the crusty bread still hot and doughy from the oven.

Hunger appeased, bravery was now simple. I walked to the rue des Pénitents, found the school, which announced itself on a brass plaque set into the high wall, and paced slowly past it on the other side of the street. I was in luck. The high wrought-iron gates, lined with sheets of metal, had been pushed open, their bottom edges scoring half-circle sweeps on the wide gravel path, and I could see in. It was the hour of delivering children to morning lessons. The white stone buildings, several-storeyed, with long windows, rose austerely in the background, looking onto a paved area edged with flowerbeds. Little groups of maids, white-capped and decorous, stood about chatting at the edge of this playground, while their charges tore up and down, running races and yelling, or jumped back and forth over swinging skipping-ropes. No one who looked like a teacher was yet visible, that my eyes could discover. I crossed over the road and came back along the pavement, making myself saunter, as though I were completely at ease. Sweat coursed down my face but I didn't stop to wipe it away. I slipped in through the gates and stood quietly under the plane tree that shaded the gravel path.

My one fear was that the boarders would not take part in this early morning recreation. I need not have worried. I saw Marie-Louise almost immediately, seated alone, some little distance away, on a stone bench, swinging her legs, her head bent, and her arms crossed over the bodice of her blue school wrapper. How removed she seemed from all the others. As though she had already begun what I would complete.

I gazed at her intently, willing her attention. She soon looked up and saw me. I smiled and put my finger to my lips. She jumped up and ran over to me. I crouched down and opened my arms and she hurled herself into my embrace. Her grip was so strong. She didn't want to let go. While we hugged each other I whispered urgently in her ear.

—I've come to take you home. We don't have to say goodbye to anybody. We're just going to walk straight out of the gate. It's like a game. All right? Come on then.

I drew us both to our feet. Still clutching Marie-Louise's hand I led her as casually as I could over to the gates and out into the street. We walked away rapidly. Nobody seemed to have noticed our departure. There was no outcry behind us, no sound of running feet, no watchman's whistle blown to summon the police. Nonetheless I quickened our pace until we had turned the corner, hurried to the end of the next street and got back into the rue Martainville. Here I felt safer, and let myself slow down.

Marie-Louise was intrigued for the moment, looking around at the old half-timbered houses whose upper storeys hung out over the street. She was swept up by the sights and smells of freedom: a cat, sunning itself on a windowsill, that she stopped to stroke; the lemony scent of a pot of geraniums on a stone ledge by a front door; a curl of white lace behind a small dimpled window. I had quickly to decide what to do next. But I felt so tired, suddenly, that it was difficult to think clearly. Lack of sleep over the last few nights was curdling my brain. I had set out to rescue Marie-Louise because it was obvious to me, from hearing Gérard read out her weekly letters home, how bitterly unhappy she was, shut up in that school. I was afraid for her, that she would suffer some damage, that something bad would happen to her as a result. She might be scarred for life. She might never recover. I had managed to get her away. But I had not thought sufficiently about the next steps I had to take.

My original plan had been to take Marie-Louise to Madame Isabelle's house and ask her to help me. I'd found her address easily enough; it was written on the back of the envelopes containing her letters that Monsieur Gérard kept in his Japanese cabinet. I had reasoned that taking Marie-Louise immediately to her uncle in Jumièges might accomplish nothing. Gérard might explain he still could not cope with a child all on his own and would therefore despatch her straight back to boarding-school again. Whereas if Madame Isabelle brought his niece home to him, he would realise how grateful he was and how much he loved them both, and how he couldn't do without them.

Perhaps he would marry Madame Isabelle, and so provide Marie-Louise with an aunt to love in the home she was used to. They would be a real family. They would be happy together and live happily ever after. Madame Isabelle would forgive me for having slept with Gérard. She would love Marie-Louise like a daughter. I would restore the child to the mother. The child would not die. The mother would not die. The damage would be mended and the breakage healed. The mother would be reunited with the daughter and they would hold each other in their arms and nothing should ever part them again. They rose up in front of me, the two of them who were one; a golden image in a secret church; not the Virgin and her Son but mother and daughter flowing together, undivided, poured and fused together, gold molten and glowing as love.

Something was getting confused. My head ached. I wanted just to lie down and go to sleep, but I couldn't, because I had the child with me, and she was starting to grizzle a bit, not frightened, but puzzled. The lath-and-plaster façades of the old shops were ceasing to intrigue her. The sun was hot. She dragged her feet and grumbled.

—Where are we going? I want to go home.

—It's not much further, I said: we'll be there soon.

The problems in my plan rose up, one by one, squinted at me, mocked me.

Gérard might have me arrested for stealing the house-keeping money. And the basket. Madame Isabelle might refuse to help. She and Gérard might be so angry with me that they would turn me over to the police, who would have me put in prison. Kidnapping was a very serious offence, I was sure of that, and I would be in prison for a long time. It would be like the orphanage all over again; those cold years of deprivation. I knew I could not bear it.

Marie-Louise tugged at my hand.

—Let's go home now.

—In a minute. Just a minute.

While I had been coaxing Marie-Louise along I had been making my way mechanically down the street without being particularly aware of the direction in which I was going. Now I felt an urgent need to get out of our hot, dusty surroundings and find somewhere quiet, free of passers-by. I hesitated, and looked around. Ahead of us was an ancient fountain, and, to the right, a stone doorway. I towed Marie-Louise in here. Suddenly we were inside a shadowy, sheltered space, a yard surrounded by old half-timbered buildings. The ground floor was made up of galleries, which were now closed in. Decorated arches rose up around us, like the frilly stone arcade of a cloister.

I knew where we were; I recognised the place from the engraving hanging in Gérard's study. L'Aitre Saint Maclou. The old plague cemetery. The charnel house. In the cool, undemanding company of the dead. They had been ill once; they had been damaged and scarred; but now they were safe, because they were dead, and their bones neatly ranged here, sorted and filed like the poem-papers in the little drawers of a Japanese cabinet.

I drew a long breath.

—Let's sit down in here for a moment. I'm so tired. Let's rest a little while. Then we'll go straight home, I promise.

Marie-Louise wandered about, her attention diverted by the grotesque carvings on the columns, showing Death dancing with the plague victims. Above them was a frieze decorated with images of grave-diggers' tools, skulls, cross-bones. She took great delight in working out what these strange motifs represented, and calling out her discoveries to me. I listened only vaguely. With one eye I watched her, to make sure she did not stray too far and get lost, and with the other I dreamily saw again the landscape of the early morning. The pink dawn sky unfurled like a sail. Nothing

had yet happened to shatter hope. Sinuous as a green serpent the river wound to the open sea.

—Look, Geneviève, Marie-Louise said, pointing at one
of the capitals.

I stretched my neck up and out like a serpent and
looked. It was so hot that my eyes were watering. I wiped
them, and concentrated, peering across to the far side of the
courtyard where Marie-Louise stood. From here, the carving the child was showing me looked just like the other
engraving in Gérard's room, the lovely sculpture from
Autun.

Eve swam gaily above my head, floating on her side, one
hand waving at me in greeting and the other pointing
towards the apple on the tree. Her little breasts were half
veiled by the spreading tendrils of her hair, while below the
waist her body was invisible, caught in tangles of greenery
like seaweed. Her good hand welcomed me and her bad
hand stretched out to grasp the forbidden fruit. Her smile
was arch, knowing.

She was the mermaid. She had come to remind me, to
show me the way.

Sooner or later the mermaid had to return to the sea,
which was her only true home. She couldn't survive on
land. She had tried her best but she had failed. No shame in
admitting that. Once before she had attempted to go back,
but it had been too soon. But now the time was right.

I would hold Marie-Louise's hand, so that she would not
be frightened. It would be a game she was used to: going

paddling in the ripples at the sea's edge. We would wade further in together, taking it very gently, giving Marie-Louise plenty of time to get used to the deep, dark green water, the buoyancy of the salt waves. We'd be laughing at our absurdity, going swimming in our clothes, watching them balloon out around us. Then she would be so tired that she would want to fall asleep, and the sea would hold us in its arms and rock us like a cradle. We would lie down together in the water and be transformed by it and take on our true mermaid shapes again and then nothing more could hurt Marie-Louise; she would be safe for evermore; and I would have finally accomplished my task and could rest and not have to wake up out of this comfort, this story.

Marie-Louise suddenly began to run, clapping her hands and shouting, past the columns on the far side of the yard, back towards the pointed stone doorway. A bat flew up, startled, a black streak whistling past her head. She cupped her hands to her mouth and made trumpet sounds.

—I'm going to play hide-and-seek like we did in the forest. Bet you can't find me.

She vanished from my sight.

I was on dry land again. Beached here in the everyday. My back had been sagging against the cold spine of a column. I was half asleep. Dazed, I sat up. Got to my feet. I staggered. I was feeling sick with fatigue, and my headache was worse, as though I'd received a blow.

—Marie-Louise, I called: Marie-Louise, come back.

My voice was feeble, cracked. She could pretend not to have heard me. I picked up my basket and ran, the basket bumping against my knees, past the skeletons and crossed bones, the grinning skulls. Apart from its dead, the place was empty. Marie-Louise was nowhere to be seen.

I hastened back out into the street, dodging through the low doorway. Sunlight struck down onto the cobbles. Doves cooed somewhere nearby. Almost immediately I decided I must have come out of l'Aitre Saint Maclou the wrong way. I'd got confused in my hurry, turned right rather than left and emerged through a back entrance. This surely wasn't the stately porch I had entered earlier. This debouched onto what seemed a different street, sunnier and more open than the rue Martainville, forming one side of a little square set with plane trees.

Then I spotted Marie-Louise. She was dawdling at the far end of the higgledy-piggledy stretch of old houses, looking into a shop window. She hadn't seen me.

I crept towards her. I gained on her stealthily, as though I were a poacher creeping up on a rabbit, tiptoeing through wet grass, coaxing it not to take fright. Oh but not to kill the rabbit, I swear, just to capture it for its own good and pop it into my basket and return it to where it belonged.

I reached her. She was studying a display of hats in the window of what announced itself to be a dressmaking establishment. I looked at the name painted in curly flowing script on the glass and sighed. So we'd got here after all. I stepped forward and rang the doorbell.

Madame Isabelle opened the door. Her black hair was loose on the red and yellow flowered shoulders of her cotton dressing-gown. She was frowning, but then she began smiling. Her smile gathered us up; we abandoned ourselves to it.

—I thought you were my sister-in-law. Thank heavens, you're not. It's rather early to be receiving guests. But since you're here you'd better come in.

She stepped back inside the hallway and motioned us to go past her. She pulled the door to behind us.

—We were just thinking about having some breakfast; she chattered, glancing into my basket: I see you've brought it with you. How kind of you to think of it. We haven't a crust in the house. Come along, we're up on the next floor.

She pushed us gently towards the staircase which spiralled up from the end of the hall. It had a polished wooden banister and wide, shallow treads. Madame Isabelle, the skirts of her dressing-gown bunched in one hand, leaped nimbly up ahead and Marie-Louise and I followed obediently. We stopped on the first floor and the stairway coiled on to the floors above.

—In here, she said, opening a panelled white door.

A tiny hallway, with two other doors opening off it, led into a long narrow kitchen which made me think of what a train carriage must be like. Sunlight flooded in through the open window, which was framed by the branches of a climbing rose, waving languidly as the breeze moved over them. The roses were round and full, white, with creamy hearts, and their scent, carried on the spring air, mingled with that of the coffee keeping warm on the little stove. The walls were tiled blue and white to two-thirds of their height, and painted white above. A table, covered in blue oilcloth and flanked by two cushioned chairs, fitted in by the window, and a white-stained wooden cupboard, with a basket hung from its handle, and more baskets piled on top, completed the furniture.

I took it all in, a second's glance around sufficing to give me a sense of the tranquillity of this clean little interior. What was completely unexpected was that Miss Milly was seated on one of the chairs at the table by the window, and looking up, as astonished to see us as we were to see her.

Yvonne

My mother used to declare how sorry she felt for Madame Colbert, having such a terrible life. It was typical of her, to stress her own superiority, that she concentrated on the difficulties experienced by others. She and Madame Colbert were neighbours in Jumièges, and a certain rivalry existed between them, just enough to add salt and spice to their relationship, which would otherwise have been flavourless and bland.

Together they put the gristle and sinews back into the soft flesh of ladies' friendships. Since they could not throw off their corsets to don shirt and breeches, and learn to fence, or follow a code of honour that encouraged the fighting of duels; since they were not allowed to swagger in gold-braided uniforms and send armies into battle, or ruin each other on the Stock Exchange; they sparred instead with domestic weapons. Combat ensued, employing whatever missiles came to hand: the earliest flowering gladioli, recipes for *sole normande,* crochet patterns, digestive problems, exploits of children and grandchildren.

Of course, if challenged, they would vehemently have denied this. A feminine lust for war was quite unthinkable. Ladies were not aggressive, ambitious and power-hungry, which qualities did harm to your reproductive organs and rendered you liable to be whisked off to the clinic in Le Havre for corrective surgery, but spent their lives blamelessly taking care of their families and doing good to all around. And so on and so on.

Both participants in the struggle wanted to be top dog in the village. Each tried to patronise the other, in the politest possible way. At mass on Sundays, they always sat in the front pews, one on the left of the aisle and the other on the right. When it came to the moment for going up to receive Holy Communion, they would wait for everyone else in the church to go up first, since humility demanded that one gave others precedence. They would emerge from their pews at precisely the same moment, to join the very end of the single file of villagers walking modestly towards the high altar with clasped hands and downcast heads. Bumping into each other having been so narrowly averted, they could then enjoy a little theatre of giving way. My mother would pause, and gesture gracefully, as though to say: after you, Madame Colbert, after you. To which Madame Colbert would respond with a little bow and flourish: no, no, Madame Polpeau, after you. After several minutes of this, one or the other would be forced to proceed and her friend could count the victory her own.

Madame Colbert would drift back from Communion as slowly as possible, in a state of exaggerated mystical rapture, her eyes turned heavenwards, her black lace veil floating around her soulful face. Down the side aisle she would pace, keeping exactly in time with my mother on the far side of the church, and then back up the centre aisle to their pews they would both come, sometimes one in front and sometimes the other. They would sink to their knees and bury their faces in their hands to make their thanksgiving, and after five minutes you could catch them peeping sideways at each other, to check who was going to raise her head first, and so prove herself the less holy.

Madame Colbert, I felt, won many of these competitions. Her widowhood raised her above common humanity, as though she were a nun. No ordinary sister, mind, but a Mother Superior. I expect you're a protestant, aren't you, rather than a Catholic? You may not know that the Church had established hierarchical categories of virtuous feminine states. It was best, really, to be sexless and dead. If you couldn't be a martyr, then virginity came next, followed by widowhood. To be a repented prostitute carried a certain cachet. But ordinary married women, such as my mother, who went to bed with their husbands and had children, were at the bottom of the list.

I was a bad child. One Sunday, having witnessed the usual performance of black lace piety and slow, ecstatic steps, I found myself, coming out of church, pressed in the crowd against Marie-Louise, and I whispered to her: your grandmother is called the Walking Corpse.

What I thought unfair was how often my father got out of going to mass. He was a believer but he had little time for priests. He was scornful of our local curé, who had grown fat as a result of so often having to eat two Sunday lunches, one at our house and the other with the Colberts. Illness can't wait till Monday, my father was fond of declaring, and off he would go to visit some stricken person on a far-flung farm, which involved a pleasant outing in the trap, and perhaps a drive through the forest on the way back. Sometimes Monsieur Gérard Colbert accompanied him. He did not go to church either, but that was because he was a strict atheist, quite a militant. One of his poems, you must know it of course, describes him, as a young man, wrestling with God in the shape of a huge raven, and finally killing him. Marie-Louise insists that the raven represents evil, not God. Well, she would.

Her uncle tolerated Marie-Louise being taken to church, out of respect for his mother. He himself steered clear not just of church but of most occasions of meeting people. Provincial life bored him. I heard him say more than once that he only lived in Jumièges because it was cheap, and quieter than Paris, good for getting on with his work. He loathed the social round of the village, such as it was, but he made an exception for my father. They went fishing together in season, or walking, or they went sailing on the river in my father's boat.

To the anxiously snobbish shopkeepers and so forth Monsieur Gérard preferred the ordinary people. The peasants and farming people. He said they were real. The salt of the earth. That was his own form of snobbery, really, and shows what a bourgeois he was himself, doesn't it? Because though he admired it in others he didn't have to do hard physical work himself. He wasn't prepared to try and change society. He wasn't a socialist. He was an artist; he kept his head down; he insisted that poetry and politics did not mix. But he respected the local people for their industry and fortitude, their honesty, which was like a physical quality not a virtue. Seeing and naming things exactly as they were, not exaggerating, then cracking a joke or swearing.

He also had a great regard for the maid Geneviève, who worked for the family for a time. She was not from a peasant background, but she gave him a lot of material for the folkloric motifs in his poems, and she served as the model for the servant in his celebrated novella *The Cook.* She came from the pays de Caux, where she had worked in a café. Her old employer, Madame Montjean, turned up in Jumièges one day, with her young son, looking for her, but Geneviève had gone off to Rouen for some reason, and was not to be seen. Madame Montjean knocked at all the houses in the village, including ours, enquiring for her. Monsieur Gérard invited her in, and then later on accompanied her back to the ferry, carrying the child for her. Treating her as a social equal was behaviour considered deeply unconventional, even bizarre.

What my mother perceived as Monsieur Gérard's oddities as a person, and indeed inadequacies as a man and a son, fuelled her complacent pity for Madame Colbert, who, with so many advantages, such as a house of her own and a small private income, had led a disappointing and disappointed life. Thirty years a widow, my mother would exclaim: and then she herself died while she was still quite young, a woman in her prime, only fifty-five or so, only a few years older than I. Her daughter dying so young; a son-in-law who vanished, leaving her with a granddaughter on her hands, for whom she was solely responsible; a son who was little consolation, involved in no respectable profession such as medicine, but a poet, which meant a layabout, a bit of a rogue, she hinted, one for the ladies, a little too much so. Madame Colbert did not approve of me, believing me to be badly brought up, a bad influence on her precious granddaughter. So I rarely spent time with Marie-Louise. And I was away so much, either at school or staying with relatives in the holidays, that I cannot say I knew the Colberts well. I viewed Monsieur Gérard Colbert from a distance. I felt he despised women such as my mother and myself. He moved

in a higher society than ours. To me he was a source of speculation and stories rather than a real person.

You probably know all those stories about Monsieur
Gérard already, don't you? They've circulated for ages.
People enjoy gossiping, telling stories about each other. It's
our way of weaving ourselves into the social fabric, I think,
of testing out our humanity, finding out what we can toler-
ate and what we can't. It enlarges our understanding of
what's possible. Just like novels do. Perhaps gossip is only
harmful when it purveys false information. Lies and fictions
are certainly best left to writers! And Monsieur Gérard, by
becoming famous, finally, was quite a hero to the village, in
the end. People were proud, eventually, of his exploits, the
amatory ones included.

Marie-Louise wrote an entire memoir about her uncle. I
haven't read it. She never published it because she was not
satisfied with it. She could not decide what to put in and
what to leave out, torn between feeling she should tell the
truth and wanting to present her uncle as solely heroic. She
might show it to you, if you can find a way of persuading
her. It's there in the house somewhere, I expect, buried in a
box in the attic. That's where Marie-Louise keeps all the
bits and pieces that don't fit the image of his life she has
constructed. She has put this composite holy portrait on
show in a series of display cases. You can study the beautiful
pink and red decorated porcelain plates off which he dined
every day, the very smart blue silk robe he wore (copying

Balzac perhaps) for composing, the handsome leopardskin rug on which he lay while in the throes of inspiration. Unlike his infinitely greater compatriot Flaubert, he kept no parrots. Unlike his infinitely more illustrious rival Mallarmé, who named his troupe *les petits académiciens,* he kept no parakeets. So there are no stuffed animals or birds on view. You can look at the bottle of lime eau-de-Cologne presented to him by his mother, his rosary, his crucifix, along with his books and all the other memorabilia, the famous pipe, the box of cigars. It's a pity, really, she hasn't included a stuffed poet, as well. It would be just as authentic as anything else.

No, you're right. I don't admire his writing. Modish, superficial stuff in my opinion, which is why, I suppose, it finally did so well. His famous novella, for example, pretends to understand women, but it idealises them in a really wishy-washy way. Some of the poems speak in a woman's voice, but to me they all sound exactly like men talking. There are several female poets of the period whose work is far superior to Colbert's, in my opinion, but of course they aren't allowed to be called great. Only men at that time were considered great writers. Marie-Louise, I have to say, bears considerable responsibility for the Colbert myth. Turning the house into some ridiculous sort of shrine and encouraging his admirers to venerate him as though he weren't just a flawed human being like anyone else.

She has rearranged the study as she claims it originally was, but in reality making a kind of stage set, stretching a

red cord across the doorway to stop the public from invad-
ing and stealing souvenirs. Across this barrier you peep in
at the Japanese cabinet, the armchair, the engravings, and
so on. There are some watercolour sketches in glass cases,
some of his letters. His collection of pornography's not on
show, of course. Though Marie-Louise was the one who told
me about discovering it, after his death. Rather fine exam-
ples of early black and white photographs he presumably
collected as a young man. One is a reproduction of a
Courbet painting *L'Origine du monde*—a beautiful painting
of a cunt. I wondered about the rest of the woman. Who she
was. Gérard's photographs of naked cunts, surrounded by
silky black hair, had the same impact on me. I wondered
who the women were.

Marie-Louise had one particular story she used to like to
tell about her uncle, in the days before she turned his home
into a temple and constituted herself guardian angel of his
spotless reputation. Because she won't tell you this tale herself, I shall. But please remember, I'm not vouching for its
truth. It's one of the legends, that's all.

Monsieur Gérard was involved, at one and the same
time, with three different women. At a certain period in his
life. Three love affairs running concurrently. Of course, I
shan't mention any names. But I dare say you know the life
story sufficiently well to be able to guess them. He had a
mistress in Rouen, who was a dressmaker; he was sleeping
with his mother's maid; and he was also involved with
Marie-Louise's governess. That sounds like something of a

harem, doesn't it? Quite a powerful position to be in. I expect he found that quite exciting, to see himself as some sort of pasha. He could play them off one against the other, if he wanted to. I think, as far as possible, he tried to keep them ignorant of each other's existence. Or significance, I should say. That way, of course, he could stay in control. His defence, I expect, would be that artists are different from other people, with complicated needs. But in my view he was no different from any other bourgeois male complacently assuming he was entitled to large doses of female adoration. He wouldn't have thought about it. He just took it as his due.

One day the three women got together, quite by chance, and compared notes. Marie-Louise claims she was there. Hers is an eyewitness account, she says. They met in a house in Rouen, behind the cathedral, in which the dressmaker had her shop premises and rented a flat. She was a young widow, rather hard up, trying to make ends meet, and so she had decided to take in a tenant. She had begun letting a room to the young governess, who had been sacked by Madame Colbert for flirtatious behaviour and general carrying on. Madame Colbert was not one for spelling things out. She liked to encourage my mother to guess the worst. The governess was presumed by the family to have gone straight back to her family in London, and to her fiancé, whereas in fact, unable to tear herself away from her hopes for the love affair with Monsieur Gérard to reach a happy conclusion, she had chosen to stay in the vicinity, find work locally as an English teacher, and wait and see what happened. She existed in a kind of dreamy state, constantly re-imagining her next meeting with the poet, and the beautiful consequences which would ensue.

Running across the dressmaker by chance in the street, recognising her from a brief encounter months before, she had renewed the acquaintance. In her desperate need to talk about her feelings for Monsieur Colbert, to open her heart to someone who knew him, she had confessed to the dressmaker, whom she knew to be her rival, that she had intercepted a packet of her letters to Gérard at a certain point and had thrown them in the river. This dramatic announcement, worthy of the most crude type of stage melodrama, amused the dressmaker rather than enraging her. Perhaps she was a little less in love with Gérard than formerly, and so able to take things with a certain nonchalance. At any rate, whether or not she was playing some deep game, trying to appear cool and keep in control of the situation, she ended up forgiving the governess her jealously interfering behaviour. The two women even made friends, and the governess moved in.

Marie-Louise and the servant-girl arrived at the house one morning by a series of coincidences, worthy of a romance, that I don't need to relate since they don't belong to this story. They recognised the governess immediately, of course; there were introductions and greetings all round, and an orgy of explanations.

Rather than spitting and scratching, as women in this situation are traditionally supposed to do, they sat down and ate breakfast together. Bread and butter and coffee. They began to discuss the predicament in which they found themselves. The three of them all interested in the same man.

The servant-woman, a rather over-emotional person, was not very well that morning. She felt awkward and nervous, clearly, in this odd situation; she was also exhausted because she had been suffering from insomnia; and she was in a somewhat agitated state. The dressmaker therefore put a generous tot of calvados in her coffee, a country habit as you undoubtedly know, to cheer and fortify her. The others all decided to partake too. Except the child, of course. Marie-Louise was only seven or eight at the time. Drinking calvados first thing in the morning, they soon became rather tipsy, which is the only explanation for their subsequent behaviour. Marie-Louise is sure they were all completely drunk. She remembers their reddened cheeks, waving hands, and raucous laughter. The servant-girl sat with a beatific expression on her face and apparently did not believe that what was happening was real.

The first suggestion was that they continue exactly as they were and simply share Gérard between them. Pass him round between the three of them. Each could be a part-time mistress. It was the dressmaker who proposed this. She was a busy woman, with not a great deal of free time. She explained that while she loved Gérard with a certain passion she didn't need him always to be there. She could love him quite well when he was not present. Seeing him once or twice a week would suffice her quite nicely. On the other days she could get on with her mending, and so on, or take a walk, or go to visit her old client Madame Flaubert of whom she was very fond, and generally enjoy herself contemplating the next meeting. And if she knew that at that very moment he was busy satisfying one of the other two, then so what? He had plenty of stamina; he had proved that often enough; and she would happily wait her turn to enjoy him.

The governess vehemently disagreed. She thought the dressmaker's suggestion cheapened the very notion of true love. She wanted the three of them to act nobly and heroically. At least, two of them should. Two of them should renounce their love for Gérard and give him up to the third. Obviously, she hoped this would be herself. She spoke eloquently about the inspiration of unconsummated love as an ideal, troubadours serenading their ladies from afar, and so on. At the same time she spoke wistfully of marriage.

The servant-girl said that where she had worked before, people often settled their disputes by drawing lots. Also they were very fond of betting.

Marie-Louise was not clear who made the final, definitive suggestion. They were all talking at once, spluttering, interrupting each other and laughing. But the dressmaker pushed back her chair and opened a drawer in the table at which they were all sitting, and took out a pack of cards. She cut and shuffled, shuffled and cut, dealt them each a hand. And so they played for Gérard. The victor would be able to say: I won him at cards.

＊ No, I can't tell you who won him, because unfortunately Marie-Louise, being just a child, grew bored with this card game that went on and on and that she could not join in. She wandered out. She went into the dressmaker's work-room and played with the contents of the button-box. She liked the little compartments, full of discs of different sizes and shapes, the stack of trays you lifted in and out, the sparkle of metal and jet and diamanté between her fingers. Composing patterns of fake jewels she forgot all about the other designing game going on in the kitchen upstairs.

Thank you. I've enjoyed talking to you too, monsieur. I wish you well with your research and I shall be glad if what I've told you can be of any use.

Poor Gérard, adored by so many women. All he wanted, you know, was to be left in peace to write his poems. And then to die before he'd begun his best work. Marie-Louise insists both that he died a hero's death and also that he didn't suffer, but how can she be sure when she wasn't there? More likely alone in unimaginable agony and terror with his mouth full of mud. Of course the telegram didn't say. It was as deceitful as any work of art or any poem.

Geneviéve

Almond green, eau-de-Nil, apple green: I didn't know what the colour was called. Sometimes I smelled it: freshly cut grass, new peas, absinthe, *thé à la menthe,* the juice of emeralds, sage.

A long, rippling crack spread across the pale green lime-washed plaster of the wall. Though it was only three inches from my face, it looked like the distant shoreline of a dearly missed country held in the vision of someone capsized out at sea and now swimming towards land. That wavering edge might be blurred by a rainstorm sweeping across, or made hazy by an afternoon of heat, but it never fundamentally changed. It was always solidly there, promising and beckoning, though often heavy with exhaustion. I didn't feel I was getting any closer to it. I swam, slowly and laboriously, towards it, and then, when my strength gave out, I lay back on the waves and let them roll me in. I waited for release, the moment when the surf would tumble me onto the beach and I could just collapse on the stones and know I'd arrived.

In more lucid moments, when I was less submerged by dreams of this far-off place called my county, to which I was desperately struggling to return, I stared at the crack and saw that it was not a line at all, but an opening into which you could insert your fingernail. The temptation was to scratch the wall, flake more plaster away, create islands and estuaries and promontories, rivers in winding loops that took you, by alternative and enchanting routes, back to your lost home. If I vanished into the crack in the wall perhaps I'd find my house again.

I slept for a week. My illness spent itself that way; it broke, a storm of fatigue that flattened me. The only thing to do was to lie low. That was how I got cured. I was asleep, and so couldn't waste my energy fretting, and meanwhile some kind of mending work went on inside. I slept with confidence and reassurance. I knew that I was in the house of friends, though I couldn't remember their names, and I knew that being ill was a way of slowing down, of stopping for a bit. Like granting yourself a holiday during which repair work can be done.

When finally I clambered out of bed and stood up my legs wobbled. I had to learn to walk again. Like the mermaid trying to hobble on dry land. But the mermaid had gone. She had swum off and I was left alone, washing my face and putting on my clothes, with a feeling of lightness. Part of that was hunger. My first day up, I was ravenous. I could have eaten the tablecloth and the cups and saucers. Madame Isabelle served up broth with a poached egg in it, and bread, and then rice pudding. She said that there were invalid foods: mild and nourishing.

—I'm not an invalid any more, I told her: I'm recovered. I've caused quite enough trouble, being ill. I'm well again.

We were sitting at the little table by the kitchen window. Outside it was raining. Summer rain in Normandy has a certain charm if you're indoors, watching it stream down the windowpane. Cool air moves over your neck; your feet are dry and warm in clean stockings; your hands curl around a blue-flowered bowl of soup; the steam tickles your nose. Outside, the world is full of water, and the view misty and green, the rain-bashed roses dangling brown-edged balls of petals above the sill, but inside everything's clear, calm. Order, and light, and peace. Like a blessing. Things are in their proper place once more. You can come back to yourself in your proper shape; no more parts of you floating off and wandering about, dissolved and unhappy, wanting to get back in but not knowing how. And so, at a nod from your hostess, you pick up your spoon and begin to eat.

I found out that I had been sleeping downstairs, in the former tailoring workshop, which was now converted into the tenant's room. While I'd been away, which was how it felt, while I'd halted, everyone's lives had gone on without me. The little flat was quiet. Miss Milly had gone back to England, the day after Marie-Louise and I arrived, to visit her parents, and to decide whether or not to return to France.

—She's been writing a lot of poetry, Madame Isabelle said: but of course I couldn't understand it because it's in English. She tried to translate some into French for me but it sounded rather peculiar.

The way she tossed out this last word told me it was one she liked. A good distancing word, like a far-off cupboard into which you put everything you didn't want to look at just now. You could shut the door on it so that you didn't have to make an immediate decision about whether something was good or bad. You could let it rest for a while, and this waiting allowed you to remain polite. At the same time you were hinting strongly that you didn't really appreciate the objects in the cupboard. Such as those wedding presents Madame Colbert never used but stored away. Elaborate vases and epergnes and frilly silver trays. Perhaps in fact to her they were simply too previous ever to belong in daily life, but to me, taking them out to dust, they were fussy and ugly. Peculiar. If ever I had a house of my own everything in it would be my best and I would use my best things every day. What was the point of keeping your best things wrapped up in the dark recesses of a cupboard like nuns in a convent? You hoped to protect and preserve them, but then you died, without having enjoyed them, and they too rotted eventually and fell to dust, and that was that. I didn't want a lot of fiddly, difficult things. Peculiar things. I wanted a few simple things with beautiful shapes and colours, that wouldn't easily break but would last through daily use. Like that white oval dish of Madame Montjean's for serving radishes; like that blue coffee-pot.

—Of course, Gérard's poems could be difficult to understand, too, Madame Isabelle was musing: but at least, or so he said, that was deliberate. I first fell in love with him after reading his poems, you know. He read them to me, I should say. That first evening, on the beach at Etretat. That was when I knew I was in love with him. That quickly.

This was a different version of events from the one she had given me a couple of days ago, when she had been chatting to me about her life, telling me the tale of her marriage. Still, she was a dressmaker. She was used to making up frocks, and now stories. I could see that she was trying on different stories for size, checking their effect, wondering which suited her best. She wasn't lying, as such. It was just that how she saw things changed from one week to another. Memories alter, like necklines and hemlines do. You choose the one that fits the moment.

She put a pan of water to boil and went on with her news. Marie-Louise was staying with the Polpeaus. Madame Isabelle had contacted the school, to tell them where she was, had sent a telegram to Gérard in Paris, and another to the Polpeaus. I was not in trouble after all; it was assumed by everyone I had meant to act for the best.

—She wouldn't have spent much longer at that school, anyway, Madame Isabelle said: thank heavens, her father's coming back from Africa very soon, and he'll want her to live with him now. He's getting married again, Gérard says. We just have to hope that Marie-Louise will be fine. Give her a chance to settle in with the new stepmother and see how it goes.

She didn't tell me off for interfering. She poured me some coffee, in a pretty cup, thin green porcelain with a gold rim, and a wide handle flecked with gold, and pushed the sugar-pot towards me. I wanted, suddenly, to tell her the whole story, of what had happened in Blessetot, and afterwards. I tried to imagine myself doing so, I saw myself opening my mouth and letting it out.

I would have to tell the truth. This would be extremely difficult. There were things I hadn't thought about yet, that belonged in the account, but which I did not know how to express, that I hardly dared say. It was one thing to stir them about by myself, in the privacy of my own head, where they existed in a comforting soup of words, hardly words at all, melting, mixed up with each other; it was quite another to fish them up and put them into sentences, into some kid of order and shape; to admit them to someone else. I heard myself stumbling and blurting. I kept going back to the beginning and starting again. I didn't know where the ending was.

And also I felt you might lose something precious by making and telling a story, because then all its part stretched out, beads strung one by one onto a string in time, tangling along from beginning to end; whereas while the unspoken words remained inside you all of them connected one to the other in a mad circling dance which was indescribably beautiful, wholly present in just one second, an eternal now. When you smoothed and flattened and straightened the story out, made it exist word by word in speech, you lost that heavenly possession of everything at once. You bumped down to earth and told one moment at a time. Speaking and telling, you threw joy away and had to mourn the loss of paradise, the shimmering eternal moment which was outside time, me and Madame Montjean together in the kitchen when no one could separate us and when we didn't have to speak to know we were happy. Perhaps Eve's punishment, thrust forth from paradise, was to become a storyteller. Not in order to defend herself but simply to have to speak. But I wasn't ready for that yet.

Nonetheless I could see that if I did tell my story then it would be done. A job completed. Like cleaning out an old shed, seeing what you've got; sacks and flowerpots and bottles of fruit; spiders' webs and dead mice and worm-eaten pitchfork handles; choosing what to keep, and what to throw away. The story would be put in order and for the moment I would be able to live with myself and it and I might feel free.

I couldn't do it. Fear of what Madame Isabelle would think of me tied my tongue in knots. Shame halted me, like a boulder blocking my throat. Like a stone door rolled across the face of a tomb. I'd been dead, and I'd sat up and walked. I'd been raised to life again. But I couldn't yet speak. That would take time. She didn't press me. She accepted my silence, and her silence was like a caress.

I have stayed on with Madame Isabelle for the last couple of days, sorting out practical things. I have cleaned her flat and shop from top to bottom, having no other way to show my gratitude; I have chopped wood for her; pressed three weeks' worth of ironing; been to the market and done the shopping; prepared our meals. She has suggested I look for a job as a cook, and has written me a reference. Gérard has sent another reference, and the wages he insists he owes me. He sent me his sincere regards. He wished me well. I kissed his signature as a way of saying goodbye then put the paper on the fire.

Before looking for work in Rouen, I am going to take the train and travel to Etretat. From there I am going to make my way, on foot or by hitching a lift, to Blessetot. I might or I might not. If I feel brave enough, I am going to go to the café and visit Madame Montjean. I might.

I have received three letters in all.

The first was from Gérard.

The second was from Madame Polpeau, who wrote to tell me that my former employer had called at her house. She had made enquiries in Etretat at the convent for me; she asked after me in the town; she discovered that I had gone off to Jumièges with a Monsieur Colbert. She came looking for me; she tried to find me; she had something to say to me; and I need to go and discover what it is.

The third letter was from Sister Pauline, scolding me for not writing to her, and saying that Madame Montjean had called at the convent a second time, on her return from Jumièges, to give her my address. Madame Montjean seemed well, and had mentioned that her husband had gone back on the road as a salesman again. Sister Pauline added that she hoped I was still being a good girl and that of course she was praying for me.

I miss the sea at Blessetot; I should like to see it again. I'd like to try making friends, now, with those village children who ran and played and shouted on the beach. Young men now, young women, but they would recognise me as I should recognise them. What happened to you? we'll ask each other: tell me. Their faces laughing and curious. Look. We're at the very beginning of our lives. Tell us a story. Inside me a jostle of voices. The voices of orphans clamouring in the dark. The voices of mothers and fathers crying for their lost ones to come home again. Crying out for all their lost words to return. I shall walk with them down onto that steep little tilt of grey-blue pebbles, in the hot sun, the sparkling light, to watch once more the waves breaking over and over upon the stones, push and tug, back and forth, back and forth, that powerful unending rhythm, that soft crash, crash of water, the salt foam tracing filigree lines of script onto the loose shingle and then erasing them, repeatedly, the sea endlessly writing its life into ours and into our stories, and all my fears of telling my story dissolving, insubstantial as sea-froth, sinking away into wet stones, in this early summer of 1914.

ABOUT THE AUTHOR

MICHÈLE ROBERTS is the author of eleven highly acclaimed novels, including *Fair Exchange* and *Daughters of the House* which won the WH Smith Literary Award and was shortlisted for the Booker Prize. Half English and half French, she divides her time between London and France.